UNDERCOVER GENIUS

A FAMILY GENIUS MYSTERY

Patricia Rice

Undercover Genius

Copyright © 2014 Patricia Rice
Book View Café Publishing Cooperative, February 2014
P.O. Box 1624, Cedar Crest, NM 87008-1624
ISBN 978 1 61138 346 1

All rights reserved, including the right to reproduce this book, or portion thereof, in any form.

This is a work of fiction. Any references to historical events, real people, or real locales are used fictitiously. Other names, characters, places, and incidents are the product of the author's imagination, and any resemblance to actual events or locales or persons, living or dead, is entirely coincidental.

Other Book View Café books by Patricia Rice

Mysteries:
Evil Genius, *A Family Genius Mystery,* Volume 1

Historical Romance:
Notorious Atherton, *The Rebellious Sons,* Volume 3
The Marquess, *Regency Nobles,* Volume 1
English Heiress, *Regency Nobles,* Volume 2
Irish Duchess, *Regency Nobles,* Volume 3

Paranormal Romance:
Trouble with Air and Magic, *The California Malcolms*

One

CARRYING a stack of library research material, I didn't see the nose-high spider web covering the mansion's front door until it plastered my face.

Startled, I juggled my loot and swatted at the tickly silk strands. Luckily for the web's perpetrator, my reflexes were quick, and I didn't drop anything. The brisk October breeze blew me inside as I shouted *"EG!"* into the towering foyer's pristine stillness.

Mallard, our spy cum butler, would never have allowed a spider within the property's perimeters. I knew who to blame for the sudden acquisition of sticky Halloween decorations.

"I suggest you repair to the turret with a broom," a dry voice pronounced from the Waterford chandelier overhead.

"I'm still not a witch, Graham," I countered our host's insult, carrying my treasure toward the basement door. "You may call me Princess Anastasia, if you're into Disney characters." The Anastasia part is actually my name. Magda, our mother—who claims to be a Hungarian princess— has delusions of grandeur and named all of her children after royalty.

Amadeus Graham is our invisible landlord. He thinks he owns our grandfather's house. Maybe he does legally, but morally, we have the higher ground. Thankfully, he lives in the attic where we never see him. We still suffer daily from his annoying commands.

Ignoring my commentary, Graham intoned in that irritatingly unperturbed deep voice of his, "Live bats appear to be involved."

Oh, crikey. Stealing one of my half-brother Tudor's imprecations, I dropped my reference material on the priceless Sheraton side table and dashed for the imposing mahogany staircase. Apparently Graham wasn't commenting on my witchy appearance for a change, but on my half-sister's behavior. EG must be testing Graham's boundaries to see what it would take to get thrown out of the first real home we'd ever known.

I have spent the better part of my life as a doormat for my evilly inventive, peripatetic mother and host of half-siblings. Under

Magda's auspices, we've been dragged around the world to live in huts and palaces, but we've never had a place to call our own.

I liked to think, since I moved into my late grandfather's Victorian home, that I was now in control of my life. Not seeing a lot of difference some days, except now I had the house's current owner breathing fire down my neck whenever my half siblings got a little too creative.

Live bats in the belfry would qualify as too creative, on the verge of dangerously destructive.

I had no idea where Mallard hid the cleaning equipment. Since our nit-picky butler wasn't here leading the bucket brigade, I had to assume EG had either chased him to the Irish pub he liked on the corner, or she had waited for him to leave on errands before populating the tower haunt she called her room.

Elizabeth Georgiana, my youngest half sibling, is the reason I ended up here in D.C. I was determined to give her the stable home I'd never had. Some days, it seemed I should have chosen a Bedouin tent rather than a mansion crammed with antiques. But I still had foolish hopes of suing for our inheritance, so I was claiming squatter's rights for the nonce. EG had to learn to live like a civilized human being sometime.

"EG," I said warningly, in my best Ruler of the Palace tone, testing the knob on her door. At the tender age of nine, EG had deliberately chosen the only chamber with an operating lock. I could dismantle it or take a hatchet to the door, but I was trying to respect her privacy, as no one had ever respected mine. The knob wasn't locked—not necessarily a good sign. "Round up the bats. I want to come in."

The door cracked open to creepy Halloween music, and my little Goth peered out. A black net blocked sight of most of the room. "They're a science project," she announced. "Bats are good for the environment. They're not hurting anything."

"Except insects and Graham's patience. Where did you find live bats and should I ask?"

"They're in the tower attic. I just opened the trap door. They're my pets!" If she'd wear her black hair in braids, she'd resemble Wednesday in the Addams family, except prettier. She has our mother's slanted cheekbones and long-lashed eyes. Today, she'd cut her hair in ragged spikes in front and colored them purple.

"You can't take bats to school, and you can't create your own haunted house until you own one. Get them out of there and close the trap door, or I won't tell you when Nick arrives."

"He's almost home?" she asked excitedly, forgetting to be a sullen brat. "Did he tear out the turd's eyes yet?"

Not a good visual. Yuck. "Bats, out," I said firmly, shutting the door before the creatures could take it as an invitation.

Having accomplished my parental duty, I trotted downstairs to return to my professional tasks. I'm a virtual assistant, an invisible researcher, and ghost writer for a number of professors and corporations, Amadeus Graham currently being my primary client. It's the perfect job for a cellar-dwelling introvert.

In addition to my normal duties, I was on a mission to save my family's fortune. Nick was about to return with the key part of the puzzle.

The business office I'd set up for myself in a previously unused corner of the cellar can nowhere compare to the electronic paradise Graham inhabited on the spacious third floor, but my needs were simpler than his. I did not know, and didn't care to guess, what our resident spook did that required equipment rivaling the CIA's. But as much as I appreciated his allowing us to live here, I really wanted to pry him out of our lives before his enemies dropped a bomb on us.

To that goal, I turned on my computer to check Nick's progress. I'm the eldest of the Hungarian Princess's brood. At twenty-five, Nick is next oldest. As a result of Magda's numerous marriages and affairs, we all have different fathers.

Nick currently works in a congressional office with EG's senator father, but he's taken a leave of absence for a family matter, ie: capturing Reginald Brashton the Snake—the executor who sold our inheritance to Graham and absconded with all our funds.

Using GPS, I'd tracked the yacht that Reggie the Snake bought with our money. We'd located the coke-sniffing bastard in the Caribbean with his off shore bank account. Nick had flown down to retrieve what he could. I didn't know the full story of how he'd bagged Reggie—Nick is a lousy communicator—but I doubt it involved law officers. That's not how we were raised.

Self-sufficient is the politest word for Magda's brood. Our mother calls herself a journalist, but I'm pretty sure she's a spy who likes hooking up with power magnates. The result is that no two of us have the same father, and there are a lot of us. Until recently, being the eldest, I'd been the one taking care of my half-siblings.

No messages from Nick were in my box, but the GPS showed the yacht had almost reached the Chesapeake. I had no notion of where one parked yachts—I didn't even drive a car. Licenses are hard to come by in the deserts where I'd taught myself to drive in jeeps "borrowed" when the owners weren't looking.

I set my latest new toy on the desk—a smart phone in which I'd disabled the tracking device to annoy Graham. I had lots of plans for the money Reggie had better be coughing up, and I was hoping Nick would call soon.

And then I returned to work researching Broderick Media, a conglomerate that Graham had taken an interest in, or a dislike to. I was deep in the bowels—bad image for a corporation called BM—of corporate infrastructure when the doorbell rang over my head. Since I wasn't expecting anyone and this was the reason we employed a butler, I ignored it.

"I'm inclined to turn her away," the desk lamp said dryly. "We have enough trouble without asking for more."

I smacked the lamp in hopes of ringing Graham's ears. He wasn't supposed to have his limitless supply of bugs in my office. "We have an intercom, you know." But I was already on my feet.

"You turned it off," Graham reminded me.

Oh yeah, well, if he had to be technical about it... I hate intrusion while I'm working. So I wasn't predisposed to appreciate whoever had dared the doorstep.

I didn't linger to have words with a lamp and was already half way up the stairs.

Graham must have used the intercom to inform our visitor that someone was coming since they weren't battering on the door or bell by the time I reached the main floor. Or maybe they were admiring the trailing pothos vine in the sphinx head that was our speaker. Graham scared off quite a few solicitors with the talking plant. If his presence didn't irritate me so much, I'd have had to admit that his eccentric habits occasionally amused me.

I opened the door. I was tempted to slam it again—just because I could and because sibling rivalry thrived—but I maturely refrained. Someone in this family had to be the adult.

"Ana, it's you! Looking lovely as ever," Patra chirped on the doorstep, before rolling her suitcase over my toe and pushing inside without invitation. Her head swiveled as she tried to gobble up all the riches that were our foyer. "And Magda grew up here? She gave this up why?"

"You could have called to ask," I said, shutting the door after noting with suppressed delight that the spider web was a little more tattered. Strands of fake silk adorned Patra's unnaturally gorgeous mop of chestnut hair. "Obviously you talked to *someone* to find the address." It just hadn't been me.

My half-sister, Cleopatra Llewellyn, had not only inherited the tall, buxom good looks, but the gregariousness and extroverted personality of our mother. Patra is also seven years younger than I am. I'd changed her diapers, so we're not exactly pals. I could admire her educated sophistication now, but she'd always been one more task on my overflowing list.

"Tudor said we all own part of this place, so I thought I'd check it out." She peered into the stuffy horsehair parlor that was actually neat without Nick here to trash it.

Since Graham had the whole house bugged, I could almost hear him growling, and I hurried to correct her assumption. "We don't own a thing. The estate executor legally sold everything before absconding with the funds. We're taking the deal to court." I threw that in with a large dollop of accusation just to keep Graham on his toes, if he was listening. "Is that all that brings you to DC?"

Sunny Patra didn't do irony or sarcasm like the rest of us. Not recognizing mine, she merely headed for the stairs. "No, I have a job offer and an interview and the opportunity was too good to pass up. Is there room for me or do I have to sleep with EG?"

For a very brief instant I enjoyed the image of bouncy Patra moving in with cynical EG and her bats, but that was the old Ana— the hermit who ran for cover because she knew a family arrival meant trouble.

I'm still a work in progress, but the mature, newly domestic Ana bit the bullet and replied, "We have room. EG has the turret, Nick the queen mother room. I sleep in the upstairs study. Beyond that, the choice is yours."

Well, except the third floor, but Patra is a newly hatched journalist. She'd figure it out.

"The place is a mausoleum!" she cried, peering into every chamber on the second floor. I couldn't wait until she reached EG's. "Oh, look, this one's in rose and green, how 70's! Do you think this belonged to Magda?" She rolled her suitcase inside.

"In her teen years, maybe," I acknowledged. Of course, Magda had only been eighteen when she'd married Brody Devlin. Would she and my father have taken another room, or maybe the third floor? I'd spent the first four years of my life in this opulence. None of my half-siblings had a memory of our grandfather. I was the only one with vague recollections of a stiff, cigar-smoking man with a mustache.

"Magda as a teen, the world trembles at the notion! I'll take this one, if that's okay. I don't have any idea how long I'll be here." Patra plopped backward on the rose satin cover of the bed and studied the wooden tester overhead. "She had posters taped up there. The tape left marks."

I was ambivalent about Patra staying, but at the same time, I enjoyed sharing one of our rare sibling moments. "Probably naked Polaroids. Or dartboards of people she hated. Magda isn't much into rock stars." I crossed over to the mantel, lifted the pastoral painting over it, and ripped out an audio wire. "Got gum?" I asked, pointing to the camera hole that remained.

Patra grinned. "Man, that brings back memories. Chip off the parental block, is she?" She sat up and fished in her humongous purse, not unsurprisingly producing duct tape.

I'd been blaming Graham for the spy holes, but yeah, Magda had probably picked up some of her perverse habits at home. Grandfather Max had been a secretive troll, although this equipment wouldn't have been available thirty years ago. It was the attitude that had been passed on. We happily covered the peephole together and returned the boring painting to its place.

Then I sat down in a rose-silk lady chair and pinned my sister with my gimlet glare.

"Now no one can hear us, tell me what really brought you here."

Two

Patra's perspective

IRRITATED, Patra glared at her older sister. "Don't be annoying, Ana. I'm an adult now, with a good shot at a staff position with Broderick Media. I don't need you to torch my boyfriend's Jag anymore."

Ana had done that, back when Patra was in high school and dating the son of a sheik. Patra hadn't known he was a jerk until he decided he'd start a harem with her, or add to his existing harem. Her sister hadn't bothered asking. Ana had simply come riding to Patra's rescue and clarified in no uncertain terms that an all-female household wasn't helpless.

At the time, Patra had appreciated the rescue. She hoped Ana was a little less aggressive these days, because Patra intended to make a career of taking down the arrogant asses of the world on her own.

"Broderick, hmm?" Ana replied with unconvincing composure. "One of Magda's buddies? I thought you were working for the BBC."

Given their mother's dubious credentials as a power magnet and Broderick's influential media consortium, Patra could see the connection. "I didn't say I was taking the job," she said defensively. "But BM paid my expenses over here. Is it wrong to want to see my family?"

"This is me you're talking to," Ana said bluntly. "The sister who spent twenty years listening to Magda's schemes and keeping all of you out of them. You don't have to tell me what's wrong, but at least respect me enough to be honest."

Patra sat up cross-legged on the bed and tossed her hair over her shoulder. Ana still wore her straight raven-black hair in braids wrapped around her head like an old lady, or Princess Leia. With Ana, it was hard to tell her intention.

"Look, I don't want anyone else involved," Patra said earnestly.

"I respect that you and Nick want to give EG a normal life. But I'm not the settling down type."

Ana shrugged. "Totally understand that. But maybe I should share a little of what I've learned in my *normal* life. Broderick Media is a privately owned international conglomerate of newspapers, broadcast networks, and publishing companies run by Sir Archibald Broderick. Archie is a notoriously amoral eccentric known to keep house slaves in some of his more exotic mansions, of which there are many. He is currently under investigation for encouraging his employees to hack the telephones of political figures with whom he disagrees, which is apparently anyone who doesn't believe Archie should do anything he blamed well pleases. And for this jewel of perfection, you would leave the BBC?"

Patra glared at her through this recitation, but finally, she relaxed. "Okay, I'd forgotten you're more Magda than Magda. Although I'll point out that anyone who reads anything except Broderick scandal sheets knows all this. But you did grab the salient points without touching the more salacious."

"And your vocabulary has grown since you called me a dirty, turdy pail of slop. Now that we've somewhat established our credentials, want to go back to the original question—what brings you here?"

"*Elizabeth Georgiana!*" a furious male voice bellowed in the hall.

Startled, Patra watched her sister fly off her chair as if they'd been attacked by aliens.

* * *

Oh crap, I'd ignored the brat too long. I dashed into the hall. Graham did not normally address anyone except me directly, but I'd cut him out of the loop when I'd cut the wires to Patra's room. The fury was probably for me.

A bat zoomed past my nose, aiming directly for the stairwell to Graham's lair. Okay, this wasn't just about me. I gestured for Patra to stand back and close her door.

EG's door at the end of the hall was shut, so the critter hadn't come from there. I located her in my bedroom, attempting to secure the window over the massive desk that had once been my grandfather's. She looked up miserably at my arrival, then donned a defiant expression.

"Why do you keep your window open?" she demanded as if this was all my fault.

"To attract your pet bats?" I suggested, leaning over to remove the rod needed to hold up the old pane. "I take it they preferred not to return to the attic."

"They were making a disgusting mess up there," she said as the frame slammed closed. "So I let them out my window. And they came back in yours."

"Lesson learned," I said dryly. "Pets make messes their owners have to clean up."

She stared at me incredulously. "I am not cleaning the attic! I didn't invite them in."

"Your bedroom could have looked like that," I reminded her. "You'd better clean it up before it starts stinking."

"Should I chase out the ones that flew upstairs?" Emerging from her room in time to dodge wings, Patra asked this a little too eagerly.

"I wouldn't recommend it unless you want to be transferred to Uganda to write about tribal mating habits," I warned. If Graham was capable of snickering, I think I heard him, but the spider in our attic lacked humor. He *didn't* lack the ability to do exactly as I predicted.

"So Patra, did you finally catch the two-timing creep?" EG asked, deliberately deflecting any return of the conversation to her. She wielded information like a lethal sword. Family trait, I fear.

"Old news, baby. I have better things to do than put up with men. Does this place have any food? Airplane fare is not what it ought to be." Relieved of explaining themselves, or even apologizing, both EG and Patra took off in the direction of the cellar kitchen. Mallard had better pray that he was back in his realm or his pristine counters would be coated in grease and flour before he returned.

I waited until they were out of hearing and hit the intercom on my desk. "Need help battling bats?"

"Only the old ones. Your sister has trouble on her tail. Find out what she's doing or get rid of her, and don't let any of her acquaintances past the door."

My eyebrows shot up, but I'd learned not to be surprised by how much Graham knew, even if he never strayed from his lair.

"I'll extend the web on the door," I told him, before hastening after my sisters and food.

I didn't know what it was like to have a real family in a real home, but I didn't mind finding out.

* * *

"I'm in Norfolk," Nick announced without preamble later that evening after I answered his ring. "I'm waiting for customs to give me clearance to sail up the Chesapeake. How would you like the toad delivered—rolled up in a rug or by the police?"

"With seventy-six trombones and champagne," I suggested, putting my feet up on my desk drawer. It was nine on a school night so EG was in bed, and I'd been working. I could take time for a little exultation. "Smooches and do you have a favorite pervert you want waiting on the doorstep when you arrive?"

Unlike Graham, Nick understood humor and knew I was bouncing with excitement.

"All good. I was thinking of tying him to an anchor and dropping him overboard until we're cleared for entry." A spate of obscenities erupted in the background. "He's been a real charmer since the drugs wore off."

"Oh, goodie. The cops are gonna love a jonesing lawyer. I've been in touch with his bail bondsman. Give me your destination, and they'll be waiting to take him off your hands. Oppenheimer filed our embezzlement charges, so there won't be any more bailing out for Reggie boy. And I mean it, Nick, you're my hero. The sky's the limit. It's celebration time."

Patra peered around the corner, and I gestured for her to come in. A celebration was merrier with more than one. My basement office didn't have the elegance of upstairs, but I preferred solid dirt and concrete around me. It offered privacy—until Graham had bugged it anyway. I'd moved a few old leather wingbacks in here to make it cozy. She settled into one and waited.

"I doubt I'll get back before morning," Nick said. "A bed that doesn't sway and a pitcher of mimosas will do it. Smooches back at you for the bondsman. I really wasn't looking forward to taking a taxi with a foul-mouthed carpet."

I laughed, nearly giddy with triumph. "Do you have the passcode for his account? A judicious fund transfer before his debtors latch onto it might be in order."

"The bastard swears Max was broke and all he owned was the house, so all that's in the account is what he got out of Graham. And he's blown half of that on the yacht and drugs. We're not buying the house back on that, Ana."

I tried not to let my disappointment show. "It's okay. You're back. One thing at a time."

Graham had only given us until we brought Reggie back before we had to pack up and leave. If we filed a lawsuit, he'd heave us out personally, even if he had to use a wheelchair to do it. I'd never seen him outside his computer chair. Of course, I'd never seen an elevator either—another reason to call him spider.

I was a little more somber by the time I hung up. I'd really hoped for millions. Patra looked expectant.

"Nick found the thief?" she prompted when I didn't immediately explain.

She'd apparently been apprised of all our activities—not surprising given that we were raised to spy on everyone, including and especially family.

I held up my finger as a signal to wait, dialed our friendly bondsman, who promised me a reward. My civic duty done, I turned back to Patra. "We have the creep, but we don't have proof that Graham bought the house illegally. Without clear-cut evidence, we have to go through the courts. We have no way of buying the place back from him."

"But you mentioned a bank account. We'll get *some* money, won't we?"

So, I'm the one with a hang-up about the house. I can see where the others would rather take the money and run. We'd had little access to cash in our lives. The prospect of dividing up half a million would cause mass drooling.

"We have to pay our lawyer out of those funds. We're suing grandfather's law firm and paying accountants to research the embezzlement. Don't count on wealth anytime soon."

She looked disappointed. And nervous. Her long fingers locked together as if to keep the manicured tips from tapping. I recognized the Magda-ism.

"Are you ready to tell me what's wrong?" I asked.

"You know about my dad?" she asked, casually studying the windowless cellar I'd claimed for my own.

Patrick Llewellyn had been a world-renowned and respected journalist. Magda had actually married him and consented to calling their daughter by the shortened *Patra* in his honor. Although knowing our mother, she had probably apologized to the Queen of the Nile for the corruption of her name.

Patrick had died reporting atrocities in some war zone. I'd have to count back the years to remember which one. Patra had still been in college, and he and Magda had long since been divorced.

"What should I know about your father?" I asked warily. I'd liked the guy, but that didn't mean I'd trusted him any more than our mother's other conquests.

Patra tapped a long nail against the wooden lion's head grip of the chair. "He wasn't shot by enemy fire."

"They did an autopsy? In a war zone?" I exclaimed. "Why?"

"I think because Magda demanded it. She never told me why. I didn't even know about it until recently, when his executor gave me the last of his effects. Dad was writing a book, and the executor finally gave up trying to sell it for Dad's estate."

She lapsed into brooding silence.

"Don't tell me— a tell-all about the power behind the power," I said dryly. "Conspiracy theories are a dime a dozen. Our grandfather was after textbook manipulators feeding fascist propaganda to kids. Don't question EG on that unless you want an earful. Magda is off on her own power trip, and so is the spider in the attic."

Patra looked irritated. "My dad may have *died* because of what he was working on. This isn't a joke. He was *shot*."

"Just as EG's dad was framed for murder so he wouldn't talk. Yeah, power attracts nastiness. Did you plan on fixing the world? Have you already attracted nastiness?"

I'd just spent an uncomfortable few weeks disentangling Senator Tex, EG's dad, from a consortium of power brokers who may have murdered our grandfather—or hastened his demise, since he hadn't been well. I was hoping Reggie the Snake might enlighten us more on that front.

I was in no hurry to pick up where a famous investigative reporter had got himself killed.

Polished, ultra-cool Patra literally squirmed in her chair. She ran her long fingers through her chestnut locks and didn't meet my eyes. "You'll make me leave if I tell you."

Shit. "I'm never going to escape Magda, am I?" I asked with resignation.

Only a sibling would understand my reaction. Patra looked miserable. "I just talked to a few publishers I knew, gave one of dad's recording to a few people. Dad's material is old, but it's pretty explosive. I just wanted to see if there was any interest in my researching his death as a finish for the book."

"And?" I raised an expectant eyebrow, although my dinner was already curdling in my gut.

"Someone set fire to his papers and destroyed my apartment." She sank deeper into the chair if that was possible.

"Someone deliberately *burned you out?*" This was why grandfather had left us this security-laden fortress, and why I would fight to the death for it. My family required armed encampments for safety. I pinched the bridge of my nose. "If the papers were burned, what can you hope to accomplish by pursuing a book your executor couldn't sell?"

"The papers they burned were mostly transcripts of Dad's recordings. I'd made audio files of the old tapes and stored them in the cloud, along with a scan of his research files. The thieves couldn't touch them," Patra said with a mulish expression I recognized well. She handed me a CD. "I've made copies of his more dangerous stuff. Just listen to this one."

I popped the disk into my old un-networked Dell, verified the intercom had been turned off and the talking lamp unplugged so Graham couldn't hear us, then hit PLAY.

* * *

"My party is prepared to support the general's request to escalate," an unaccented, arrogant American baritone said.

"The weapons lobby backing you?" a cynical, less grammatically constrained American voice asked. *"Or the oil industry? Or both?"*

"Unless we want terrorists controlling the world's oil supply, my request for escalation is the only solution," a crisp, commanding voice said. *"But the media will raise hell unless we have all our ducks in line."*

A bored Brit drawl intruded. *"The Arabic station is ours. We can feed a propaganda frenzy whenever it's needed. Just be certain all your pawns are in place, because once the rioting starts, there will be no stopping civil war."*

The arrogant American responded. *"We've acquired newspapers in France, Greece, and Germany. These things take time—and caution. The American media will take longer to convince, but we have officials in place who can pull the right strings, and our own mouthpieces to start the shouting. We'll be ready."*

"Freedom of the press isn't all it's cracked up to be over the pond, is it?" the Brit asked mockingly.

"Everything can be bought for a price. But there are still a few obstacles," the authoritative one said. *"That's what I brought you here to talk about. You have a wild card in your deck who needs to be dealt with. He's been snooping where he shouldn't—"*

* * *

The voices on the CD quit speaking after a knocking sound in the background. I reached over and ejected the disk.

"A *general* is talking about manipulating governments and bringing down a foreign regime through propaganda and the *media!*" Patra said in indignation. "They've bought the media— TV stations, newspapers, radio! Just to keep oil companies and weapons manufacturers afloat. Millions of people died for their greed! I think this reflects part of the conspiracy my father was writing about. If Dad taped this, and anyone learned about it, they may have had him killed. I need to hire someone with voice recognition software."

Danger, Will Robinson was the first idiocy leaping to my mind.

I didn't need any more conspiracies on my plate. Rich politicians monopolizing the textbook industry had nearly cost me EG and had almost certainly ended our grandfather's life. Greedmeisters buying up international media to put their own puppets into place—probably in oil rich countries—was business as usual as far as I was concerned.

So I rolled my eyes at Patra's suggestion. "You want the kind of fancy software they have on woo-woo shows where the cops compare voice patterns to identify the baddies? Not happening, babe. No database."

"They can do a spectro-analysis of the voices in that file. All we need to do is provide recordings of potential suspects for comparison. Once we find matches, we can positively identify the speakers through science," she said stubbornly. "I sent a copy of that file to an analyst recommended by a friend of mine, and he's pretty excited about it. He thinks I'm on to something."

"But the analyst needs money for the analysis," I finished for her, beginning to see the light.

"Yeah, but all the men I want to record are here in D.C," she said with more excitement. "We can do this, Ana. We can prove some pretty powerful men are manipulating the media for their own immoral purposes, and they killed my dad to cover up his findings!"

Ah, the innocence of youth. Did I have any right to burst her bubble with my apathetic cynicism? I gave up fighting for causes long ago—probably before I was EG's age, since my father had been killed when I was four. Survival was the name of my game.

Except I was learning that family was why we needed to survive, and I knew her pain. "How much?" I asked in resignation.

She named a sum that left me sputtering and glad EG had a scholarship to her private school.

As reluctant as I was to do it, for the kid's sake, I had to roll out the big guns. "And if your thieves discover you still have evidence, will they come burn us down too? Or just put a period to your existence?"

Instead of moping, Patra sat up straight, donned her best Magda superficial smile, and tapped her pretty chin. "What, little ol' me? How could anyone think I'm dangerous? I'm too dumb to use a smart phone."

Three

  WE BOTH stayed up too late. Patra made copies of her audio file, then started researching the names of every VIP who might have been in the vicinity when her father died. Back then, Patrick had apparently been slipping in and out of Mideast war zones by way of any country he could bribe his way through. With no date or location for his tape, Patra had her work cut out for her, but she was like a pit bull on her quest.

  Our best guess was that the power moguls on the recording wouldn't have done the shooting. Our only real clue was that one spoke English with a hoity Brit accent, two others were American, and one was a general.

  Neither of us had spent much time in the States. We couldn't identify regional inflections, but one of the American accents sounded professionally blended by a good speech therapist. My bet was on a politician, but I was prejudiced that way.

  I spent the evening researching our options on the voice analysis. Even though I could buy software and save money, I concluded if we wanted a professional job, we would have to pay professional prices. But we might be able to sort out the unlikely suspects and narrow the speakers to be analyzed, thus reducing cost. Patra emailed her friend Bill with the go-ahead for spectrum analysis on the voices we already had and told him we'd give him comparisons as soon as we could.

  I sent him a down payment out of the family account we'd established a few weeks ago with Nick's gambling winnings. There are only so many casinos on the eastern seaboard, and he'd be banned from them all if he took any more hauls like the last. I doled those funds carefully. Our family had learned at an early age about the dark undersides of life. Even if we had to eat peanuts for dinner, we always kept an emergency stash.

  I was accustomed to long hours with no sleep. Patra had jet lag. She eventually dragged off to bed and left me to arrange an automatic fund transfer emptying Reggie's offshore account into the fake business account I'd set up a few weeks ago to catch a money launderer. Ah, the irony! I now knew how to launder my own money.

Since it was legally inherited, I wasn't hiding anything from the feds. I had to hide it from Reggie's creditors, of whom there were many, most of them unsavory.

I'd darned well let the lawyers work out inheritance taxes on embezzled funds. We now had half a mil at our disposal, although technically, it needed to be divided among all of us. I was still thinking of it as the house fund, since the house had been left to all of us, too.

I was up in the morning in time to see EG off to the alternative school we'd found for her. The school encouraged the use of iPads instead of ancient encyclopedias for research, provided a variety of resources, and satisfied EG's genius level of world knowledge. No more complaints about right-wing propaganda and textbooks that ignored Darwin. That didn't mean she didn't complain, but we'd eliminated her legitimate problem with her other schools and now merely dealt with her conjured ones.

Since Nick still hadn't put in an appearance, I refrained from mentioning his arrival before school. EG would want to stay home and have one of our celebration parties. I figured Nick would prefer to crash first.

The intercom in my office sat ominously silent when I returned to my office. As careful as I was, I had little hope of hiding anything from Graham for long.

I loved this house with its connection to a time when I'd felt secure. If Graham already knew we'd found our lawyer, he could be plotting our imminent departure. A man who had never had the human decency to come down and introduce himself was capable of anything.

I'm not much at suffering in silence, but I wanted to see Nick safely home before confronting our resident ogre about our continued residency.

Organizing my files on Broderick Media, I concluded I ought to read Patrick Llewellyn's notes in case there was anything pertinent to my project. Patra's father had worked for a legit news organization and not Broderick's sleazy tabloids, but he still might have some interesting insights into the competition.

I hesitated before opening Patra's files on my computer. Graham had access to anything I did on the Whiz, the fancy computer he'd bought for my use and networked to his. Patra hadn't given me permission to share. If I loaded her files into my non-networked Dell, I'd have to use my mobile device to follow links, and it didn't have the power of Graham's spooky satellite accessibility.

And then I realized Patra had left both the CDs and her USB drive on the table where anyone could pick them up. I wasn't convinced Graham had the ability to leave the third floor since I'd never seen him do so, but Mallard was his flunky, and our butler was home now. The old Victorian's kitchen was in the cellar, just down the hall from my office. He had a suite right next to it. With a good lock pick, he had access to my office.

As a precaution, I ran Patra's files through the Dell, verified there was nothing obviously explosive, then uploaded them to the Whiz for a more thorough investigation.

"I was wondering if you'd trust me with that information," the intercom said dryly.

This is the reason I usually turn off the machine. Admittedly, I have trust issues, but I'd conquered a few of them where Graham was concerned. He'd let us stay here when he didn't have to. He'd helped us save EG from a kidnapper. While I resented his high-handed authority, he was currently on the Good Guy side of my list—except for that owning my house business.

I sat back and began scrolling through the pages that Graham was apparently reading as we spoke. "Trust? What does trust have to do with it? They're Patra's files. Her privacy is the concern here, not your nosiness."

As usual, he ignored my snark. "Patrick Llewellyn was a brilliant man who despised Broderick. You won't be able to run your usual search on his private data. He learned coding from the British army. I'm sending you links to several databases that might help unlock the code he's using."

My eyes might have popped out of my skull except Nick chose that moment to arrive home. I could hear him singing overhead and cheerfully greeting Mallard. He'd apparently found better libations than the fresh orange juice and champagne I'd asked Mallard to have ready for him.

Since the intercom light had gone out, I assumed Graham was

done with me. I made a mad dash for the stairs. Nick was waiting for me with a big grin. Even though he was wearing grubby cut-offs and a fishy-smelling polo, I flung myself into his arms and nearly bowled him over.

We might not do affection in our family, but enthusiasm comes with the drama queen territory. He swung me around in circles until he staggered.

"That was fun. When can we do it again?" he asked, dropping me back to the floor under Mallard's unsmiling reproof.

"The staggering or the Caribbean?" I inquired.

"The catching of sniveling thieves. The bondsman you sent was a hunk and a half, thank you!" Tanned to a golden brown, with new gold highlights in his disgustingly blond hair, handsome Nick looked as if he'd been born on a yacht. Knowing Magda, maybe he had.

"I didn't think you were into blue collar hunks, but whatever works. I hope next time you go sailing, we can all go with you."

Nick shook his shaggy hair. "I've found a buyer for the *Patsy*. If I never have to sail it again, it would be too soon." He held out the front of his striped shirt with disgust. "Verify the value of the yacht, if you will. I have a cash offer of half a mil. And now I'm off to bed to sleep for a week. Or until I go back to work in the morning."

He stumbled toward the stairs, met Patra coming down, gave her a hug and an air kiss, and ascended in a cloud of *eau de poisson*. Fish and lack of dry cleaners would explain his dislike of yachting. Nick favors tuxes and delicate sauces flavored in fresh herbs with veggies. Fish that stinks isn't his forte. If he had to gut his own meals these past weeks, we'd be going on a no-seafood diet for a while.

Petra stared after our normally sartorial perfect half-sibling in astonishment. "What happened to him?"

"I'm assuming he sailed without crew to protect his prisoner. I'm sure we'll have the whole story later. Your father's files may be coded. Eat while I start looking into them."

I dashed off, trying not to gloat too much over the cool mil we'd soon have in our coffers. I, of all people, knew money corrupts. I'd much rather have the house. But it takes money to run a house like this. No mixed feelings here, no, sir.

I began sifting through Graham's code websites using various seemingly innocuous documents from Llewellyn's files. While the programs did their thing, I had time to start ticking off my to-do list.

Grandfather Max had left everything to his daughter Magda's children—which divided our funds worse than was immediately apparent. Five of us had more or less grown up together. A sixth, who would be a couple of years older than EG had he lived, had died in a fire-bombing I hadn't been able to prevent. Poor little Antony was the reason I'd gone ballistic when Magda had become pregnant with EG. We couldn't protect the kids she already had. Adding another to the menagerie had been more than my heart and soul could bear at the time.

After that, I'd sworn off all religion along with my parents' Catholicism and walked out. I eventually flew to the U.S. and hid, until EG had found me.

And now here was Patra, leading trouble straight to our doors again. All of which left me debating whether I really ought to provide the home we'd never had—or just parcel out the funds and be done with it and them.

I really wasn't liking that last idea, but I hadn't been appointed ruler of the world either. And there was still another issue that I wasn't entirely certain the others realized. As the oldest, I'd always been Magda's secret keeper, and she had more secrets than even I knew.

But I knew about the twins. They'd been born in the eight-year gap between Patra and Tudor. Patra might be too young to remember. Nick had been off getting educated in England, courtesy of his lordly father. Magda had been living in the Rand outside of Johannesburg with a South African diplomat. The twins had been adorable, more coffee colored than white, a boy and a girl. They'd been kidnapped by their father's family, and I hadn't seen them since. They'd be about twenty now, and I saw no reason they shouldn't be included in our bounty.

Magda never spoke of them, but I was betting our Mata Hari had never stopped looking for them. Magda isn't an airhead by any means. She was tenacious and she was smart and as underhanded as the devil. If the twins were alive, she'd know where, and if she hadn't gone after them, it would be because she'd decided they were better off where they were. Money might change that.

So for now, the funds would only be used to pay the lawyers for the sake of the whole family. I researched the yacht as requested, and learned Nick's offer was less than Snake Brashton had paid but a fair enough price. I should have asked Nick if he'd coerced the thief into signing over the yacht title so we didn't have to bring in cops and lawyers. My bet was on Nick's smarts, but I added the question to my list.

Then I returned to the de-coded documents on my screen. Negative. No coding found. I plugged in some more pages from different folders, and started looking for more coding programs. If Patrick Llewellyn had thought it necessary to use very obscure codes to hide his work, he'd been playing with nuclear material.

And home-burning thieves probably had lots of incentive to be hot on my sister's trail.

* * *

Patra's perspective

Patra ate the amazing breakfast Mallard laid out for her and almost forgot her agenda. Their family had a butler! And a mansion. Well, maybe they didn't own either if she listened to pessimistic Ana, but all this splendor had belonged to their *grandfather*— a man she'd thought existed only in Magda's fairy tales. They could have been living like kings all these years instead of running one step ahead of creditors or bumming off whoever was unlucky enough to invite them in. She'd like to hear the real story behind Magda's exile.

But at least the family's roller-coaster upbringing had made it possible to move in any circle and survive anywhere, which she would need to do if she were to fill her father's very large shoes. Had he finished his book on the atrocities of war, and the real reason they'd been committed, he might have single-handedly put an end to the Mideast conflicts. He certainly would have exploded a lot of erroneous patriotic beliefs.

It was too late to stop the damage already done. Her journalism degree was just a piece of paper in comparison to what she'd learned from her father.

Not that she'd ever spent a great deal of time with the late, great Patrick. He'd always been traveling. But his papers were an insight into the man she wished she'd known, and the journalist she wanted to become, so he hadn't died in vain.

To that end, Patra couldn't keep relying on her big sister for answers. She had every intention of infiltrating Broderick's insidious conglomerate and proving that it was cynically and deliberately manipulating information to achieve an agenda that looked blacker and nastier the deeper she dug into it.

She'd ace the interview with Broderick. And then the fun would begin.

Four

HEARING the ancient plumbing gurgling through the pipes over my head that afternoon, I finished up what I was working on and dashed up to the ground floor for Nick's grand entrance.

EG was home and almost bouncing with excitement by the time he sauntered downstairs after his beauty nap—which meant she was reading the encyclopedia and glancing at the stairs every three minutes. Patra had been out all day and only just returned home. She, too, looked up eagerly from her paperwork.

"What did you do with the toad?" EG demanded the instant Nick entered. "Torture him into returning our money? Are we rich? May I have my own computer now?"

Nick rolled his eyes and looked to me for help. He's not too much into family decisions. I nodded at the front door, prepared for this. "Celebration time! Get your jackets, we're going out."

Last time we had celebrated, we could only afford gelato. Not this time. This time we had *money*. I was practically dancing in my sandals.

But my main goal in going out was to keep family business in the family. That wasn't possible in the house with our omniscient landlord. My secondary goal was to give EG the kind of family experience the rest of us had never had.

I'd booked a table at a new Cajun restaurant down the street in Dupont Circle. We'd eaten Moroccan food in Casablanca and Greek food in Piraeus, so we didn't need an ethnic dining experience, but we'd had very little American cuisine. One of these days we might make it to New Orleans, but for now, this place would suffice.

The zydeco music was catchy as we walked in, and the table was as private as I'd requested. Admittedly, my siblings were dressed a little better for the occasion, but my denim skirt and T-shirt weren't all that bad. I worked in a basement and didn't need to dress for the public. Well, except now.

"Interesting choice," Nick said mockingly, scanning the menu.

"Mind if I skip the gumbo?"

"Blackened everything for you," I agreed. "Next time, you choose. We can still order champagne if you like."

"I think this is cool. I particularly like the red satin shirt." Patra nodded approvingly at a roving fiddle player with dark eyes and thick curly hair.

Nick glanced over his shoulder. "Greek, not Cajun. Met him in a bar last month," he said dismissively.

"Will you quit stalling?" EG said impatiently. "Are we rich? Can we buy our house?"

"No and no," I told her. "But we have a nice nest egg that gives us options. Let's hear Nick's story. He's the hero of the hour."

We ordered a pitcher of beer and a pitcher of non-alcoholic punch and Nick took great pleasure in regaling us with his adventures. He could have just called our thieving lawyer a drugged-up pushover and been done with it, but where was the fun in that? So over our meal we heard about Snake Reggie's wild orgy aboard the yacht that Nick had crashed. The party had ended with the crew mutineering and Reggie trussed in the hold while Nick sailed off one step ahead of the authorities. No one cared enough about Reggie to rescue him or his yacht.

"Do you think we can nail him for Max's murder?" I asked as the tale wound down. "He was the only one who could have delivered the poisoned envelopes."

A few months back we'd arrived too late to save our grandfather's life or our inheritance. We arrived in time to uncover Reggie's embezzlement, and for EG to be kidnapped by a rogue from a mysterious political cabal called Top Hat. I'd been rescued by a hunk in a tux and diamond cufflinks after I'd wiped the floor with the baddies. Reggie had been part of the mess we were still cleaning up.

Nick shrugged. "Reggie was sobbing so badly by the time I turned him in that his lawyers can probably beg him off on an insanity plea."

"He can't afford lawyers. We have our money back," I said with the satisfaction of knowing the funds were safely transferred back to our account. "He'll have to be assigned a public defender. I don't think he has any family left who cares what happens to him."

Karma paid off. Reggie had hurt a *lot* of people. It was time he paid the price.

Patra's phone tinkled, and she held up an apologetic finger as she answered. Her excitement as she talked caught our curiosity. When she hung up, we waited expectantly.

Unaccustomed to this much family interaction, she hesitated.

"Our new family motto is all for one, and one for all," I informed her.

"That's a stupid motto," EG retorted. "Who's the one and who's the all?"

But Patra had had time to consider, and she beamed obligingly. "That was Bill. He's been playing with the audio file I sent him, and he thinks he's found a match for one of the speakers already. I told him to meet us over here."

I didn't like mixing dangerous business with family, but at least she wasn't bringing her contacts home. "Try not to let your friends know where we live," I warned.

Nick and EG waited to be filled in, but it wasn't my story to tell, and Patra returned to admiring the wait staff. Annoyed, EG resorted to her best attention-getting device. "If you mean Bill Bloom, he's a loser. You won't get anything useful out of him."

"So says our very own Cassandra," Nick said, lifting his glass in toast. "Anyone into making wagers on the outcome of this charming prediction?"

"Not me." I was on to EG's pessimistic prophesies. "She's already run a dossier on all Patra's connections, and *useful* is a subjective judgment she gets to call."

"Bill's not a loser," Patra said with irritation. "He's a geek who knows more than schools can teach him. He took this project and ran with it on just the promise of payment."

Speaking as an independent contractor and someone who would have given her eyeteeth for a chance at college, I thought that spelled loser, but again, the call was subjective. I'd wait and see what he produced.

"Let's celebrate by going to the mall again," EG demanded.

Nick didn't look as interested as usual, to my relief. Weeks at sea and he'd probably arranged a hot date for the evening. Patra was looking at her watch. I hated disappointing the kid—this was a poor sort of celebration— but I despised the mall.

Tentatively, I suggested, "What if we look at Macs on-line and study what you need first?"

EG lit up like the Washington monument. "You mean it? You'll let me have my own computer? Can I have a Macbook?"

I'd known it was the Apple store she wanted at the mall. Nick and Patra looked suitably impressed that I'd pushed the right buttons. And then the hunky fiddle player strolled over, and the real celebration began.

A sumptuous repast and pitchers of ambrosia were consumed. Patra swirled between tables, learning zydeco dancing from the appreciative staff. Nick flirted with the wine steward.

A screech of tires and bloodcurdling scream abruptly blared over the racket of the accordion. I looked up from letting EG admire the new Mac desktop on my smartphone. We both glanced to the distant windows, but this was the city. Accidents happened. No one else seemed disturbed, even when sirens wailed. We went back to our own selfish concerns.

Not until the bill arrived, and Patra had returned to the table, frowning that her contact hadn't arrived as promised, did we notice the police near the entrance. We hadn't been among the diners placed on display in the front window, so we weren't of interest to the policeman currently interviewing restaurant patrons seated there.

"Would your Bill have reason to dodge the cops?" I asked uneasily as I signed off the meal on the family credit card. With our experience, the cops outside seemed the most reasonable excuse for the no-show.

"None that I know of. Let me call him before we leave." She punched his name on her phone and wrapped a colorful Pashmina around her bare shoulders, while watching the action on the street.

Other diners were starting to glance around, too. Cops inside pricey D.C. restaurants are not common. The men in blue were being circumspect, but the flashing lights outside had become obtrusive. An ambulance screamed to a halt in the middle of the street, and I was glad we'd walked. A D.C. traffic jam was a spectacle to behold.

"Maybe we should look for a rear exit?" Nick suggested, eyeing the mob gathering outside the door. "That's looking like a pickpocket's paradise out there."

My infernal nosiness really wanted to know what was

happening, but practically speaking, Nick was right.

"Ask your steward friend about an exit," I suggested. "I'll see how bad it is in front." As a family, we preferred avoiding authority. As a professional researcher, I liked having information. I lived a life of internal conflict.

I heard the persistent ring of a phone before I reached the front door.

I didn't like coincidences. My trouble alert radar clamored as I glanced back to see Patra frowning and still holding her phone to her ear. I hurried and caught sight of the street just as a policeman directing traffic located the ringing phone in a pile of leaves in the gutter.

I froze as he lifted it to his ear. If we'd been in Africa, I'd have swung around and herded my chickies out a rear entrance and into the nearest plane right about now. Self-preservation relies on strong instincts.

But this was the United States of America, and we were having an innocent family dinner. I had no reason to expect terrorist plots on our doorstep. But I knew, even before Patra's expressive features screwed up in horror, that the man she was talking to was the policeman outside. I had less than thirty seconds to decide whether we should get involved.

Graham had warned me about Patra's friends. Patra's apartment had been burgled and burnt. And that was her contact's phone at the site of a possible crime scene. One and one often equates two.

I blocked her path as she rushed toward the front door. Yanking her phone from her grip, I swung her around. "Take them out the rear exit," I warned. "Let me handle this."

The childhood habit of obedience in times of terror must have kicked in. She didn't argue but hurried back to Nick and EG, following Nick's steward friend to another exit and safety.

I hurried out in my long skirt and braids— looking small, wide-eyed, and innocuous—to meet the policeman waiting for Patra. "What's wrong?" I asked anxiously, not having to work too hard at appearing worried. "Where's Mr. Bloom? Why do you have his phone?"

Three cop cars and an ambulance blocked the street. I knew the news wasn't good. I was too short to see past the crowd and the medics crowding around a stretcher, so I focused on the officer who was stepping up to replace the traffic cop.

"I'm Sergeant Cobb, miss. Your name?"

If the phone was Bill's, he'd have Patra's name in it. I took a chance. "Llewellyn," I replied, looking more anxious and straining to see the ambulance. "I was supposed to meet Mr. Bloom here. Why did you answer his phone?"

"How well did you know Mr. Bloom?" the sergeant asked, still not answering my questions.

"Not at all." That wasn't lying. "He was to meet me here about some speech work I'd requested. Why?" This time I focused on the cop and donned my suspicious expression.

"Would you be able to identify him?"

There it was, the news I didn't want to hear. But I maintained my impatient business mode. "Of course not. I've only spoken to him on the phone." I should be an actress. I opened my eyes wide as if I'd just understood his implication and asked in horror, "Oh, you don't mean... Has he been in an accident?"

"Hit and run. Your name and address?" The sergeant had his notebook out.

I didn't want my family dragged into whatever Patra was doing, and Graham would most definitely go ballistic if the police started invading his private hideaway. The authorities needed to believe this was just an accident, even if I thought otherwise.

"Oh, my." I held a hand to my heart as if I might pass out any minute. "How is he? Where are they taking him? This is terrible! We just spoke. He said he was running late, and oh my..."

Don't get the wrong idea. I detest dramatics, but I'd grown up with drama queens. At this point, Magda would faint, and some striking gentleman would rush up to carry her away. I refused to faint, and I had no striking gentleman in my ballpark, although now that I thought about it, we weren't too far from Mallard's favorite pub where a certain reporter hung out.

I glanced up, and sure enough, there was Sean O'Herlihy, God's gift to the Irish and snoopier than I am. While I can admire his curly-haired good looks, I had no desire to be carried off in his arms. He was just ever too conveniently around when I didn't need him.

"I'm sorry, Miss Llewellyn," the officer said sympathetically. I must have looked appropriately pale—not difficult since I seldom see the sun. "Mr. Bloom apparently jaywalked across a busy street. In these cases, it's often a drunk who hasn't the reflexes to stop quickly and flees for fear of being charged with driving under the influence."

I didn't agree. This narrow road was packed with traffic all night long. No way could anyone speed or flee while drunk. It would take impeccable timing and an oddly convenient opening to build up enough speed to kill, and then get away. I concealed a shudder. What had Patra got herself into?

"Oh, dear, oh, dear," I managed to gasp. "Did anyone catch a license plate or describe the car? His poor family! I'm so sorry." I had to slip away before he asked my address again, but I'd rather collect information now than hack it from computers later.

Sean was pushing his way through the throng. I wasn't in a mood for explaining Patra or her problems.

"We have partial plates and a description. We'll find him," the officer said confidently. "Now if—"

No, they wouldn't. My bet was that the car had already been reported stolen. Just call me cynical. I interrupted his request. "This is dreadful. I'm feeling faint. I have a small heart problem…" I held my hand to my chest. "I need a glass of water."

I retreated into the restaurant and out the back exit. I had a notion it was time to circle the wagons around Patra.

Five

MY FAMILY had scampered for home, leaving me to deal with the cops, then find my own way back alone. Since I'd been known to maim armed bandits with my feet, this wasn't carelessness on their part.

I circled the block first, keeping an eye out for loiterers or other suspicious characters. Our Victorian home has a lovely landscaped backyard with a wall around it. A sprawling carriage-house-like structure surrounded by a security fence occupied the lot behind the wall, providing additional protection beyond Graham's security cameras.

Not detecting anyone more dangerous than the drug dealers on the corner, I slipped down into the basement entrance, then upstairs into the antique-furnished fortress I called home. I adored the scent of wax and flowers that always greeted me. After years of living in musty basements and malodorous tents and tenements, I wanted this place just for the aroma.

Nick and EG were nonchalantly playing chess in the front room. They didn't fool me. They hated chess. Patra was nowhere in sight, and she was the one I needed to talk to.

"Is Patra in her room?" I demanded from the doorway.

"What happened?" EG asked. She's still young enough to be straightforward and blunt.

"Hit and run, drunken driver." I didn't want her involved in the family business. But I wasn't giving her any fairy tales either.

Nick frowned, but maybe he was learning a few maternal instincts because he didn't argue. "Patra said she had to go out. I gave her my phone since you have hers."

Crap. In our earlier days, when Magda was still finding her feet, Nick and I had to learn self-defense the hard way. Our younger siblings, on the other hand, had grown up with the security of nannies and bodyguards. Patra was naive enough to think the guys on the corner were hanging out, looking for girls.

EG, unfortunately, was much too perceptive. I didn't want her seeing how worried I was. I nodded in recognition of Nick's generosity in loaning his phone. I transferred family numbers from my new toy to the one Patra had given me, and handed Nick my phone so he could hit the streets or whatever he had planned for the evening. I called Nick's phone as I headed for my office.

Patra answered instantly. "How is he?"

One thing about my family, we didn't waste time with niceties like polite greetings. "Dead. The cops think a drunk. I'm not buying it. Get your rear back here before you end up the same way."

"Why not a drunk?" she asked defensively.

"Let me count the ways—after you haul your tail back here." I shut her down and turned off the phone. If she was out playing kissy face with a waiter, I was heaving her out. I was *not* assuming the role of mother hen again.

I unlocked my office, turned on the Whiz, and checked my email. Only my immediate family had my phone number so I never had voice mail. Since leaving Magda and my siblings behind, I'd narrowed my world to a computer monitor. EG's arrival was changing that, but not completely. I had access to the entire planet at my fingertips, so I wasn't lonely.

No work orders from Graham awaited. Only a few documents from my researchers. I started sneezing half way through my mail. By the time I'd read it all, my eyes were streaming. Confound it, Graham knew not to let his damned cat loose.

I could never figure out how the creature got through locked doors. Maybe this was our host's idea of revenge for the bats. I'd have to hunt for allergy pills. As I stood up, my usual sensitivity to my environment belatedly checked in. I'd felt safe in my basement hideaway and didn't usually bother with extra precautions. But something was wrong.

It took me a minute of careful analysis of what was on my work table now and what had been there when I'd left, but I worked it out—Patra's DVD was no longer in the stack of library microfiche where I'd stuck it.

I'm pretty good at two and two, even if there's a big old minus in between like how a man who never leaves the third floor had broken through my locked barriers and how a cat with no opposable thumb had opened doors. I saw no reason to beat the walls hunting for hidden elevators and secret passages when I could simply go straight to the source.

The problem, of course, was that we were here on Graham's charity. He claimed he owed our grandfather a lot, and as long as I helped his research in lieu of rent, he'd tolerate us. But until we could buy the house back, we were one temper tantrum short of the door.

Most of the time, that kept my fury and frustration from pushing him out a window. Oh, and the fabulous gym on the third floor really helped me express my hostilities. But cats, theft, and chicanery breeched all my barriers. I was in need of a face-to-face showdown with the sneaky bastard.

I'd installed Patra's information on the computer so Graham could see it. He had no good reason to steal the disk. Or send Mallard to steal it. I marched back up the stairs and noted Nick had already departed. EG was in my study, on the laptop, and I ordered her to bed.

"There's still a bat in my room," she said, looking for a way around my orders.

"Then don't expect Mallard to clean your room until it's gone. It's a school night. You're going to bed." Because of her brain, it's hard to think of EG as a child, but nine-year-olds need their sleep. I watched her drag to her room at the end of the hall. Once she closed the door, I continued up to the next floor.

I wasn't sneezing anymore. In my mood, I took that to mean the cat hadn't come down by way of the main staircase. Somewhere, the house had hidden stairs—which would explain a lot.

Graham's office door was open. He'd been expecting me. I stopped in the doorway to let my eyes adjust to the darkened room lined with wall-to-wall computer monitors.

The screen Graham sat in front of displayed grainy video footage from the street outside the Cajun restaurant. I'd have admired his ingenuity if I hadn't wanted to bash him over his handsome head. I'd never seen him out of his chair, so I tended to think of Graham in terms of Christopher Reeve, the broken Superman, with his dark hair, massive shoulders, and strong, cleft jaw. But Graham wasn't a patient, kind-hearted Superman by any means.

"They set up a roadblock at the intersection," he said without preamble. He scrolled the grainy footage backward to show a Hummer stalled in a turn beneath a stoplight, blocking the one-way street in front of the restaurant.

He expected me to know what he was talking about without explanation. He knew me too well. The appalling video drew me in like a crocodile to water. Instead of dumping fish guts over his head, I edged closer, straining to make out details. "How did you get this? Do the police have it?"

"Of course not," he said impatiently. "They're looking for a drunk driving a black Cadillac."

The aforesaid black Cadillac sedan appeared down a side street, lingering at a stop sign until a chubby, long-haired male in jeans took advantage of the temporary break in traffic to jaywalk in front of the restaurant. At which point the sedan accelerated from zero to sixty in race car seconds.

"How could they humanly plot this?" I asked. "It couldn't have been more than an hour between the time Patra told him where we were and the accident."

"The *murder*," he corrected. We watched the sedan ram the chubby geek, flinging him into painful backflips like a broken doll. As he crumpled to the blacktop, the Caddy vanished down a different side street. The Hummer miraculously came unstalled and rumbled off out of sight of the camera. The pent up traffic at the intersection didn't have time to get up to speed before screeching to a halt near the bloody victim. At least they hadn't run over the body a second time. Graham halted the footage as Good Samaritans ran to the victim's aid. "I suggest you ship your sister back to the BBC."

I didn't ask a second time where he'd stolen the video. He never revealed his sources. I'd learned he was former CIA with presidential affiliations, so he could have taken it from spy satellites for all I knew. Although hacking a security company's cameras was more likely. "I need a copy of this to show her."

"Would you return to England after seeing this?" he asked dryly.

He had a point. It didn't matter. "Patra deserves the truth. She needs to know what she's up against. It took one impressive organization to pull together an operation like that so swiftly. How could they have known Bill was on to anything? We need to search his office to find out what he learned."

He clicked the screen one shot forward. The Good Samaritan was rifling Bill's pockets.

"Crap," I muttered. "They have his evidence, address, and keys to clear out any backup. I repeat, what kind of organization is this well prepared? Besides you," I added snidely.

"Top Hat."

Had I not known better, I could have taken this as an enigmatic brush-off and crowned him with his keyboard. But *Top Hat* was burned into my synapses. My grandfather had been allegedly poisoned by a mysterious cabal of power brokers that called themselves by the code name Top Hat. *Allegedly* being the key word here. We had nothing but my grandfather's last message to me and the admission of a scam artist murderer to base our theories on.

I tried out-waiting him in hopes my silence would force him to say more. Stupid ploy, but it gave me a chance to process a few facts.

When Graham continued playing his computers as if I weren't there, I pushed harder. "Broderick is part of Top Hat, isn't he? He's a Brit, but his media network over here supports Senator Paul Rose." As did the senators behind the now-defunct textbook propaganda scheme. Everyone in politics has an agenda. My agenda was to steer well clear of megalomaniacs who think they can rule the world. They inevitably cause a lot of grief and come to a bad end. The world is seldom improved in the process.

If I had believed in the devil, I'd have made him a politician.

"Send your sister home," was all Graham said.

"Stay out of my office," was my retort. "You had no right to steal her DVD. And if that blamed cat gets near me again, I'll start ripping out walls to find your sneaky passage."

He gave me a middle finger salute, hit his keyboard, and zoomed in on some Mideast carnage.

Really, if I wasn't worried that he might actually be a cripple, I'd turn Graham over in his chair.

If he hadn't smelled so damned good, I might have lingered to torment him more. The sad fact was that Graham tortured my hormones as much as he messed with my mind. I really should have returned the favor. Oh, wait, I already had. I was just too lazy to dress up to do it often.

I stalked out in no better mood than I had arrived, but with vital information in exchange for the stolen disk. Graham had weird ideas of fair trade, but at some base level, we understood each other. A very base level. You will notice we did not discuss anything normal like the million dollars and the lawsuit pending to get our house back.

Patra still wasn't home. I vowed to learn to track GPS chips in phones.

* * *

Patra's perspective

Patra was standing outside Bill Bloom's apartment, watching a thug systematically work the place over. She had a cozy dark corner of the doorway across the street and one of the best zoom lens cameras on the market. Every time the thug passed Bill's curtainless front window, she snapped. She'd called 911 and reported a burglary in progress. She needed to make friends with someone on the force. She wanted inside that apartment. Only she knew what her father's enemies sounded like or what to look for. The cops sure as hell wouldn't.

A long black Escalade limo pulled up to the curb in front of her. Patra realized the drawback of her hiding place immediately. The door behind her was locked. She had no escape.

Six

WHEN Patra didn't return as ordered, I had no choice but to hack into Graham's GPS network and track Nick's phone. The coordinates led me to the address I'd already ascertained as Bill Bloom's. Stupid idiot. That was the first place the bad guys would look. If Patra persisted in this investigative nonsense—and in our family, it's really hard to avoid—she would have to learn a few basics.

I changed into black leggings and knee high boots—better for kicking than sandals—and grabbed a Metro to the exit nearest Bloom's crappy tenement. His neighborhood was quite a few Metro stops from ours, but a taxi would have made me a rich target.

Flashing cop strobes caught me as I rounded the corner to Bloom's front door. I picked up my pace. I didn't want to find any more abandoned phones in the gutter, especially not my sister's. I was counting on this being a different precinct and a different set of cops, but if anyone started putting together the hit-and-run with this address, we'd have officialdom breathing down our necks.

At this point, I was more concerned about Patra.

I breathed easier when I saw her leaning against the building, chatting with a familiar figure. Damn O'Herlihy. He either had a Sir Galahad complex when it came to our family, or he thought he would learn more about Graham by spying on us.

"Graham is still off topic," I told Sean before he could speak. I turned to Patra, biting back my big-sisterly fear, and sticking to business. "Unless you have a way into that apartment, you should not be here."

"I could have got in, but someone beat me here," Patra protested.

"And then she had a run-in with a limo until the cops ran them off. Are you going to introduce us?" Sean asked with interest.

My eyebrows reached my hairline as I swung on Patra and ignored the nosy reporter. "What kind of limo and what did they do?"

"Black Escalade, tinted windows, very men-in-black. They blocked me from taking photos, grabbed my camera, and then the cops showed up, and they moved on. I have a partial license plate number. The street light isn't working so I couldn't get more. The guy who took my camera looked more like a hired thug than government, though— bald, massive, over forty, wearing a shiny suit. If I see him again, I'm picking his pocket. That camera costs."

"You really need to keep a better eye on your siblings," Sean interrupted, wearing an impressive frown. "She's too young to be running around DC alone. I assume from her accent that she's not local."

I swung back to the critic. Behind me, Patra choked on a laugh. I'm just too predictable, but nobody criticizes my family except me. "Patra has robbed thieves in Singapore and driven elephants in India. DC is not the problem. Patra's imitation of her damnable father is the problem. Are you covering burglary reports these days? Bit of a come down from political reporting, isn't it?"

"I got hired at the BBC because I don't have an accent," Patra protested, interrupting my rhetorical and irrelevant question. "All those years of traveling wiped it out. Anyway, nosy here followed me from Dupont. I figured he was a cop, he was so bad at it."

Sean shrugged, leaned back against the brick wall, and followed the activities across the street. "I had no reason to hide."

Single-minded Patra ignored this. "Do either of you know anyone on the force? I really need to see inside Bill's apartment. He might have left notes about my father's recording. I need to know what he was so excited about."

Moral judgments did not happen in my world. I let the slippery slope of breaking and entering slide by and returned to the practical. "Catch anything with the camera phone?" I didn't think Patra would miss any opportunity, and Nick's phone was a dandy.

"Probably not much," she said, confirming my suspicion. "Look, I really need to get inside. Any suggestions?"

With a sigh of exasperation, I answered her plea by morphing from Basement Mouse into Kickass Ana.

Keeping an eye out for familiar faces I needed to dodge, I crossed the street and took the stairs up to where all the activity was. I didn't like it. If the beat cops had learned the apartment owner had just been killed, I was opening a can of worms.

Conversely, if dangerous thugs were on Patra's heels, I needed to know everything.

Four apartments to a floor, I noted as I emerged on the third where two men in blue were scribbling notes. "Hello, officers," I said, swinging my legging-clad hips as I noted door numbers and located Bill's. Patra and Sean were right on my boot heels. "Neighbors been beating up on each other again?" I reached for Bill's doorknob as if I belonged there. We were in luck, the door hadn't been shut.

"Wait a minute," one of the officers looked up from his note-taking, "That your place?"

"Of course not. Have you seen inside that dump? We're just here to help Sean shovel out his stuff. Why?" I donned my best puzzled innocent expression as I pushed open the door and scoped a glance. The apartment had been trashed, as feared.

"We had a burglary report, found the place unlocked." The note taker held up his pad while the other cop tried to block our access. "You got any ID?"

"I don't know what good it will do you." I rummaged in my bag. "I don't live here. Hey, sis, what did you do with my wallet?" I called as Patra sauntered past the cops.

"In the car," she replied blithely, pushing the door open wider and grimacing at the contents. "I borrowed your Amex. Where are the garbage bags?"

"Shoot." I handed the policeman a business card with my mailbox drop address and my fake schoolteacher ID. "Will this do? You think Bill's place was burgled? How could anyone tell? These guys live like bums."

"Does he always leave the place unlocked?" The cop noted my fake name and address. I might have to think about changing them.

"We only have the one key. Sean, didn't you lock up after that last load?" I obligingly lingered in the hall entertaining the officers while Sean and Patra did a quick reconnoiter inside.

"I thought I did," Sean called back, emerging from the kitchen area with a box of trash bags.

That was good—loading up the burglary bags while the cops watched. Sean's father had been friends with my father—both good Irish IRA lads. Family experience made him about as trustworthy as

I was, which wasn't much.

"I don't see anything missing," he continued. "TV is still there."

"You didn't see anyone in the apartment?" I asked the policemen with mild alarm. "Not that there's anything worth taking except the computer, but we'd hate for Bill to blame us."

"No one here when we arrived." The note taker put away his book. "Show me a key and we'll be on our way. Next time, make sure you lock up."

"Sean, where's your key?" I peered around the door to see Patra sweep a stack of disks into her purse. I could see a couple of computer monitors, but not the hard drives.

"Right here." Absent-mindedly patting his jeans pocket, Sean emerged from the bedroom with a stack of file folders under his arm. "I can't find my good shirt. I know I left it here. If that butthead took it with him..." He dumped the folders in a garbage bag, then dug a ring of keys out of his pocket.

"Then he's wearing a shirt two sizes too small," I said, playing along and taking the keys from him.

One of the officers was already taking another call while the note taker waited impatiently for me to sort through keys. "All these things look alike. Which one is it?" I shouted back at Sean as he meandered off.

"Domestic dispute around the corner," the officer taking the call reported. "Anyone here filing a complaint?"

The note taker looked impatient. "Look, all of you, get out, take your keys, and I'll close this place up. If you don't see anything taken and don't want to file a report, we'll be moving on."

"Anything missing?" I yelled at my looters. "If not, get thyselves out here and find the damned key."

Patra and Sean ambled back to the hall, arguing over the key ring as the cops turned the flimsy inside lock, shut the door, and hurried off on their next call.

"You're good," I commended them with reluctance. I'd never had partners in crime before, unless Nick counted, and he tended to do his own thing. "Did you find what you needed or do we have to get back in there?"

Sean handed his garbage bag of files to Patra. "Computers are gone. These are the only recent files I found. What are we looking for?"

"Skullduggery," Patra blithely answered. "You're a good person to know." She pressed a kiss on Sean's cheek and swung off down the hall toward the stairs.

Sean raised questioning eyebrows at me.

"Patrick Llewellyn's daughter, and that's all I'm telling you." I hurried after her.

Behind us, Sean whistled. As a journalist, he knew precisely what I'd just told him, and could infer the rest. I expected he'd spend the rest of the evening learning who owned this apartment and would be three steps ahead of the overworked cops before dawn.

* * *

"Do you have dibs on him?" Patra asked as we emerged from the Metro down the block from our grandfather's home.

"Who, Sean? He's occasionally helpful, but I don't trust him. He's spying on Graham. I'm not risking irritating the beast in our attic for a nosy reporter." Carrying the trash bag of paper files, I unlocked the now spider-web-free front door and made a mental note to have a key made for Patra.

"You're awfully protective of that beast in the attic," she observed with interest.

"I have issues, okay? I protect what's mine and so does he. Move on." I gestured for her to go in.

"Sean's cute," she said, changing back to her real interest, "and he might be able to help me find my way around the local talent. You don't mind if I use him, do you?"

"You sound just like Magda. *Tell* Sean you're using him and don't go giving him ideas. Let's pretend we've learned our lesson." I handed over the bag and aimed for my hideaway.

"I think if he's using us, he knows the score," she called after me. "And thanks for hunting me down."

"It would be easier if you'd tell me where you're going," I muttered back, but she knew that. Then I stopped and nodded at her bag. "Let me know if there's anything on those disks?"

She grinned and hefted her stolen goods more tightly under her arm. "Will do. That was a pretty good caper."

"I refuse to bail you out if you repeat it," an irritable male voice growled from the chandelier.

I waved at the camera in the cornice. "Same to you, lover."

That shut him up. I do love Graham's thunderous silences.

We didn't *need* Graham's bail money, I realized. We had our own little nest egg. I liked having that cushion of cash to fall back on.

I trotted downstairs to finish up a few projects I'd left hanging. I needed to start a separate file on Broderick Media as related to my family. Would BM actually offer the daughter of Patrick Llewellyn a job or had they lured her here so that arsonists could destroy the rest of her father's notes? Not that I was jumping to conclusions, mind you. Cough.

The Bill Bloom incident had compounded my wariness. I booted up the computer and remembered to turn my phone back on. *Patra's* phone. Dang, I'd have to run upstairs and trade with her.

Even as I read the message on the screen, I heard her racing back down the stairs. Nick had texted both of us.

YACHT BLEW UP.

Our yacht blew up! I almost cried at the stupid message. I wanted to put my chin up and say *easy come, easy go*, as I would have in the past. But Nick had risked his life going after Reggie to salvage that damned thing, and my heart broke with his.

At least Nick had been alive to let us know, which meant he hadn't been aboard, but probably nearby. I ran upstairs punching in a message and met Patra in the foyer.

"What does he mean?" Patra shoved my phone at me. I handed hers back after I sent a reply into cyberland.

"Unless we've forged insurance papers as well as titles, it means we're out half a million dollars and someone doesn't like us very much," I said, my hopes dashed lower than my cellar floor.

I couldn't tell if it was gloom or triumph emanating from the spider in the attic. I could be enslaved to him forever, or out on my ear tomorrow. If I didn't have to trust the man, I'd suspect he'd planted the bomb himself.

Seven

TRAGEDY had haunted my life so long that I knew the best remedy was to return to work rather than weep or rage over what couldn't be changed—no matter how much I wanted to fling myself on the floor and throw a tantrum to end all tantrums.

The last time I'd been this furious and heart-broken, I'd walked out on my family and disappeared for years. I liked to think I was older and wiser now.

With resignation, I climbed up to my room while flipping through the phone photos Patra had taken. I found nothing more elevating than the rear end of a black Escalade. It had been a sedan that ran over Bill. I had no evidence other than common sense to prove it was the same people.

I didn't sleep well that night. Dreams of providing cozy houses/trailers/tents for all my siblings kept exploding into fire and ash. I'm sure the dreams weren't that explicit but my memory of them the next morning was Freudian enough. I was getting soft. I should have been forging fraudulent insurance papers before Nick returned.

But I'd stupidly hoped I could provide an honorable example of good citizenry and its rewards to the rest of my family. Stupid, stupid, stupid. We all grew up understanding that the rest of the world lacked integrity and the best liar won.

Nick was at the breakfast table looking as haggard as I felt. He glanced up with shadowed eyes, shoved a file folder at me, and returned to inhaling Mallard's mean cappuccino.

I sipped fresh-squeezed orange juice, thinking maybe slavery wasn't too awful if I could always be fed like this. Flipping open the file, I perused the yacht title signed over to us. Brashton was a lawyer, after all, and knew how to handle these things even coked out of his little mind. The insurance and assorted other documents were all still in the name of Reginald Brashton. He'd insured the *Patsy* for the same amount as he'd paid, which was more than we'd been offered. If he collected the insurance, he could hire lawyers and get out of jail free.

"What happened?" I asked with a hint of grimness, fighting my Magda tendencies to call in neutron bombs.

"The cops believe Reggie was transporting drugs and his suppliers blew it up in retaliation for their losses." Nick gloomily poked at his Canadian bacon.

"Feasible, if he wasn't profiting from the loss, which he will be. Maybe drug dealers are too stupid to know about insurance. Your thoughts?"

"Same as yours," he said with a morose sigh. "Either Reggie learned how to make bombs from jail—or someone didn't want us to sell the yacht."

Since we were living in the house of one of those someone's, who could hear everything we said through the bugged candelabra, we didn't attempt guessing the names of our enemies. They were undoubtedly legion, but my money would be on current enemies and not the sheiks and KGB agents we'd tweaked in our childhoods.

I tried to fit Broderick Media and Patra into the picture, but it wasn't happening. Yet.

"Talk to Oppenheimer," I concluded, naming the lawyer who was suing Reggie's old law firm over our embezzled inheritance. "Since the yacht was purchased with stolen funds, maybe he can make a case that the insurance proceeds belong to us."

Which probably meant an interminable court fight in which we'd come out with a pittance at best, but we were constitutionally incapable of doing nothing.

Nick brightened a little at having something to do, which proved my point. Had we been trained to politics à la the Kennedy dynasty, we'd be on our way to running the world by now. Magda had reasonably avoided her father's political machinations by removing us from temptation. She couldn't change our genes, unfortunately.

I heard EG on the stairs, so I switched topics. "How's Senator Tex doing now that he's a lame duck?"

Nick worked for EG's senator father, who'd been outed as not exactly a family values candidate after he'd acknowledged EG's existence. He had been married and already had a kid when he and Magda had their impetuous fling.

"Tex is pushing his own agenda, which won't go anywhere without the power of his cronies behind him," Nick said with a shrug. "I think he's planning on staying in D.C. with one of the local law firms when his term ends, so EG will still have a daddy. I'm not sure he quite grasps my orientation yet, so I'm lying low while keeping my eyes open for a safer position. Wonder what it takes to get on an ambassadorial staff?"

"Knowing an ambassador?" I suggested as EG slid into her seat. "You mean you want to return to roaming the world instead of lounging in our little corner of paradise?" I had to ask. I hated the idea of taking full responsibility for EG turning out normal.

"I meant like getting on the Brit staff here. I have dual citizenship."

"I like that thought," I said, immediately feeling more cheerful. "Let's research current staff and see who we know. Can you talk to your dad about your desire to be a humble civil servant? I'm betting he'll be happy to help. Beats gambling for a living."

Nick shrugged. While Nick's dad had paid for his bastard son's education, Lord Terence Arbuthnot didn't like acknowledging his youthful indiscretions. He'd ditched Magda so long ago that even I didn't remember him, but he and Nick checked in with each other every few years. I had no idea if their relationship included calling in favors.

"I want the MacBook Pro," EG announced into the silence.

"You have an iPad. You don't need another portable device. Look at the low end iMacs. I want it out where I can see what you're doing." I'd promised her the computer when I'd thought we were millionaires. I couldn't renege on my promise now that I was feeling cranky and less generous.

"I'm not a baby," she argued. "You don't need to watch over my shoulder."

I gave her the old gimlet eye. She'd gotten herself kidnapped a few weeks back by emailing the universe of evil. Guiltily, she went back to crunching cereal.

Patra clattered down next, wearing what might be called a power red suit, except the skirt was about a foot too short for professional. I'm a lousy judge of style, but human nature I understand. Patra was not sending the message she ought to be if that was for her Broderick Media interview.

"They're hiring hookers?" Nick asked for me. Since he's our family arbiter of fashion, his words spoke louder than mine.

"I'm getting that job," she said, throwing her portfolio on the table. "I'm not an idiot, okay?" she said defiantly at our incredulous looks. "But if Bill died for me, I owe him the respect of finding out why."

The three of us familiar with the Power of the Candelabra waited expectantly for Graham's opinion of that news. The silver remained oddly silent. Or ominously, as the case might be.

I raised my eyebrows and shrugged. "Are you sure the people interviewing you are men?"

Patra sent me a look of scorn. "It's Broderick. What do you think?"

"Point taken, although it's a point against working for the sexist pigs."

"If Broderick had his way, women would be barefoot and pregnant and never seen in public. Al Qaeda has nothing on him. I'm going for the modern harem girl look." Patra admired the platters of eggs on the buffet and helped herself to a healthy portion of everything in sight.

"Magda," Nick and I said in unison.

Patra slid into her seat and unfolded her linen napkin. "Whatever works," she agreed. "If men are too stupid to change, why should women, when we have them by the..." She threw EG a look and cut off that particular Magda-ism. "I know what I'm doing."

"I doubt it." The candelabra finally spoke.

Patra's fork fell out of her hand. She hastily chased it under the table.

"But if you insist on emulating your notorious mother," Graham continued in that deep voice that always rattled my gonads, "at least go in with a knowledge of the power brokers and questions only they can answer. Ask Ana for the document."

The speaker gave that infinitesimal click that said it had gone dead again. The Wizard had turned to other interests.

"If I land this job, I'm hunting for an apartment," Patra announced, taking a clean fork from the buffet. "I don't know how you live with that nut job."

Nick and I smirked. Just let her find an apartment with a better location and amenities than this place. On a reporter's salary, she'd be lucky to find a leaky cellar and live off ramen noodles.

"And welcome to slavery, twenty-first century style," I said. We could move out anytime we liked. I just refused to do so.

I got up and ran downstairs to see what Graham's nocturnal messages had delivered to my office.

Flipping on the Whiz, I printed out a document that had appeared overnight in Graham's networked folder on Broderick Media, not my private one on my personal computer.

Before taking anything to Patra, I skimmed down the sheet. I recognized half his list of names as stockholders and upper management at BM. Further down the list was local editorial staff for the Washington edition of the newspaper, which was pretty much the same personnel for the local broadcast station. Congress had severely limited the objectivity of the fourth estate when they'd allowed media conglomerates to buy up all the journalistic real estate in major cities.

Graham had added lovely touches like "Ted Tuttle, married with a Vietnamese manicurist mistress," and "Bernard Black, silent partner in Virginia casino." He didn't have to add *No Jews, Muslims, or people of color*. Not a Cohen or Jabal on the list. And as expected, only two females, pretty far down the tree. Broderick had worked hard to earn his reputation as a crooked, conservative, sexist bigot loved by all for his money and power.

At the end, Graham had appended suggestions. *For Patra's consideration: determine if wire-tapping, cell phone surveillance, and hacking still encouraged. Ask if Paul Rose is still a favored candidate and indicate your enthusiasm. Mention your involvement with the Righteous and Proud and ask if they'd be interested in human interest stories on members.*

Broderick Media was the official mouthpiece for the stick-up-their-ass Righteous and Proud. Graham might as well tell her to join Al Qaeda for White People. I crumpled up the suggestions and flung them at the wastebasket before whacking the intercom keys. "I am not involving my sister in your paranoid conspiracy theories."

"Then send her home," he grumbled.

He knew perfectly well I wouldn't do that, no matter how much I'd like to consider it.

* * *

With all my chickies out of the house, I settled down to my own work, but disentangling the corporate web around Broderick Media did not hold the personal appeal of learning what might have got poor Bill Bloom killed.

Let me make this perfectly clear—I am not a sleuth, not of the detective/trained investigator sort. I'm a hired researcher, yes, a virtual assistant with international connections, but not a cop. Just think of me as a rat terrier who sinks her teeth in and keeps shaking until something useful falls out.

Bill Bloom was my starting place, if only because he'd told Patra he had information just before he died. I needed his telephone records. Logic said if that information had got him killed, then he must have told someone about it besides Patra.

I could have eventually cracked police files, but why bother when Graham's extensive spy network could go directly to the phone company? And probably already had. I shuffled through our networked computer files and found the records without tapping anyone. Graham had been snooping and had left the results where I could find them, should I look. The spook was always testing me.

Not knowing exactly when Bill had identified any of the voices, which is what he'd said he'd done, I arbitrarily chose the entire day of his death. Bill had been a busy little beaver that day. The day prior hadn't been quite as active. Using the reverse directory, I determined that he'd made three calls to a Carol Bloom—his mother, if last name and gender were any indication. His on-line statistics had revealed he wasn't married, and until recently he'd lived with Carol Bloom at the address for that number. Carol was old enough to be his mother since she'd owned that house for decades.

Moving on… He called his dentist, two men who were listed as friends on his limited Facebook profile, three companies who might be clients, a female name not listed on Facebook— and just about every media outlet in the city.

Looked like Bill had been doing a little investigating of his own. On the assumption that he was looking for comparison voice clips and not giving out secrets, I focused on his last call—a local independent news website that called itself Intrepid News.

I scrolled through the website to be certain they didn't have any late breaking news about Patra's tape or anything relevant, but they hadn't even reported Bill's death. Apparently uninhibited by advertisers, the on-line rag played a pretty heavy left wing game.

If I was political, I'd probably call myself liberal because I'd lived in countries where men can legally kill women as if they were roaches, and that kind of chauvinism scared the heck out of me. I didn't want anyone dictating what I could do as a female, particularly not narrow-minded sexist morons—which was how I identified conservatives, since I'd never had money and knew nothing about the economy.

The liberal website Bill had phoned seemed quite gleeful in pointing out any laughable faux pas of the conservatives. They'd even caught a clip of a leader in the R&P movement stating that our founding fathers were all good Christian men. Check that out on Google some time. Even with my limited education, I knew better. Half the men signing the Declaration of Independence didn't belong to churches, and the better known among them called themselves Deists, intelligently disassociating themselves from the religious turmoil of the old countries they'd fled. The only thing those good old boys had in common with the R&P were that they were white and male.

I found the Intrepid News phone number and called but only got voice mail. I left a message letting them know of Bill Bloom's death, in case anyone was interested, then asked for a return call at a number I could pick up on my computer. Fiber optic was my friend.

Then, overcoming my scruples about snooping through my sister's room, I ran upstairs to locate the files Patra had lifted from Bill's apartment.

Eight

Patra's perspective

PATRA cruised past Broderick Media's lobby security with the free pass of an appointment with executive vice-president David Smedbetter. She recognized the name from her father's papers. Broderick liked to hire ex-military men, and Smedbetter had once been in the army.

His office confirmed her interview, and she was directed to the third floor.

The reception area she entered from the elevator featured a world map with out-sized pins indicating headquarters in every English-speaking country and smaller pins for bureaus with foreign correspondents. An enormous vase of artificial flowers occupied the coffee table by the area's one sofa. The dust on the flowers suggested that they had been there since the office's initial opening.

Patra smiled confidently and refused to take a seat as directed. She was impatient to have this interview over, and an annoyed receptionist would get rid of her sooner than later. Pacing the lobby, Patra admired each and every ancient photo, the trophy display, and the dusty flowers again. A bespectacled male wandered in and nearly tripped while ogling her legs. Word spread quickly, and the lobby turned into a busy intersection, until the receptionist nagged someone into removing her. Patra bit back her grin of triumph.

She ought to be ashamed of her sexist tactics, but she was entering a world that only saw a woman's body and feared her intelligence, so she merely gave them what they wanted. Ana might think she was a spoiled little college girl, but Ana hadn't been around when Patra had started touring the media outlets in every country Magda dragged her through. She knew damned well what was what.

Following a beauty queen secretary through institutional

corridors, Patra smiled at heads lifting from cubicles and offices along the way. She counted two women in the cubicle farm, none in the offices.

The secretary left her with a Human Resources drone, who had her fill out enough forms to complete Wikipedia. Half way through, an executive assistant arrived to tow her to Smedbetter's office. Patra sat in another reception area occupied by still another secretary while she finished filling out her forms. Just as she was wondering if she ought to invent a few more addresses for her nomadic teen years, the secretary signaled that the Great Man would see her.

Smedbetter hadn't given up his Army background. With military-buzzed iron gray hair and bull-like shoulders, he looked like he had a steel pipe up his spine. He studied her with a vague air of suspicion when she entered, but her skirt must have done its trick. He picked up her application and took his time examining it.

She tried not to yawn while he inquired, in a boring monotone, about her education and experience. She began swinging her leg impatiently by the time he reached her BBC credentials. He glanced over his reading glasses occasionally, so he wasn't oblivious to her looks. Finally, she decided it was time to take the bull by the horns.

"The BBC is a great place," she acknowledged with a dismissive wave, "but it's so my daddy's kind of place, you know? They're still analyzing wars and bombs when everyone knows the real battlefield is socio-economic. Corner the oil market, and you win. I really want to work with an organization that understands this."

Smedbetter scowled and raised his graying eyebrows. "You have extensive experience in foreign countries."

"Naturally. My father was a foreign correspondent." Who hadn't taken her with him anywhere, but impressions were everything. "I have international contacts, but I was hoping for an assignment in the states for a while, because this is where the action is."

Smedbetter's phone rang, and he lifted a finger to indicate that she wait—as if she had any intention of walking out. Patra fiddled with the V-neck collar barely concealing her best push-up bra and hid her smile as her interviewer glazed over and began nodding without speaking. No wonder these toads feared women if they were so easily led by the balls.

The VP hung up and made a few notes. Patra obligingly put

both feet on the floor and her hands in her lap.

"Your credentials have already been approved by upper management, Miss Llewellyn, congratulations. You can start Monday at nine in the entertainment department, if you'll check in with Human Resources, they'll show you around. It's been a pleasure meeting you."

He stood up dismissively. Patra rose and held out her hand to shake. Had she been interested in a career move, she would have laughed in his face and told him where to shove his offer. Entertainment, her foot and eye. They wanted her to hack celebrity phones for gossip for Broderick's scandal sheets.

But they were also putting her in a position to hack their internal files, and that's what she wanted. This was Friday. Next week, she'd have them by the short hairs. She accepted Smedbetter's finger-smashing handshake and sashayed back to the corridor.

Voices from a meeting room down the hall drew her like an ant to sugar. Pretending to be absently checking over her employment papers, she leaned against a wall and listened.

"Look, we've got her where we want her. All we have to do is tap her phone. Leonard is a schmuck. Why haven't we retired him yet?"

Patra raised her eyebrows. She was pretty certain that sounded like Broderick, The Man, himself. Whose phone? She listened harder.

"Leonard's got useful connections," a different voice replied. "And he knows where too many bodies are buried. Let's just see if she knows anything or if that damned twerp sent Smit's files to anyone else."

"Now that he's had a chance to size her up, I'll set Smedbetter to locating Smit's files. Billy Boy, have we got anything on the girl's family? Can we have her discredited if she still has copies?"

Billy Boy—Broderick's son and next in line to the media estate. And if they were talking about *her* family, they could find enough to discredit a few presidents, kings, and prime ministers. Might make for good reading.

Someone closed the meeting room door. Damn. It sure had sounded like they were talking about her. That pretty much verified this interview had been the set-up she'd suspected.

Who was Smit?

* * *

Sitting in my basement office, flipping through the file folders Sean had lifted from Bloom's apartment, I decided they were mostly old client files. I set aside a few on politicians talking to local crime bosses like Salvador DeLuca. That could make interesting reading. I returned the rest to their sack.

The disks Patra had smuggled out in her purse weren't helpful since I didn't know speech analysis. They were all carefully labeled audios of people I didn't know. We needed a new analyst, but I was reluctant to add another corpse to the count if we were the reason Bill had died. Maybe I'd look for labs in Seattle.

I was glad we'd made copies of Patra's recordings because Bill's copies weren't here.

Which led to the interesting question—if we assumed Bill's death was related to Patra, had he been killed to prevent telling Patra what he'd discovered? So now did the Bad Guys think we'd been rendered harmless?

Anyone who knew our family knew better than that.

I checked the time. I had a few more minutes before I needed to tune in to my on-line English lit class. Now that I had a home and a little money, I'd resolved to take the classes I'd always wanted. My watch confirmed I had ten minutes to spare.

I called the Intrepid News website again. This time, I got a harried female.

I adopted the alter ego I used on my fake business cards. "Hello, I'm Linda Lane, a friend of Bill Bloom's. I'm trying to finish up some of his cases after his tragic death yesterday." I paused, hoping for a lead to follow from the person on the other end.

"Bill?" the voice asked in shock, apparently not having heard the voice mail I'd left earlier. "Bill's dead?"

"I'm sorry, I didn't mean to break the news to you. To whom am I speaking?"

"Sorry, this is Carla. Bill and I go way back. We worked together on some projects in college and keep in touch. How did he die?"

"A hit and run accident on Dupont last night. The cops suspect a drunken driver."

A telling silence followed. I waited.

"You worked with Bill?" she finally asked, sounding wary.

"Yes, and he was on a fascinating new case, which is what makes this more tragic. He could have put his name in headlines." I dragged out the bluff, hoping she'd take the hook.

"He said something about working on a death threat," she said even more carefully. "I sent him some audio clips. I keep a file of asinine things politicians say."

"That's what I needed to ask you," I said sympathetically, hiding my eagerness. "Bill filed those clips under their names, but I have no idea which names in all this mess are the ones you sent. Do you have a list?" That was such a blatant stupidity I feared she wouldn't fall for it, but it was the best I could invent on the spur of the moment.

"I just sent copies…" Her voice trailed off as she apparently hunted through her computer. "Here's the email. Don't you have a copy of it?"

Stupidity number one and she'd caught it already. "I don't have his email password, just his networked files." Damn, but I was getting creative.

"Oh, of course. I can't believe he's gone, a human life, poof, just like that. You don't think… that his death had anything to do with these files?"

"Who would know he had them besides you?" I asked blithely. "And yes, it's quite frightening to recognize our mortality. Makes me want to live every minute as if it's my last." I'd lived like that most of my life, but my version meant avoiding the dangers of living. "You could just forward the email to me, if that's easier," I suggested.

"Okay, I guess," she said dubiously. "Are you finishing up all his cases?"

I gave her my Linda email address. "I hate for his clients to think he left his office in this state. I'm just doing what I can. I don't know what else to do. It's not as if he cares about the help from where he is."

"Do you know his mother? I'm sure she appreciates what you're doing," Carla said. "I guess I better send a sympathy card."

"We were just computer colleagues. I never had the pleasure. But that's a thought. I'll send a card, too. Anyone else I should send a card to?" I was just fishing for information. I could see her email with the attachments in my box already.

"He has a brother and sister, but I don't think they were real close. Bill was a lot more open-minded, and they're… kind of midwestern-minded," she finished lamely, probably realizing she didn't know my level of *open-mindedness*.

"Righteous and Proud people?" I said cheerfully.

"White and Proud, more like it," she said bitterly. "My mother's Hispanic and I wasn't allowed at his family's table."

Crikey. That wasn't proud, that was stupid, but I only had a few more minutes before class, so I wasn't getting into human behavior. "It takes all kinds, I guess. Thanks for the information!"

I wanted to dive into the audio files but I satisfied myself with opening the attachments and reading labels while I signed into the website for my on-line classroom. The titles were too cryptic to translate with accuracy, although I chortled over *Rosesmells*. Given Carla's liberal leanings, that was bound to be a Paul Rose boo-boo.

I listened with half an ear as the on-line professor pontificated on classic essay structure. I could see Magda's point—this wasn't precisely relevant to life as I knew it. Lectures on economics, civics, technology, and history would be far more useful, but I suppose that a day could come when I needed an essay.

I reduced the professor to a corner of my screen, zoomed in on the textbook, and highlighted passages he mentioned. Bored, I started opening the audio files. Graham was probably itching impatiently to see what was in them, so I might as well pretend I was working.

Bill had apparently asked Carla at Intrepid for files on every politician in D.C. connected with the Righteous and Proud organization. Interesting. Was he feuding with his siblings or did he have a deeper motivation? A couple of the men on the list had powerful connections to Paul Rose and his conservative textbook committee, which made them candidates for Top Hat.

But if Bill had been working on Patra's tape the day he died, I didn't understand the connection to R&P and certainly not to Top Hat. As far as I was aware, neither group had anything to do with the old wars that Patrick had been killed in. So maybe Bill had been working on something else—and that's what got him killed? Not Patra?

I heard Mallard greet Patra in the foyer above me just as the professor was giving the homework assignment. I jotted it down and signed out. It was almost lunch time. We needed to talk.

I jogged upstairs and met her on her way to her room. "Lunch?"

I asked. "At the Irish pub without the talking candelabra?"

She glanced disparagingly at my ragged T-shirt. "Not if you're dressed like that. Honestly, Ana, Nick's right. You look like a ragpicker."

Since Nick had shredded the bib overalls that I once wore to hide the holes in my favorite shirt, I shrugged. "My business contacts can't see me, and there's no one at the pub to impress except a bunch of old men."

"Sean said he'd meet us there," she corrected. "He's too old for me, but he's just your type. Clean up."

I opened my mouth to correct her but then decided it might be a good idea to steer her clear of the nosy reporter by making her think I was interested.

"He's a hunk," I blithely agreed, before running upstairs and contemplating my nonexistent closet. I had taken my grandfather's study as my room and used his file drawers for my undies.

On a hook on the back of my door I had the fancy clothes Nick had made me buy a few weeks ago. The file drawers contained my Goodwill purchases. I owned very little in between. The weather was cooling off, so the cool spandex halter top and capri outfit weren't working. Unless...

Minutes later, I had my knee-high boots pulled over the capris and my black blazer over the halter top. Accessories, Nick had always said, made the outfit.

Patra had changed out of her power red suit and into jeans and a long-sleeved knit top with half its top buttons undone.

"I want one of those," I told her, eying the form-fitting, cleavage-revealing top with envy.

"It's a cheap Henley, for pity's sake. Don't they have them at Goodwill?" She studied my improvised outfit and rolled her eyes. "He'll have to just imagine what you look like, I guess. Why don't you get your hair cut?"

"Did I ask for your opinion?" It wasn't as if Nick hadn't told me the same a thousand times, but I hated hair stylists, and short hair required frequent visits, ergo, I didn't need short hair. Besides, I didn't *want* Sean taking an interest in me.

I continued to tell myself that half an hour later as I sat across the battered wooden table from him. Despite Patra's disparagement, Irish Boy didn't seem to be having any problem seeing me. I wore my long black braid over the front of my blazer, but I didn't think it was my hair he was admiring. I sat next to Patra, so it was obvious I wasn't as bountifully endowed as Magda and Patra. Yet it was me Sean focused on. My neglected hormones performed a tango.

"You really think this speech analyst was killed for investigating the Righteous nutwings?" Sean asked in incredulity. "That doesn't even come close to making sense."

Admiration apparently only went so far. "Well, maybe his mother killed Bill," I said with a shrug, dragging a tasteless fry through ketchup. The food here was close to inedible, but the fries and burgers wouldn't cause ptomaine. "I would have if he called *me* three times a day. The media numbers he called weren't direct to anyone, but I suppose the operator could have connected him with someone who didn't like his agenda."

"Wiretap," Patra said through her hamburger. "If his phone was tapped, everything he said to anyone would have been heard by some person we don't know."

"And the king of illegal wiretap is...?" I asked pointedly.

"Why I mentioned it," she retorted. "Broderick is the most likely suspect. His media act as the mouthpiece for R&P, and he's the only one wealthy enough to pull off that operation last night."

"Paul Rose and his cronies are," I reminded her.

"And Graham," Sean added for good measure.

I sent him a withering look. Patra looked interested.

Nine

OVER lunch, I listened in boredom as Sean and Patra discarded Bill Bloom theories and dived into uninformed speculation about Amadeus Graham. Sean delivered all the punches about the Icarus who soared too close to the sun and had his wings scorched in a terrorist attack. I didn't need to hear the painful story again. Graham was still a brilliant man, even if events had turned him into a paranoid nutjob, possibly a handicapped one.

After learning what I could of Patra's morning and trying to believe she was safe in BM's halls, I left the two of them to gossip. Restless and not ready to settle into my cave once I returned to the mansion, I dashed upstairs and changed back to my grubbies. I needed to spend more time on Graham's tasks, but everyone was entitled to a lunch break. I'd only taken half of mine.

After suffering stirred-hormone syndrome from Sean's lascivious glances, I needed quality time with the upstairs gym I'd been neglecting lately.

The third floor was sound-proofed. That's the only explanation I know for never hearing Graham coming or going. And apparently no one could hear me when I tore into the heavy bag with feet and fists. My old therapist had told me I had a lot of suppressed anger, and boxing was better than beating up thugs. He'd been right. I now had carved biceps and could tear the throats out of thugs through the internet. My hostility issues are deep-seated.

So were my sexual frustrations. Maybe I ought to pick up Sean, if only for the relief.

I sneaked down the carpeted corridor. All the third-floor doors were closed, indicating Graham wouldn't welcome my presence—but he'd given me permission to use the gym.

He hadn't posted times for that use. I saw no reason to knock—until I shoved open the gym door and saw a half-naked, heavily muscled man beating the tar out of a boxing bag.

I nearly dropped my teeth.

If that was Graham, he wasn't a cripple. Faaaaar from it. Those were a runner's solid legs.

He'd apparently thought me still at lunch with Sean. That proved spying didn't pay.

He shot me a scowl that should have scorched my hair, but I'm made of sterner stuff than that. Ask me sometime about my months in Atlanta's inner city gyms.

Scowling right back, I donned the gloves he'd bought for me—so I wouldn't steal his. And then I proceeded to kick and punch the stuffing out of the heavy bag until I was as hot and sweaty as he was.

It was oddly soothing and unsettling at the same time—my steady pow, pow to his fast whackety, whackety, *whack*. We developed a kind of rhythm that built with our awareness. At least, I was aware of the powerful masculine body emitting enough pheromones to knock out a female squadron. He gave no indication that I existed—until he spun gracefully and walloped the side of his foot into the heavy bag, sending it swinging in my direction.

"O'Herlihy is a gnat," he growled in that deep bass that always shot straight to my girly parts. Definitely Graham. No question about that. And very probably the diamond cufflink man who had rescued me from a mob. *Don't swoon now, Ana. Breathe.*

Sean was the reason he was beating up sawdust and leather? That was insulting to all of us.

I counterattacked. It wasn't easy. I wasn't used to having a partner, and I was off balance just realizing Graham was a whole man, but I kept my momentum in slamming the bag. It was hard to keep up with his powerful return kicks, though. I was easily distracted by chiseled biceps and thick quads and abs to die for. I was so fascinated by his muscle movement that I really didn't absorb the scars covering him until my strength began to flag.

I assumed they were burn scars. I know nothing about medical deformities, but I'd heard he'd raced into a burning building to save his wife. And failed. PTSD caused erratic behavior after that, and he'd been very publicly fired from his presidential advisory position in the years following.

Then he'd wiped himself off the map. He doesn't exist in computers anymore. I've looked. Most people, except annoying gnats like Sean, thought he was dead.

But Amadeus Graham was pretty damned real right now. He

must have worn some kind of gas mask when he'd entered the inferno. I could see an ugly scar along his currently ragged, damp hair line. The rest of his face was just as intensely Superman gorgeous as I'd suspected. I'd noticed that American politicians often start out as beautiful as Hollywood stars. Graham would have been JFK presidential material on his looks alone.

He had a Don't Tread On Me snake tattoo winding up his left bicep, over the ugliest scar tissue. Right now, with his dark hair damp and smeared to his head, he looked like a worse thug than Sly Stallone—definitely not a presidential candidate. Deepset, dark blue eyes pinned me as he gave the bag one last punch.

And then I was up against the padded wall with all that gorgeous male muscle pressing into me and hot lips sucking my breath away, and I didn't give a damn who he was as long as he kept on doing what he was doing.

We both apparently had a lot of frustration to express. I practically climbed his leg after he crushed my breasts in long-fingered hands. Crotch met crotch and we would have been doing it up against the wall if Patra hadn't started shouting my name in the hall below.

I slid out of his grip without a second thought. Id and libido shouted angry epithets, but my ego wins every time, probably because I lack a super-ego. Freud only got it half right. I lack morals but reality gives me a roll.

"Really bad idea," I think I muttered.

I heard him swearing like a pro as I ran for my room.

* * *

"We need a plan," I told Patra later, after I'd taken a cold shower and returned to my office. "We're dealing with Broderick, a man who has been accused of shoving his wife off his yacht. He owns a corporation that condones mass murder in the interest of foreign oil. He's our best candidate for ordering the death of your father. If so, he could be guilty of hiring Bill's killers and arsonists to burn down your apartment. You cannot simply start rifling his company files without a cover."

"Broderick's father was killed by a hit-and-run driver," the intercom intoned.

This time, I didn't smack it. My lips still throbbed from the volatility of Graham's kisses, and just his voice turned me on. Smacking the intercom would indicate I cared. "That's how he started his conglomerate, on daddy's little newspapers?" I asked with my best professional interest.

Patra grimaced and nodded.

The intercom didn't answer my question directly. Instead, it suggested, "A decent position has opened at CNN in Atlanta. I can arrange it for you."

I didn't waste time getting my hopes up. Patra was already shaking her head.

"If the monster ordered my father's death, I'm bringing him down, and then I'm publishing dad's book on media encouragement of war for profit," she said defiantly.

"Meaning *Broderick's* media," I corrected. "No other network or chain of newspapers has so vociferously backed the military as Broderick's. If he has any hint that you still have Patrick's files, he'll bring you down like your father."

"Like Bill," she added.

"I'm not entirely convinced that's true. Bill's personal conflicts might be equally dangerous. Unless we can find the connections, that's a dead end street," I warned. "We need to hire another voice analyst."

Patra looked mutinous, but we'd discussed my little foray into Bill's phone calls. She knew I was right. "BM supports R&P," she argued, reducing our problem to acronyms that could be translated as *shit supports death*. "Bill could have been proving the connection."

"Broderick supports anyone stupid enough to promote his agenda," I corrected. "Stupid people don't question what he tells them. That's not the same as *caring* for what the Righteous stand for, not any more than he cares for our boys in uniform. Evidence is required to prove that R&P has any interest in helping BM or vice versa."

I kept waiting for Graham to intrude, if only for the sound of his voice, but after his offer was rejected, he'd apparently moved on. I needed to rebuild the distance between me and our reluctant landlord. Exchanging saliva—no matter how much fun—was not the solution.

"I can't plan anything until I get inside and know what

resources I can access," Patra explained. "The U.S. office won't be the same as the London one, but there ought to be connections I can ferret out. In the meantime, I need to work on my cover. They're putting me in entertainment. Who do we know in Hollywood?"

"Ask Nick. But you'll have a hard time looking up war zones while covering celebrities being naughty in the Caribbean. Have you gone through your father's files to see who he knew? Maybe you can start with his friends?" I suggested, reminding myself to get back to the code programs to see if her father's papers really were coded or if Graham had sent me off on a wild goose chase.

Patra brightened. "Dad had an affair with that old Welsh actress, Rhianna Mattox. Good idea!"

Even I knew who Rhianna was—only one of the best known Brit actresses on stage and film. She'd have a human shield two blocks deep around her. I rolled my eyes but didn't discourage her fantasy. "Broderick will wet his pants if he thinks you're hooking up with her. But be careful and don't let anyone hear you asking about your father."

"Don't patronize me. We have the same mother, and I know the same tricks you do." She rose, taking my collection of Bill's files with her.

Fortunately, I'd already scanned them into my computer. I had a few years more experience on dirty tricks that she could figure out on her own.

I built a computer folder six layers deep on all Broderick's subsidiaries but still hadn't found any connection to the textbook companies and Top Hat, my particular goal.

Then Oppenheimer, our lawyer, called.

I checked the clock, almost time for EG to get home. I couldn't go far, but I couldn't discuss our inheritance problems with Graham listening to every word. I didn't care if he looked like Superman. The man was still a predatory spider. I jogged up the stairs and out the front door with my cell to my ear, listening to the lawyer's recital of all he'd done since we'd last talked.

EG's silk cobwebs hadn't reappeared since Mallard had removed them from the entrance. I passed through, unscathed. Outside, I leaned against the wrought iron fence separating sidewalk from three inches of lawn and watched up the street in the direction of the Metro entrance while I talked.

"Brashton is still claiming the house transfer was legal between the executor of the estate and an objective third-party with no collusion. He claims the sale was necessary to cover debts," Oppenheimer was saying. "Without his cooperation, the burden of proof is on us and the courts will drag their feet."

"The *contents* of this house are worth more than Graham paid. The house itself is worth an easy ten mil, if not more. No one is that stupid. Tell Reggie boy we know about the poisoned envelopes, and if he doesn't come clean, we'll be talking to the cops."

"Poisoned envelopes?" Oppenheimer asked in alarm. "Actual poison, not drugs?"

"Graham isn't likely to give us his chemical analysis if he knows why I'm asking, but yeah, actual poison. Brashton killed our grandfather. Proving it in court might be tricky, but Reggie ought to cave before it comes to that, right?"

"Holy Lord Almighty," Oppenheimer muttered. "I knew you'd be trouble, but this..."

I envisioned him shaking his shaggy head as he made notes. Oppenheimer was a wheeler-dealer, but he was damned sharp, and he was enough of an outsider to be willing to go up against Reggie's respectable old D.C. law firm for our case. I didn't have to like him, just respect his ability.

Oppenheimer asked questions. I explained how my grandfather received an order of personalized envelopes from Reggie's office, envelopes that had been in Max's bedroom and could have been licked by anyone. While we talked, I watched EG stroll down the street with Mallard. I tried not to look shocked.

Mallard did not often play bodyguard for us. What the devil was going on?

I scanned the street with more awareness as I hung up on the lawyer. Once upon a time, I would have done this automatically. I was definitely getting soft.

I observed workmen on scaffolding across the street and a city bus pouring diesel fumes. This narrow residential road had no parking—everyone parked in the alleys behind the buildings. Most houses had ornate fences around their postage stamp patch of green turf. I had a completely clear view of the street—no good hiding places. Until now, I'd felt really secure here.

My gaze drifted back to the scaffolding and the vacant windows of the house across the street. The windows were open. Was there one last workman up there?

I jogged down the street to walk on EG's other side. Graham's paranoia was contagious.

Ten

I'D ALWAYS thought of Mallard as built like a brick house, sturdy and thick. He dressed the part of butler in a formal black suit, starched white shirt, and black-on-black embroidered vest. He'd been my grandfather's employee in my childhood, so my suspicion that he's former CIA had no foundation other than family instinct. My grandfather was not a kindly old businessman, appearances to the contrary. Paranoid Graham was his protégé. Mallard was more like their aide-de-camp than any butler I'd met, and I'd met a surprising number over the years.

"Hanging out on street corners these days?" EG asked with suspicion as I approached.

"Talking to Oppenheimer," I said cheerfully, working on that normal childhood routine. Unfortunately, in our family, normal is relative to the politics of a third world country. "Have you decided which features you want on your iMac before we place the order?"

"All of them," she demanded, as expected. "If we're rich, we shouldn't need to cut corners."

"We're not rich, you only get a very small percentage of that money, and you need to learn to budget for college. You have no need of a giant screen, extra speed, or more than one drive. You'll have to decide if you'd rather have more memory for programming, or high-end graphics for gaming. You can't have both."

This discussion got her in the front door without further questioning of why we were walking her home. Not that I had any answers for that either. I sent her upstairs to consult my laptop and make her wish list fit my bottom line. Then I followed Mallard to his downstairs hideaway, conveniently placed at the other end of the low-ceilinged cellar from my office.

"What's up?" I demanded, strolling into the cellar kitchen and catching him grating cheese as if he hadn't just behaved more oddly than my family on a good day.

"Nothing, of course. It's a lovely autumn day and I strolled down to the corner for a breath of fresh air."

"You should respect my intelligence. You were not down at the pub. You always smell of cigars and beer when you come back from there. You're not carrying shopping bags. And your timing was too convenient. If my sister is in danger, I want to know about it."

Mallard did not appear the least perturbed by my analysis. "If you lie down with snakes, expect to get bit. I saw no reason why a child should be put in harm's way."

"Fine, then I'll check out that vacant house across the street on my own."

"Ana, I would not advise—"

I wasn't taking advice from someone who refused to answer me in clear English. I jogged up the back steps into our narrow, walled backyard and slipped out the rear garden gate into the cement yard of the block building behind us. I waved at Graham's camera. Being able to envision the man I was waving to ought to halt my mischief, but it only made me more reckless. I'd kissed Superman and survived. I could do anything.

Or maybe I was daring him to leave his lair. My mind is as warped as anyone else's.

I trotted past the ugly building to the street behind us. I hurried up to a corner, where I blended into a crowd getting off a bus. I followed the crowd past our street, to the alley behind the houses across from us, a round-about route that was almost a complete square.

The alleys behind the staid old Victorians on either side of our street really weren't meant for modern vehicular traffic. A horse and buggy might rattle down the cobbled dirt, but it would rip the heck out of a Porsche's undercarriage.

The vacant building was easy to locate. All the windows in back were boarded. A workman had propped open the cellar door with a can of paint, presumably to let in some fresh air. The French doors on the deck had been boarded up. I had no choice but to enter downstairs.

I'd spent the better part of my life exploring on my own, without supervision. No sense in changing my habits, although now that I knew Graham wasn't immobile... It freaked me out. I admit it.

Entering from the bright outside, I lingered to let my eyes adjust. I smelled cigarette smoke and fresh paint, but in the light of one dangling dim bulb, I didn't see anyone lurking in the cellar. Unlike my basement office, this underground floor was essentially unfinished. It was a dismal coal cellar with the remains of an ancient kitchen, which had been reduced to a pantry for storing canning jars or whatever.

The stairs were in about the same place as our house. I took them slowly, using the sides to avoid squeaky treads. I could hear workmen cursing and joking. Sounded perfectly normal. I should have just turned around and left, but my obsessive need to protect my family wouldn't allow it.

I located the voices in the front room, so I stayed in the back, taking the servants stairs up. My theory was that anyone spying on us would choose an upper story. Maybe I could see what Mallard or Graham had seen from this height.

I was wearing cheap Keds, so my soles were soundless as I explored the second floor. The racket of power saws and drills drowned out the squeak of boards under my feet. My real problem was the scaffolding. I needed to look out the windows but didn't want to end up staring a startled painter in the face.

So I steadied myself on the second-floor hall wall and peered into each bedroom as I passed, checking things out. I spotted no workmen, inside or out. I saw no telescopic rifles or lurking men in black.

Starting to feel a trifle foolish, I took the back stairs up to the third floor. This would have once been nursery, children's rooms, and servants' quarters. In our house, Graham had turned this story into offices and his suite and the gym. Looked like construction had knocked out a lot of the walls up here, and it was being reconfigured into open family space. I studied the area cautiously. Still no workmen, but I could tell this was where the outside crew had been working on windows. Modern thermal panes were being installed, carefully crafted not to change the exterior appearance.

I could continue to the attic or abandon my ridiculous search.

I'm damned thorough and not in the habit of quitting.

I opened all the closed doors, finding nothing more than closets, plumbing, and construction garbage that needed hauling to a Dumpster. I really didn't know what I was expecting to find.

Idly wondering if we could buy an unfinished house for a million and rejecting the idea in favor of stubbornly wanting our grandfather's life for my siblings—possibly over Graham's dead body— I took the stairs to the attic.

I was truly off guard by the time I stepped into raw unfinished storage space, or I wouldn't have let the lurker catch me so easily. As it was, he came up from behind and tackled me as I was turning to the dormer windows. He was twice my weight, so I went down.

He clambered back up, apparently intent on escaping, but I had questions. I kicked at his ankles, caught my knee around his leg when he faltered, and yanked, unbalancing him. Yeah, I know, it would have been smarter to let him go, but I react badly to surprises. And I didn't like the humiliation of getting caught.

I grabbed a handy two-by-four and came up swinging. He was still intent on running. I disabused him of that notion by aiming at his well-padded midriff.

I connected just enough to make him grab his belly with a *whoof*.

I could have broken his kneecaps, but it had finally dawned on me that this wasn't a dangerous muscle man but a middle-aged, out-of-shape idiot. He'd probably been as surprised as I was and had taken me down by accident. That *really* irked.

The binoculars around his neck upped my irritation. "Who sent you to spy on us?" I demanded.

"Bird watching," he gasped, bent in half and holding his flabby abdomen.

"Fine, then show me your ID and I won't call the cops." Like I had any more right to be here than he did, but in my experience, idiots respond to authority.

"Not hurting anyone," he protested, still gasping for air.

"Trespassing, stalking..." I groped for more crimes, but he held up his hand to stop me.

"We investigate all new employees," he said, hauling himself upright by using the stair rail. "Standard procedure. No reason to be hostile. I have permission to be up here."

"Yeah, they think you're bird watching. Who is 'we' and what new employee?" Although given my research, I'd already worked that one out. I just wanted to hear him admit it.

"Broderick Media," he coughed up, giving me a cross-eyed scowl. "Patra Llewellyn. Who the hell are you?"

I leaned on the two-by-four and studied the cretin. He didn't look like an arsonist out to burn Patra and her papers. Even if he did, I couldn't heave him out a window without evidence. There were drawbacks to living in civilization. "Broderick sent you to spy on Patra? I ought to whack you upside the head just for that alone. What kind of creepy company is that?"

He looked alarmed at my tone. "We're very cautious in our new hires. The world is full of terrorists who would love to bring down one of the most powerful pillars of the free press."

I'm not sure how he said that with a straight face. I couldn't keep the smirk off mine. "Free press? Is that what you call spinning propaganda these days?" So, if I couldn't whack him physically, my suppressed anger issues went verbal. Who knew?

He indignantly dusted himself off. "All patriots must be cautious in these troubled times. I don't need to stand here and argue. I'm here legitimately and can leave anytime I wish."

I bowed and indicated the stairs. "Please do. And don't come back or I won't be so polite."

He scampered. I watched out the window as he appeared in the side yard, followed by another man who looked more like the thug I'd been expecting. Interesting.

I was more accustomed to taking out bad guys with trickery than using toys. So I was a little late in remembering to pull out my phone. By the time I found the camera app, I had to really zoom in to snap a couple of pathetic pics.

Since EG's little kidnapping episode, I was wary of thugs in alleys, even if they called themselves reporters. I watched this pair head for the Metro and out of sight before studying our house across the street from this fresh perspective. Mallard kept all the downstairs draperies closed. I liked my second-floor windows open except at night. Nick and Patra's rooms overlooked the back yard. The other bedrooms on that floor were closed up. EG's turret was draped in heavy black. The kid wasn't dumb.

I checked Graham's third floor lair, but he existed in a dark computer room at the back. The front rooms had shutters. They could have spy holes for all I could tell. Trying not to think about Graham over there, staring back, I hurried down the stairs, no longer trying for silence. If the workmen allowed in nerdy birdwatchers, then I was the neighborhood pigeon lady.

I slipped out through the cellar but directly crossed the street without taking my earlier roundabout circuit. Since it was a crisp, sunny October day, I cut through the side walkway to admire the garden and descend into Mallard's domain. He was busily whacking up a naked chicken with a short-handled ax.

"Thank you for looking out for EG," I said, proving I had no fear of angry men with sharp instruments. "I'll try to meet her from now on."

"It was my pleasure," he said stiffly. "I will continue to meet her. Your grandfather would have wanted it that way."

"We can't pay you," I pointed out. "Unless you want us to pay your tab at the pub. We could do that."

He almost smiled. "You're more like him than you realize."

"Probably not in a good way." I clicked my camera roll so he could see the photos I'd taken. "The trespasser claimed to be from Broderick, but I'm not certain about his pal in the alley. Living with my family is a twenty-four-hour security problem."

Mallard studied the photos, then nodded. "Dinner will be at six, as usual."

I didn't know if we'd ever earn his respect, but I was satisfied with his dinners.

I returned to my office to put faces to the names on Broderick's employee list. Let's see how Birdwatcher took to being cyber-stalked.

Eleven

I PUT on my blazer and pretended to look normal when I went upstairs for dinner.

Waiting for the rest of us, Nick gazed admiringly on the resplendent meal Mallard had laid out. Once I arrived, Nick took his chair at the head of the table. No one had nominated him as master of the household. He simply assumed the position as his birthright, just as I took the other end as eldest.

EG propped a textbook next to her plate. No one objected. We knew she could listen and read at the same time.

Patra stacked crisp new file folders next to her place, but she was happily filling her plate with lemon chicken and risotto and not inclined to part with any findings as yet.

"I mentioned to the senator this afternoon that Patra is applying at Broderick," Nick said after sampling the chardonnay. "Tex is a conservative, so I thought he'd approve."

Patra merely lifted an elegantly arched eyebrow and continued chewing. I was the only one considering the implications of Nick speaking to the senator about a war-mongering media conglomerate. Tex had been a reluctant part of Top Hat for a while. Nick was thinking conspiracy.

"Did Tex offer to call Broderick and personally recommend Patra?" I asked, just to prevent Nick from dropping the topic to dig into his repast.

"*Au contraire*, he recommended the CNN position in Atlanta. Our prosy senator ranted about BM being a dangerous collusion of oil magnates and the military industry hiding behind the social reform of Righteous and Proud. EG may have inherited some of her pessimism from him."

"It's called intelligence, dumquat," EG said from behind her book.

"Intelligence that predicts doom and gloom creates a society motivated by fear," Nick warned her. "No positive action comes from fear."

"Military industry?" I derailed EG's derailment of the topic. "I thought he was into oil."

"Makers of guns, tanks, and military equipment," he clarified. "Broderick likes *all* rich men."

"Old news," Patra said with an airy wave. "Broderick would be emperor and own gladiators if he could. Soldiers are nothing more to him than avatars in a video war game with bigger and better booms. Irrelevant to my position."

"But not irrelevant if your father was against war and had evidence to prove Broddy was corrupting news to foment revolution in order to enrich his military and oil buddies," I corrected. "Motive is half the puzzle. The men on that recording are just the sort to support Broderick Media. It's a lead of sorts."

"I met David Smedbetter today. I'm pretty sure he's in my father's files. I listened in on their boys' club but heard nothing conclusive and haven't found anything else interesting," Patra said in disgust. "I'm still looking."

The name Smedbetter meant nothing to any of us, but I added it to my to-do list. I needed to get back to the de-coding software and find another speech analyst, but unless I uncovered something, I saw no reason in raising her hopes. "You do realize your new boss is spying on you, don't you?"

Patra shrugged. "That's to be expected. I spent the afternoon at the library, so they must have been bored."

I produced the cell phone images and showed them to her. "Broderick has to know who your father is. You'd better play total innocent or you'll end up like Bill," I warned.

"Now who's a pessimist?" EG asked, not lifting her gaze from her reading material.

Patra studied the images and shook her head in non-recognition. "These creeps are way off base. I'm providing entertainment like the gladiators," she said mockingly. "I have an interview with Rhianna."

I tried not to let my eyebrows soar off my face. Patra was damned good if she'd wormed her way through the actress's security in one day.

Patra blithely continued as if she hadn't accomplished the impossible. "She remembers daddy with fondness and has promised to help his little girl contact any other entertainers looking for a little publicity. Why should the poopmeisters suspect me of anything?"

"Because you're a Maximillian, and Broderick hated your grandfather as well as your father," the candelabra said.

I sighed and resumed eating. Even though he made my hormones sing hosannas, Graham still had a way of dampening any convivial conversation.

"Keep your enemies close works both ways," Nick said cheerily.

Perspicacious, Nick, I realized. Graham was doing a damned good job of keeping us close. I studied the expensive dinner on the fancy dinnerware that we'd simply accepted as our birthright, just as Nick had taken the head of the table. Technically, none of this was ours.

"I'm working for Graham to cover the costs of our rent," I said, derailing the topic even better than EG rather than discuss enemies. She even glanced up from her book to watch me with interest. "I think we need to start paying for our food. Maybe the two of you could throw a hundred each a week from your salaries into the kitchen kitty."

"Socialism," Nick muttered ungratefully, but he cast a considering look at the silent candelabra as he said it.

"Fair enough," Patra conceded, "but if I'm staying in D.C., I'm finding my own place."

"Good luck with that," Nick and I both said in concert.

After that, we returned to the business of eating. We'd never really gone without, but we'd shared enough meals of ants and grubs and porridge to appreciate good food when we had it.

I sat down with EG after supper to order her new Mac. It was Friday night, so Nick had a hot date. And even Patra, who had just arrived in this country, was heading out. I was the non-social introvert in our family of cuckoos, so I got to babysit.

After we completed our order, I let EG play with my Dell in my basement office while I used Graham's Whiz to hack into Broderick's personnel files, looking for the sneak I'd caught across the street. As I suspected, company paranoia required photo IDs. They had enough info in their employee files to order up birth certificates if they suspected someone hadn't been born on the right side of the border.

Patra hadn't. To the best of my recollection, she'd been born in

Algeria, at an American military facility since the country was in the middle of a civil war at the time. But Magda is a totally American blonde, and Patrick the Brit had been there to claim his daughter, so her birth certificate was well documented in Algeria, the UK, and the US. Confusing, but legal.

Patra's personnel files weren't recorded in Broderick's computer yet. I couldn't search "middle-aged" or "tubby" or any of those few things I knew about the spy who'd irritated me. I tried "American" and "reporter" but the search list was still tremendous. The firm had a *lot* of employees. Too bad I couldn't do a photo ID match with my camera images, but if Graham had that kind of software, he hadn't given me access to it.

I uploaded my phone images, just in case.

I scanned the files for David Smedbetter, just out of curiosity. He was a vice president, hired a few years ago. Like many of Broderick's employees, he had military credentials. Nothing singled him out as interesting, including his photo.

Deciding we'd had a long week and had worked hard enough, I downloaded the old flick of *Fahrenheit 451*. EG and I spent the evening scaring ourselves imagining a world without books.

After I saw EG into her tower—the bats had apparently departed to a better home, leaving behind a faint smell I'd rather not identify—I settled restlessly into my own chamber, closing the window and shutters. I'd covered up the camera behind the portrait of John Adams weeks ago, after amusing myself by tantalizing Graham with my bare legs.

At the time, I'd imagined a wheel-chair bound invalid suffering sex-deprived voyeurism. Now I knew Graham had the ability to come down here and throw me through a window if he so desired.

I had mixed emotions about that. Torturing an invalid had been mean-spirited but well-deserved under the circumstances. Tormenting a man who could throw me up against a wall—that was just plain stupid. But enticing a man who intrigued me more than any other mortal in the world... that was pure Magda. I refrained. But I still couldn't help throwing occasional looks at John Adams as I worked on my laptop until midnight.

I occasionally peered through the shutters at the house across the street, just to check if someone was sitting over there, waiting for Patra to come home. I saw no lights. Patra didn't come home.

Neither did Nick. I finally gave up and went to bed.

Saturday morning and it was still just me and EG. For years, it had been just me, and I hadn't minded at all, but today, I was a bit pissed. If I couldn't have sex, I needed action. I'd been debating making a little visit to Bill's mom and finding out more about his family and their connections, but I couldn't very well take EG with me.

Sitting at the computer running decoding programs didn't help my restlessness. Patrick's papers weren't responding to anything I'd tried so far. I located a new speech analyst on the other side of the country. I needed to email him from an anonymous address using a computer at the library to prevent anyone from knowing where I was sending Patra's sound tracks.

I also needed to know that my family was safe from spying intruders across the street. *That*, I could do something about. By mid-morning, EG and I were on the Metro heading for the spy museum. I love D.C. I could indulge EG's eagerness to learn everything and pick up a few essentials in a gift shop at the same time.

EG cleaned out the museum's bookstore. I acquired a few useful toys. I could have ordered more professional equipment on-line and had it shipped, but I wanted to monitor movements in the house across the street tonight, not next week.

Nick and Patra's doors were closed when we returned, so I could breathe easier. I made a lousy mother figure, but this sharing the same roof business dredged up old memories.

After lunch, I left EG with Mallard and set off on my spy mission across the street. I took the back approach to hide where I was coming from. The cellar door was still open. Workmen still gabbed inside. I wore binoculars around my neck and took the back stairs to the attic as if I belonged there. Who would suspect evil of a hippy-looking twerp, even if they noticed me? Which they didn't.

I ran a few trip wires. I saw no evidence that any work was being done in the attic, so anyone coming up here was just being nosy. I hooked up my wireless device and the silent alarm and camera. Basic tools of the trade.

Returning to my office, I worked up my next plan, which would involve deserting EG yet again, now that Patra and Nick were in the house. Feeling guilty, I checked with her in the kitchen. "Will you be okay doing your homework while I run out for a while? You can pester Nick or Patra if you need anything."

"I'm good," she declared, hopping down from a stool where she'd been cleaning up on cookies. "Can I use your laptop?"

"The Dell, in my office, where Mallard can check to be certain you aren't ordering drones to intercept missiles."

She made a rude noise. My sister might be a genius, but she's still only nine.

For my expedition into conserva-burbia, I opted for khakis and blazer and wrapped my braid around my head. I couldn't look more innocuous if I'd worn glasses. I waved at the camera on the landing as I strode down the stairs. I never knew if Graham was watching or if he even cared what I was doing, but I figured if I was ever kidnapped, he'd have a record of the time I left and what I was wearing.

I stopped and bought a sympathy card and a little potted plant before I hit the Metro.

Carol Bloom, Bill's mother, lived far enough out of the city to not be easily accessible by Metro. I took the line as far out as it went, then called a cab. One of these days, I'd have to buy a car and obtain a driver's license, but I wasn't spending money until I knew had an income. Working for Graham didn't pay in anything except room and board. And my other clients were getting short shrift these days.

I'm a world traveler, but I hadn't spent a lot of time in suburbs. All the little brick houses looked alike to me. Some had covered their immaculate yards with flowers and ornaments. Others hadn't mowed their grass. Carol Bloom's house was somewhere in between. The yard needed mowing, but she had pots of bedraggled flowers on her concrete porch and a climbing rose straggling up the wall.

The woman who answered the doorbell actually wore a faded, flowered housecoat like those on TV matrons from the fifties. Where does one buy such a thing? She was stout, short, and graying but she didn't look particularly grief-stricken.

"Mrs. Bloom, I'm Linda Lane, a colleague of Bill's," I said. "I can't tell you how sorry I am to hear of your loss. He was a good, good man."

She opened the storm door and allowed me in. No wonder so many people get robbed. They'll trust anyone bearing presents.

She set my houseplant and card on a coffee table in the living room. I didn't see any similar tokens. "Not too many people have been by," she said stiffly. "Bill was like a stranger to us lately. I knew the city would kill him."

"Have the police caught the driver yet?" I asked, assuming that would be the natural thing to ask.

"They found the car, but it was stolen. Would you like to take a seat? I can bring you some coffee."

I didn't think she meant a Starbucks mocha latte, so I declined. "I don't know if he ever mentioned me," I ventured with a question in my voice. "We often shared files. I've been trying to finish up some of his cases as a gesture of respect. He often spoke of you, so I thought I'd let you know, in case you were worried."

"That's kind of you," she said, but her expression didn't display gratitude. She just looked irritable. "Bill was always the oddball of our family, hanging around with misfits and weirdoes. It's good to know he worked with decent people."

I didn't think I'd call myself decent, but I suspected that was a code word for white and/or conservative. I egged her on, just a little. "The city is full of all sorts," I agreed. "You have to take work where you can get it. Did you know any of his clients?"

"No, no, I didn't. After he brought that Spic home to meet us, he hasn't been back. I blame her. Those lousy Mexicans are taking over the country. We'll all be speaking Mexican if someone doesn't do something." She tugged agitatedly at a crocheted doily on her recliner arm. More echoes of the fifties.

"I understand your concern," I said sympathetically. "You know about the group called the Righteous and the Proud, don't you? They're trying to help."

She nodded, relaxing a fraction. "Me and my other kids belong. Bill told us we were puppets for the Man. I don't know where he gets...got...those ideas."

The Man—as represented by Broderick Media, et al? Or just a general term for the One Percent? I wish I'd known Bill better. "I never thought of Bill as the rebellious type," I said sympathetically. "I wonder if he had anything in his files that Dr. Smythe should look into? Bill was terribly good with his recording equipment."

My brief research had turned up Dr. Charles Smythe as the leader of R&P, if a mob could have leadership.

A frown formed over her nose. "The police brought me all the boxes they took from his apartment. Ken went over and cleaned the place out but said Bill didn't have anything worth keeping. He said he'd give it all to Goodwill when he had time to truck it over there. Reckon I should look at those boxes? I didn't know what to do with them."

"They're probably just client files. I can't imagine there's anything bad in them. I can look them over if you like, see if there's anything Dr. Smythe should see." I was positively brimming with excitement but I played it cool. Easy to do since I had no car and no way of hauling away the files.

"Would you?" She still didn't look relieved but as if she were worrying over some new crisis. "I'd better ask Ken, first. He said he might want to burn them like we did his dad's papers after he died."

Brother Ken cleaning out the apartment and burning Bill's files might strike me as symptoms of guilt, paranoia, or a need to wipe his brother off the planet, if it hadn't been for the bit about burning his *father's* papers. The guy could just be a firebug, but it seemed weird to ritually burn all family history.

"Oh," I said, "I'm not sure I'd realized Bill had lost his father. I'm sorry. Was it recent?"

Carol shook her head with sadness. "We lost Ernest almost five years ago. The boys were grown by then."

That didn't seem exceedingly relevant but just in case, I kept up my fake sympathy. "That had to be hard. Was it a serious illness?"

She shook her head, turning non-communicative.

Not willing to push my luck too far, I pulled one of my fake business cards from my purse. "I shouldn't keep you any longer. If you decide you'd like me to take a look at the files, you can send them to this address or just let me know, and I'll have someone pick them up. I don't know all Bill's clients and couldn't notify them, so if nothing else, the files might help with that."

She took the card and nodded absently. "Thank you for stopping by. I do appreciate it."

Poor Bill, I thought, pulling out my new phone to call a cab company as I walked down the street. Just when he started living an interesting life, he'd been taken out and erased in a mundane fashion. In honor of his memory, I'd have to find out why.

Twelve

I REVERSED my travel process, taking the cab to the Metro and the Metro to home. It gave me time to think—and to check my email, thanks to my handy new toy.

I had turned off the phone while talking to Mrs. Bloom. The chimes rang the instant I switched it on. The screen also flashed a warning that I had a dozen voice mail messages.

Since they were all from Nick, I called.

"Where the devil are you?" he asked in irritation. "We have a situation, and as usual, you're the cause."

"Just for that snide remark, I think I'll go shopping." I kept my voice low so as not to annoy my fellow riders. Nick was such a drama queen, I waited for real news.

"We'll have the cops out here if you don't come back and settle this now. Your mouse trap caught a rat, and we don't know what to do with him. Mallard seems in favor of slicing and dicing him and serving him up on rigatoni."

I heard a protest in the background, but I was translating Nick's metaphors and didn't know whether to laugh or frown. "I'm just a few stops away. I trust you've prevented squealing."

"Just come straight home." He punched off—so less satisfactory than a slamming receiver in my ear.

If I'd translated correctly, my fun with spy toys had tripped up a nosy reporter. The alarm going off must have been exciting. I wondered who had been in my office monitoring my equipment. That was a foolish question. EG had been down there while Patra and Nick slept upstairs. But EG couldn't hogtie a grown man. That would be Mallard's involvement was my guess.

Patra was furiously pacing the front room of our abode by the time I arrived. She shot me an angry glance, but EG was eagerly bouncing to tell me her part in the escapade and no one else could get in a word edgewise.

"And the alarm went off while Patra was in the shower," she was saying. I'd tuned out on the prelude of what she'd been doing in my office but tuned back in again when we got to the real news. "And I told Mallard we'd caught a spy, so we went over there and Mallard decked him! One blow and he was out! We had to tie him up!"

"You left him over there?" I asked, already turning toward the door.

"They couldn't carry him across the street," Patra said dryly, finally breaking into EG's moment of glory. "I can't go over there. I don't want Broderick suspecting I have anything to do with my insane family's depredations."

"Are Nick and Mallard over there slicing and dicing?"

"I believe they're discussing whether rats belong in Dumpsters," the lamp on the table said. "Please return Mallard so dinner won't be delayed."

I was almost positive I heard amusement in that sepulchral voice. "I'm happy the gladiators entertain Caesar," I retorted before heading out. I had to turn and point EG back inside. She glared, but she knew better than to disobey She Who Owns the Computers.

The work trucks were gone. Presumably the construction crew only worked half days on weekends. I wondered how the rat had got in if the door was locked. I checked the imposing carved oak front door. The crew had done due diligence by locking it. I trotted around the house and found a board removed from one of the side windows. I assumed the rat had entered there. Since I couldn't imagine portly Mallard or elegant Nick wriggling through that entry, I continued around to the back.

The plywood covering the French doors had been neatly removed and lay on the deck. The glass in the doors was cracked, but probably not in the process of opening them—the door lock had been jimmied by an expert. Mallard and Nick were professionals.

I stepped inside and took the front stairs up, admiring the light wood finish on rails and floors. This place would be far more modern than my grandfather's mansion when they were done.

I heard muffled protests and kicking before I reached the top. That would be the rat. Mallard and Nick were probably cleaning their nails and waiting for my appearance.

Keeping in mind that I looked like a shrimpy librarian in my blazer and khakis, I removed brass knuckles from my shoulder bag. I never used them. A roll of coins was legal and just as lethal. But sometimes I needed accessories to get my point across.

It was still daylight so the attic was filled with enough gray light for them to see my approach, if they hadn't already heard it.

I let the rat see me don the knuckles as I climbed the last step. He was on the floor with a tie stuffed in his mouth and his hands tied behind his back. His eyes widened. I didn't smile but lifted a black eyebrow over my gimlet glare. Small and dark can look deadly with a bit of effort.

Mallard held a baseball bat at the ready. Nick was leaning against the wall, polishing a wicked looking switchblade. Neither of them had a hair out of place. Well, Mallard didn't have many hairs to muss. Nick's shirt was missing a tie.

"Have you called the cops yet?" I asked.

"We thought you might like to question him first," Nick said with a threatening undertone that was probably more for me than the rat. But he wouldn't yell at me in front of strangers.

I leaned over and released the necktie holding our intruder's mouth shut. "Hello, again," I said, recognizing yesterday's culprit. "I think you'd better give me your name this time so I know where to go looking for you."

"Puddin'n'tame," he taunted. "I'm going to have the lot of you arrested."

Yesterday, I'd been outweighed and in no position to investigate our spy. Today, I had him where I wanted him.

I tugged the worn billfold from his back pocket. His license labeled him as one Leonard Riley, living on a street I didn't recognize. I removed my nifty smart phone from my pocket. "Well, Leonard, it's this way. You're trespassing. From the looks of that window downstairs, I think we can charge you with breaking and entering. And even if Patra isn't aware of your existence, I can assure the police that you've been stalking her, hence our little trap. I warned you yesterday that we take care of our own. Did you not impart that information to your employer?"

"Assault and battery!" he countered. "I'll have your two thugs behind bars for years."

I glanced up to Nick. "Hear that, dear? He thinks you're a thug. What do you think the senator will say about that?"

I deliberately title-dropped. A real reporter or spy would already know who lived across the street and where they worked. I didn't think Leonard was good. I wanted him to know right upfront that we had as many or more connections than he had. That tactic usually assures that pestilences like Lenny don't annoy me later while they work for the information.

"Tex would say that I couldn't hurt a flea if my life depended on it," Nick said with assurance. "He would be proud that I've defended my home and family from a worthless no-good lying reporter."

"Excellent. And I'll vouch for Mallard. He was only protecting poor little me." I rubbed the knuckles for effect. "Perhaps you didn't quite comprehend my message yesterday, Leonard. My sister is harmless. You go back and tell your boss she's actually eager to be a reporter for the biggest news agency in the world. And then you might mention that the rest of Patra's family is plumb out crazy with connections so far-reaching that we can remove you from the planet without anyone the wiser. Are you getting all this?"

The rat was sensing defeat. His nose twitched and his gaze darted around the room. And I had tried to sound so reasonable, too. I left the knuckles on while I began photographing every piece of paper and card in his wallet.

"How do I know your sister isn't as crazy as the rest of you?" the rat demanded.

"It's all a matter of perspective, isn't it?" Nick asked, strolling over to cut the ropes around his prisoner's feet. "We think Patra is crazy for wanting to work for an asshole. But if that's what she wants, we'll see that she gets it. We're giving her your photo and ID. If she sees you anywhere near her, she's to call the police without question. She's a good girl. She'll do exactly that."

Mallard just tapped his bat impatiently against his shoulder, a man of few words.

"You rich, privileged asses will get your comeuppance," Leonard growled. "I'm not letting this go."

Nick and I looked at each other and laughed. "Rich!" Nick said with shades of meaning.

"Privileged." I nodded agreement. "We probably should start a trust fund."

I finished up by snapping a photo of our nosy prisoner. I had him now, although I didn't think I would mention how I could make his life a living hell with his entire identity in my hands.

I threw the wallet back after Nick released his wrists. Leonard was still massaging blood into his hands and didn't catch it.

"Just think of my grandfather as Mafia and you'll understand us better," I said sympathetically. "He's not with us any longer, so the younger ones are making their own way in the world. But Nick and I, we know the connections, if you take my meaning. Be a good spy, do your basic research, and then go back and tell your boss that Patra is as clean as she looks."

"Or else what?" the rat snarled, but I could tell it was a half-hearted retaliation.

I shrugged. "Depends. Your credit may disappear. Your dog may take flight. You might meet with some unpleasant uglies in a dark alley. Do you really want to find out? Do your research instead of spying on pretty girls. You'll understand."

We could probably do all that and heave a horse's head on his bed if we were feeling mean enough, but our usual retaliation tended to be behind the scenes. Unlike Graham, Nick and I hadn't erased our pasts. And since our mother had consorted with everyone from the CIA to the rulers of foreign countries, we'd run tame in palaces. Riley could fill a book on us with almost no effort.

An uneasy feeling rolled over me as I realized we'd been able to hide behind our mansion walls these last weeks, but now our address was in the hands of one of the biggest bullies of them all, thanks to Patra. Graham would be very unhappy if more creeps showed up.

"Oh, and one last bit of advice," I said with saccharine sweetness, hoping to put an end to this once and for all. "Patra is a good person to have at your back. You really don't want her for an enemy."

He snarled and escaped the crazies. Now that I had his name, I could search in BM's computers and see if he left a report. It could be entertaining reading.

I looked out the window to see if the coast was clear. Sean O'Herlihy, the gadfly reporter, was leaning against our wrought iron fence, studying the house where I was standing. Had Patra called him or was he following Leonard? The interesting point was that when Leonard emerged from the alley into the street, the rat caught sight of Sean, and scampered in the opposite direction from the Metro to avoid him.

Score one for O'Herlihy. The rat not only knew him, but was

afraid of him.

After giving the house another thoughtful look, Sean sauntered off in the same direction as his fellow reporter. Not dumb. The good reporter sensed a story.

I gestured for departure by the stairs. "Job well done. Coast is clear. Even O'Herlihy has gone away."

I'd had my suspicions about Sean and his motives in the past, but as far as I'd determined, he really was after Graham's story and nothing more. Mallard seemed to trust him, which had to be enough for me.

Mallard reset the trip wires. Still scowling, Nick sauntered down the stairs, examining the construction project as if he owned the place.

"The place looks like a McMansion," he said in disgust, gazing around the over-sized family room.

"You prefer dark and dingy?" I passed him and headed to the first floor. "With EG's bats maybe?"

"Elegant," Nick corrected. "Our original woodwork is sophisticated and elegant and doesn't look like a nursery."

"Thanks for stepping up to the plate while I was out," I offered. "We don't need any more spies than Graham."

"Getting friendly with the spider in the attic, are we?" Nick asked testily. "He'll throw us out as soon as Oppenheimer files the lawsuit on the house."

"We should buy this place and aim telescopes and satellite dishes at him," I agreed cheerily. "Is Oppenheimer getting any closer to Reggie? Are there hidden funds we don't know about?"

"My guess is that Reggie spent years siphoning off Max's money for drugs and we'll never see a cent," Nick said gloomily. "We won't be able to afford house upkeep even if Oppenheimer can get it back."

"One day at a time, grasshopper." I located the unboarded window, sat on the sill, and decided the distance to the ground was negligible. "Maybe we'll grow on Graham and he'll let us stay."

Nick's laugh followed me out. Sooner or later, we'd been thrown out of most of the palaces and tents we'd occupied.

Thirteen

Patra's perspective

PATRA stood on the corner, waiting for Ana's spy to stomp past. She'd seen Ana in action enough to know her sister had probably raked the jerk over the coals a few times and threatened him with their powerful connections.

Sometimes, if she was feeling generous, Ana would offer the jerks a bit of cheese to tempt them in another direction. Patra was curious as to that direction. The creep didn't look happy.

Sean showed up a moment later and fell in step with her. "His name's Leonard Riley. Used to be an investigative reporter until he got locked up for wiretapping and other stupidity. Now he's either too old or dumb to learn the technology, so Broddy uses him for small snoop jobs. What's he doing hanging around?"

"Spying on me. I'm trying to decide how to use him," Patra said, watching as Riley stepped into a bar. "But if he's a drunk, he's not worth the trouble."

"We all turn into drunks eventually. How else do we anesthetize ourselves to the shit we see around us?"

"By acting on it instead of complaining. Isn't that what you think you're doing by spying on Graham? What did he do to you?" Deciding Sean was more interesting company than a drunken sneak, Patra leaned against a lamp pole to talk.

"Way back when we were toddlers, my dad and Ana's dad were friends. Her dad got killed. Mine got sent to jail. And Graham rose out of the ashes. He keeps doing that. Let's just say I'm curious as to how."

From beneath lowered lashes, Patra studied O'Herlihy. For an older guy, he was more than attractive. He probably had more than ten years on her, which put him nearer Ana's age bracket. She'd never met Graham, but she'd heard Ana's complaints. Their host was probably in his thirties as well. She'd learned conspiracy theories at her mother's knee, but she was only interested in the one involving her father.

"Old news," she said dismissively. "Times have changed. Ana's father was a terrorist before Ireland got rich. Now they're bankrupt again, along with everyone else. The IRA is driving around in rusty BMWs. Muslims are the enemy now, not Protestants. Once they run out of oil in the Mideast, war mongers will move on to Africa. Historical cycles, doomed forever to repeat themselves."

"A Maximillian through and through," Sean said admiringly, before catching sight of someone or something down the street that made him frown. "Riley has called in the heavyweights. I wonder if he got permission from BM to pay hired help."

Patra cast a casual glance over her shoulder. It was a mild Saturday evening. The neighborhood was a mix of offices, row houses, and boutique hotels. The street bustled with pedestrians and traffic. She wasn't as adept at sorting out Americans as she was Europeans, but she assumed the people in gaudy shirts were tourists. The ones in jackets and blazers were a little more DC.

The six-foot, three-hundred pound gorilla wearing a narrow tie and shoulder holster under his shiny gray suit coat would be recognizable anywhere.

"Charming," she muttered. "Looks like the guy from the limo, except this one's bald. Did Riley put a hit out on me or on Ana?"

"Your whole family, if his employers can afford it. He needs his job and it appears as if someone is interfering in it." Sean looked entertained.

Patra wondered if she should call Ana and Nick, but she was a grown up now. Calling on her older siblings shouldn't be necessary. She didn't think this goon could have burned her London apartment, but it had probably been one like him. Thugs were international.

"I have a college education. I ought to come up with a better trap than sex," she grumbled, snapping a few quick photos of the gorilla and shooting them off to Ana as a precaution. Then she straightened her gauzy, low-cut tunic, tousled her hair, and smoothed a wrinkle from her cropped leggings.

"There's nothing better than sex," Sean said laughingly. "Just ask your mother. But I don't think you'll get far with this creep."

"I don't need to get far." With a lazy saunter, Patra strolled toward her target. He didn't even cast her a glance. She *tsked* under her breath, pretended to stumble on her high heel, and fell into the gorilla's arms.

He caught her with brute instinct. He would have brushed her off, but she grasped his coat sleeve.

"Oh, thank you, sir. My feet are so tired, I can scarcely lift them. I really don't need bruised knees too." She lifted a leg clad in tight knit and wiggled her toes at him. "Let me buy you a drink. I was just headed for Maxine's here anyway."

She took his arm, limped a little, and he silently dragged her into the dark bar.

Patra had seen her mother perform this next act so many times, that she could repeat it in her sleep. In fact, she'd used it more than once through college, adapting according to her purpose. She squeezed the thug's arm, lit up like a lantern, and as if totally surprised by the company inside, cried, "Mr. Riley, what are you doing here? This is so exciting!" She tugged her baffled escort in the same direction as his pal. "I never thought I'd have a chance to meet you."

She settled cozily on the bar stool next to Riley's and held out her hand. "Patra Llewellyn, sir. It's a pleasure to meet you." She gestured at the gorilla, who took the stool on her other side. "This gentleman just saved me from an ignoble fall, and I'm about to buy him a drink. Could I buy one for you, too?"

Riley gaped. Really, he was getting too old and slow for his job if he bought that act. Beside her, the gorilla shrugged his hefty shoulders and ordered a whiskey neat.

At the sound of the door opening, Patra glanced at the bar mirror. Sean slipped in and headed for a dark corner. She sparkled even brighter to provide him entertainment.

"I'll just have a tonic and lime," she told the bartender apologetically. "I have a lot of prep work to do for my new job, and I don't want to be fuzzy. How about you, Mr. Riley? Another round? Now that I'll have a salary, I'll be able to pay my credit card again."

He nodded, quit gaping, and donned a suspicious expression. "Patrick Llewellyn's daughter?" he asked in a surly tone, not responding to her best innocent smile.

Patra upped her Brit accent. "You know daddy? Oh, that's terrif!

Did you work on any stories together? The world has changed so much since he was alive, I don't think he'd recognize it. He thought Dick Tracy wrist watch phones were ridiculous, and now look at where we are." She pulled out her smart phone, snapped a shot of the three of them together, and sent that off to Ana, too, just to jerk her chains. "May I upload this to my Facebook account? It's just so exciting meeting you this way."

"Dammit, no!" Riley finally found his tongue. "Broderick hates for us to expose ourselves in social media. You'd better take that account down."

"Oh, no, I can't do that. I'm not an important investigative reporter like you, but I have fans already. It's the greatest way to build an audience. I'm certain Mr. Broderick will understand marketing. How about you, Mr. Riley, what have you been working on lately?"

She pulled out her shiny card case to hand him her business card, then dropped the case. "Oops, I'm clumsy when I'm tired." She waited expectantly.

Riley glared but picked the case up and handed it to her. She carefully tucked it into her purse so she could have his fingerprints pulled later. Maybe Ana knew someone who could dust Bill's apartment for prints. She'd have to steal the gorilla's whiskey glass if she had a chance.

"I'm retired," Riley said grumpily. "We all write our memoirs at this age. Did your father have notes for his?"

"Oh, daddy just had boxes of notes and dusty old disks. Even his lawyer said they were worthless. I lost them all in a fire. You must have exciting tales to tell about politicians you've met. That's what I aspire to, interviewing the president and the prime minister!"

Riley wanted to know about her father's memoirs, interesting. Did he suspect there was dirt in there? Or was he just fishing? If so, he wasn't very good at it. An interviewer had to show interest in his subject. Riley looked as if he wished she would drop dead.

"It's a dangerous world out there for little girls," Riley said with scorn. "You ought to stick to interviewing movie stars."

"Oh, I'm sure I will for years and years, but I can wait until opportunity knocks. It was so good to meet you, sir." She waved her credit card at the bartender. "But I really must do my Rhianna research before I talk to her Monday. Such a fascinating woman!

Good luck with your memoirs." She leaned in to touch gorilla's coat and confiscated his empty glass while he was distracted. "And thank you again, sir."

After signing off on the tab, she sauntered out without her unpleasant companions even thanking her for the free drinks. She'd like to think it was because she had them so baffled that they couldn't react, but she figured it was because they were jerks.

Sean lingered in his dark corner booth without looking up at her departure. *Go, Sean.*

Still, she located a dirty alley between buildings, climbed over the feeble gate, and hid against the wall between garbage cans to see what happened next. She watched the bar entrance in the traffic mirror reflector on the corner. The gorilla lumbered out a few minutes later, heading in the direction of her new home. Patra didn't worry too much about the gorilla knocking on Graham's door. Ana had his photo and a gargoyle glare that would scare varnish off wood.

Riley appeared next. He looked up and down both sides of the street, studying everyone before stepping out onto the sidewalk. Apparently satisfied that he was safe, he trotted in the same direction as Gorilla Boy. There was a closer Metro stop in the other direction. Really, could one man be so stupid?

She fell in a block behind him and Sean joined her.

"We really should quit meeting this way," she told him, not looking at him.

"I wasn't sure you could take care of yourself as well as Ana does. After you left, the thug and Leonard had a brief discussion. Money was exchanged. My bet is that someone is a target for gorilla-boy's automatic. Want to place any wagers on whom he's about to threaten?"

Patra snorted. "Sexist pigs like that will think they don't need automatics to scare Ana. They'd think a good shovel would work. So my bet is petty revenge on Nick or Mallard or both."

"Very astute of you, if not spyboy." He shoved a hand in the pocket of his tweed trousers as he watched Leonard turn a corner. "Did you indicate you had something that might be of interest to Broderick?"

"Old news," she scoffed. "Leonard wants to know if I have my father's files, which probably means Broddy wants to know. If they try to look for them inside the Monster Mansion, they'll either be dead or behind bars for a long time."

"Graham's that good, huh?"

She finally shot him a quick glance. Sean looked determined as well as interested. And interesting. Excellent jaw. Cute curly dark hair. Nice shoulders. But did she really know the man? "You're kidding, right?"

Sean shrugged. "A guy can only try. Why do you protect Graham? He could be a pervert and a terrorist for all you know."

"So could you, for all I know. Graham has the benefit of offering us a house to live in. He leaves us alone, and we return the favor, to the best extent possible, leastways. One doesn't muddy one's own nest. Look, Leonard is taking the street behind ours and Gorilla Boy is casing the front. Obviously, they didn't learn. Surely they don't mean to commit murder on a public street. Threatening seems more their speed."

"Do I call the cops now or wait until there are bodies?" Sean asked dryly.

"The bodies would be the gorilla and Leonard, and that comes under messing the nest." Patra texted Ana and Nick. "Really, I don't know how old-fashioned hoodlums think they can keep up in modern times unless they recall technology exists."

"Do we watch and wait or incite war?" He studied the gorilla's position beside the house under construction, apparently unfazed by murderous thugs or Ana.

He really ought to be worried about Ana.

"On my own, I'd go for war, but EG's inside, and that comes under messing the nest, too," she said with regret. "I really need to get my own place. This level of monitoring is beyond all tiresome."

"Leonard's had an opportunity by now to discover the old carriage house on the other block. Shall I leave you here while I check on him? I can video you the result."

Laughing, Patra looked up at him. "An older man who gets technology. Good for you, sport. Go at it. I want to see how Graham protects his rear."

Sean all but snarled and trotted off around the corner. That should get him out of her way before she started shooting.

Fourteen

I GLARED as my no-longer new or amusing toy beeped with still another message from Patra. My sibling was showing off, metaphorically strutting her stuff by sending photos of the nosy reporter and his cohort in a tavern. If Patra wanted to try the mossy tactic of cozying up to the enemy, it was her time and money. But I supposed it was considerate of her to let me know where she was.

I was monitoring the coded file slowly emerging from the current document I'd fed into the software. Graham had been right. Patra's father had coded some of his papers. Figuring out which ones was the trick. He'd played dirty pool by encoding what appeared to be meaningless office memos and expense reports instead of his journal entries.

I hit the phone for the image coming through at the same time as Graham snarled through the intercom.

"Send your sister back where she came from. I don't need those termites snooping around my back door."

"Because that's where you keep your Batmobile?" I asked, just because.

The image appearing on my phone showed a gorilla-sized goon with a shoulder holster leaning against the wall of the house across the street. And Graham had spotted a termite at the back door? Not good, Patra.

Graham didn't waste his breath responding. He'd got his threat across with his snarl. I grabbed my phone as it rang with a forwarded photo—from *Sean*? What the hell was Sean doing out there? I trotted to the kitchen to show Mallard the image of Riley at the carriage house.

He recognized the location behind us and grabbed a meat cleaver.

"Protect yourself and EG with that," I warned. "We don't take violent offensive."

As if Mallard would take orders from me. He glared down at me with scorn and took the kitchen stairs to his backyard herb garden. Assuming Patra was somewhere outside, I ran up to the second floor and EG's tower aerie.

I knocked politely. "Tower surveillance needed. Coming in."

Her door instantly popped open. She had our newly purchased spy telescope in hand. "There's a man with a gun in the alley."

"Yeah, Patra is out there sending live action photos. Have you spotted her yet?"

EG had lowered the top half of her shades so she could stand on her reading chair and look out. I had a little more height, but not enough. I took the spyglass, climbed on the desk chair, and worked it like a skateboard, looking for the best position.

The big goon with a gun was on the east side of the vacant house across the street. Patra was stationed on the west, watching something on her smart phone. Sean must be sneaking around with a camera, and she was forwarding his images.

I turned to look out the rear tower windows, but the warehouse or reinforced carriage house or whatever that was behind us was a solid mountain obstructing the view. I couldn't even see Mallard.

Nick wandered in, dressed in his best Saturday night duds and smelling like an expensive whorehouse. "What game are we playing?"

"Patra's out there with a hitman," I said, handing over the glass. "We're wagering on whether she brings him down before or after Graham does. And Graham reports a termite at the rear."

"Oh, goody, can I have the termite?" he asked facetiously, checking out the thug in front. "The goon is totally passé. Patra really ought to look for a better class of enemy. A good strong fire hose would bring him down. I think Mallard has one in the basement."

"Mallard has gone after the termite with a kitchen axe. Since Patra's been following Leonard Riley, I assume he's the termite. We're waiting for the fireworks before bothering with the goon."

A recorded voice began broadcasting from the speakers in the hall. We all obediently trudged out to decipher the staticky broadcast from Graham's lair.

"Perennial bad boy, Reginald Brashton the Third, died unexpectedly in his jail cell today after being extradited to face drug and embezzlement charges. An autopsy has been arranged. Arnold

Oppenheimer, lawyer for one of the plaintiffs suing Brashton, had visited with Brashton earlier in the day. Speculation is rife in the legal community."

In frustrated fury, I whacked the telescope against the speaker. The one at the other end of the hall continued with the news report, but I didn't have to listen.

Brashton. *Dead*! After all our efforts to return him alive.

I couldn't summon any grief over a spoiled rich boy who'd murdered my grandfather. Fear and fury warred inside me instead. This was worse than losing the yacht. I pounded my heel into the wood paneling in a fit of frustration.

Damn Reggie! Even in death he was a pain in the rear.

Unable to fight this devastating blow, we grimly retreated to EG's room to spy on the spies.

"News van at three o'clock," Nick reported, gazing out the shaded windows without need of chair. "The media has figured out who the plaintiffs are." His voice had gone from cheerful to flat. All his work bringing Reggie back alive—for naught.

Nick and I gloomily contemplated the many ways we could have tortured our grandfather's lawyer if we hadn't been trying to play legal. Was Reggie's death in a jail cell the justice we wanted? It didn't feel like it.

"Thugs to the left of us, termites to the right," EG said helpfully. "Now what do we do?"

I sighed. Pouting wouldn't get us anywhere. We might as well deal with what was on our doorstep.

"Nick, check on our favorite termite journalist. Tickle Riley's fancy any way that makes you happy to chase him away so Mallard will put down his axe and go back to fixing Graham's dinner. We have a news van out front, blocking our goon's aim, so I'm guessing we don't need the fire hose. I think I'll go pull a few daisy petals and see what happens. I need to get back to work and this parade of imbeciles is in my way." I stalked off, simmering.

I was back in my grubbies—long cotton skirt and tie-dyed t-shirt—so I wasn't exactly camera fare. Which was precisely the image I wanted to project—dull, uninteresting, unnewsworthy. If gorgeous Patra of the short skirt got out there first, the media would never leave us alone.

So I took the stairs two at a time while texting Patra to tell her to stay the hell out of sight. She objected. I told her I'd lock her out of the house. She sulked in silence.

When I reached the front door, I slowed to a mosey. The cameraman was at the front gate by the time I let myself out. Instead of going to meet him, I ignored him. I sat down on the front step and began looking for four-leaf clovers in the patch of lawn. If there had been daisies, I would have plucked them.

Apparently Mallard had locked the gate while wielding his meat cleaver. Smart man. The camera whirred and a reporter leaned over the spiked wrought iron fence to shout, "Miss Maximillian, did you know Reggie Brashton was murdered in his jail cell this afternoon?"

I picked a blade of grass, chewed on it, eyed him skeptically, then returned to playing with the clover. I wasn't giving him credit for identifying me. My long black braid is pretty distinctive, and I'd stirred up an ant's nest of reporters just a few weeks ago. I looked for the gorilla goon across the street from the corner of my eye, but the van blocked the house.

The reporter tried again. "Your lawyer was the last person to see him alive. Will Brashton's death help or hurt your case?"

Oh, the little boy had read his press copy. Very nice. I chewed my grass some more, then looking past him, I nodded as if to a friend. The reporter and cameraman swung around, maybe just a little afraid. I doubted that they knew Graham was inside, so maybe it was just their surroundings that made them jumpy.

From his street-side position, the cameraman must have spotted the hired goon with his telescopic lens. Instead of jumping in his van and leaving, he started filming the goon.

I pulled out my phone and called Patra. "Is the baddie leaving yet? Want to be on entertainment news or come in the back way?"

I'd seen her across the street, so I knew she was watching the whole scene. I trusted she was keeping an eye out for Gorilla Boy, who should be making his escape down the alley about now.

"Entertainment news?" she asked warily.

"Brashton is dead and apparently the media thinks our lawyer killed him. Can you think of any *good* questions they might ask?"

I waited for her to run that scenario through her encyclopedic knowledge of the media and reach the same conclusion as me.

"Probably not," she agreed. "I'd rather be the one asking questions. Is Nick out back?"

"Yup. He'll escort you through the kitchen garden."

With the reporter still shouting questions at me and the cameraman now filming the whole street, I got up and went back inside. Riley and friends wouldn't risk a film crew.

I jogged down to my office with my heart in my throat and my head pounding. I needed to find out all I could about Reggie's death.

It would make a great deal of sense for our enemies to kill Reggie and blame our lawyer at the same time. I knew Graham would benefit since it was his house we wanted. Reggie's old law firm would benefit because we fully intended to drag their esteemed East Coast asses through some very murky mud. And number one on my list of suspects—the shadowy Top Hat organization that I suspected of ordering Reggie to kill Max. Reggie had had stories to tell, names to name. I should have seen this coming.

I wished I had Graham's banks of computers at my fingertips. I didn't like it that people around us were dropping like flies.

"Riley ran when he saw Mallard coming," Nick announced with disappointment, clattering down the stairs with Patra. "They don't make good hoodlums anymore."

The phone rang.

I waved everyone to silence while I answered the phone. Oppenheimer's secretary was on the line.

"Mr. Oppenheimer regrets that he will be unable to pursue your case," the poor secretary said. I could tell from her voice that she hadn't wanted to call us—for good reason. I wasn't about to be reasonable.

"Tell Oppenheimer not to be a chicken-hearted turd. We've paid him a substantial sum, and we're not letting him off the hook. He can help us find out who really killed Reggie and why. Tell him to hire a detective if he's incapable of asking the right questions. We're not taking no for an answer." I hung up and smiled wickedly at my listeners. I didn't have to let them know how worried I was.

"And now we start hunting Reggie's murderer as well as Bill's," I told them.

Fifteen

MY DECLARING we were about to become detectives didn't deter Nick from heading out for the evening. Nor did it stop Patra from exchanging notes with Sean at the fake Irish pub on the corner. Heaven forbid that I should interfere in their social lives just because I didn't have one.

Before I started my own detecting list, I located EG in my bedroom, pecking away at my laptop. She had a clear view of the street from my desk and her slightly battered spyglass beside the computer.

"I don't suppose you're doing homework?" I leaned over her shoulder. She was Googling Broderick Media.

"In one sense of the word, yes," she said in a clipped snotty tone. "If this is to be my home, then I'm working to protect it."

"I don't see any Gatling guns. So, are we chasing Reggie's trail or the beanbrain who's been spying on Patra?"

"Leonard Riley, investigative reporter, fired by Broderick Media after being convicted *and* sued for invasion of privacy over telephone hacking the vice president of the United States. Apparently the Secret Service was displeased. That was back before 9/11." She called up a back issue of the *Washington Post*. "There's a different media conglomerate in the UK currently sued for tapping the phones of public officials. They must have picked up a few tips from BM."

I quickly scanned the story. "I don't think Leonard's little misadventure begins to compare with the English variety," I pointed out. "The UK media directly hacked the queen and the prince and everyone down to the baby sisters of rock stars through some antiquated phone system. It's tougher to hack U.S. phone systems. If he actually tapped the vice-president, he needed someone with equipment on the inside. Different sort of operation."

"That's what I thought." EG brought up another tab with the image of a portly, white-haired gent wearing a shit-eating smile that made my guts grind. *Dr. Charles Smythe, leader of the Righteous and Proud*, read the caption, but I would have recognized a sleazy snake-oil salesman anywhere. Half the members of Congress wore that expression. The other half just weren't as pretty. Not that I'm prejudiced or anything.

"Why Smythe?" I asked.

"Dr. Smythe, *a former aide to the vice president of the United States,* recently appointed to the R&P's newly-created executor's position," she read aloud. My own personal evil genius pointed to a figure in the background of the photo.

The figure looked like our rotund reporter, a few pounds lighter. The story date was roughly ten years ago—way beyond our concern. I waited for explanation.

"Dr. Smythe has resigned his position at the White House to work as head of the Righteous and the Proud," she read further into the story. "Shortly prior to Leonard's arrest," she added, tabbing back to Riley's page.

"Why on earth..." I tabbed back and forth, skimming the articles.

Smythe had resigned from the White House not long before Riley was arrested for tapping the veep's private phone. The two of them were shown together in a publicity photo—so presumably Riley knew Smythe? As well as Broderick, because Riley had been working for BM when he'd got arrested and fired.

Had the R&P rewarded Smythe with a paying position after Riley had gathered inside information from the vice president's private phone line? The correlation of place and time were there, but not much else.

"And after Lennie left prison, he collected a small pension from B&M, according to his credit report. The credit bureaus list him as an independent contractor," EG added.

"Independent contractor could mean anything. Lennie could just be doing exactly what he said," I reminded her. "Investigating new hires is not unknown, although Riley could be putting his own spin on it for whatever reason. I'll dig in a little deeper. You did good, grasshopper, now go take your bath and read a book about bats."

"Once I have my Mac—"

"You'll be dangerous, I'm aware. But we have to give Nick and

Patra a few things to do, so you can clock out now. Give the brain a rest." I shooed her out of my room, feeling a mother's heart tug at recognizing her child was a chip off the old block.

Except EG is my sister and she emulated Mata Hari Magda, and that really was not a good thing for any of us.

* * *

Patra's perspective

Patra leaned against the wall and sprawled her legs across the booth seat in the dark pub. She sipped her beer and returned to tapping through her smart phone. "Why aren't you quizzing me about Oppenheimer and Brashton and all those fascinating things all reporters want for this week's gossip?"

On the bench across from her, Sean shrugged and sipped his own beer. "Investigating a dead druggie isn't my kind of story unless it leads me to Graham and whatever he's up to these days. I'll be your media mouthpiece on Reggie, if you need it."

"Not happening unless Ana gives the word. You do not want to get on Ana's wrong side." Patra showed him the text that had just arrived. "She's found another speech analyst for my father's tape and is sending him all the audio files we confiscated from Bill's place."

Sean already knew about Bill's files and had done nothing with the information. She had to trust him if she wanted insider information. But she didn't mention that Ana had figured out part of the code in her father's papers. That was private. "She's scary good."

"I agree with the scary part." Sean eyed her text with skepticism. "But your father is old news. What's the point? The world's moved on. That war is done."

"My apartment was incinerated a month ago, and Bill may have just died for that *old news*. If I'm earning a Pulitzer before I'm thirty, I can't ignore any story that comes my way. Bill was murdered. We don't know why. The cops aren't looking. I will. Simple. Now are you with me or not?"

"The whole family is crazy," Sean muttered. "Do I get to share the Pulitzer?"

"Sure, why not?" she waved her hand and shut down her phone.

"Ana says the rest of Bill's papers are with his family. I want them. I have tomorrow off. How about you?"

"It's Sunday," he pointed out. "Even the media has the day off."

"Yeah." Patra sent him her sexiest grin. "That's what I'm counting on."

* * *

Sunday morning, I woke up from a hot and nasty dream of a sweaty, very naked Graham on top of me. I was so far into the dream that I actually contemplated going upstairs and experimenting with another of his steamy kisses. I'd have to do something about getting laid soon, but family complicated my life. I hit the shower instead.

I took time to study my wardrobe after I got out. I'd spent my earlier years as my flamboyant mother's inconspicuous shadow. My comfort zone had always been with invisibility. Disguise served a similar purpose. I was planning on visiting a jail today. I didn't think prison orange was the look I was after.

So I opted for lawyerly. I really needed some black-framed eyeglasses but sunglasses were all I owned in that department. And I owned nary a single suit. Blazer over a tank top and khaki skirt had to do. I pinned up my braid at the back of my head and hurried down to the dining room for breakfast.

"I thought Sunday was family errand time," the candelabra said with a distinctly ironic tone as I filled my plate.

"And so it is." Since none of my family was down here for Graham to eavesdrop on, I was perfectly comfortable talking to a hunk of silver. That he recognized my street clothes ought to chill my bones. Instead, the fact that he noticed gave me a cheap thrill. "Saving my family home comes under family errands."

"Give it up, Ana. You can't afford to run a place like this. I own the house. You can have use of it. Your family needs to find their own lives."

"I'm not content with *having use of it*, your royal highness. I want a *right* to it. So go back to bed. I'll let you know if you can stay when it's my turn." I sat down to a lovely breakfast of English muffins and poached eggs while Graham growled and clicked off. That's what he got for fogging up my dreams.

EG wandered in all sleepy-eyed and carrying a text on chiropterology.

I raised my eyebrows. "Rodents kept you up all night?"

"Bats are not rodents," she said scornfully. "They're mammals and more closely related to us than rats. Scientists ought to be using them for experimentation instead of mice."

I figured I ought to get credit for guessing that her text was about bats, but arguing with a nine-year-old is batty. "Nice. I know a few mammals I could suggest for lobotomy experimentation. Why mutilate poor bats? Did you get the one out of your room yet?"

"I think he's hiding in my closet." She dropped the book beside her plate and poured juice. "What are we doing today?"

"You and Nick are doing laundry. I'm helping Oppenheimer win our case. We ought to send Patra grocery shopping just to keep her out of trouble." I savored the last sip of my tea and wondered if donuts were an appropriate bribe at a jail. I'd never been inside an American one.

"They have a traveling bat exhibit at the zoo," EG said, intruding upon my reverie.

And that was the kind of family expedition we were supposed to have on Sundays. Properly chastised, I grimaced and got up. "Okay, do the laundry, tell Patra she's going with us, and we'll check it out this afternoon after I get back."

We were hardly the modern American family, but our time division involved the same kind of choices. Did I work long hours to keep our lavish home, or find a cheaper place and stay home with the kid on weekends?

I wasn't any more temperamentally suited to staying idle than Magda was. I really had to quit blaming her for our miserable upbringing.

The D.C. Correctional Facility was on the opposite end of our mansion-studded area of town. I took the Metro to challenge my navigational skills. I'd already researched the facility and knew the only way I was getting inside today was by being a lawyer. I'd made a few phone calls. It's amazing what a little advance legwork can do.

Because he was a lawyer, Reggie had been given a private cell. Or maybe because someone needed him alone to murder him, which might implicate jail employees in his murder. Not a happy thought.

A few months ago, I'd found a backdoor into police files, and I'd used it this morning to read the report on Reggie's death. He'd been poisoned with cyanide—a really crude choice.

According to the police report, Reggie's collapse had been public and noticeable. Cyanide poisoning is nasty. If Reggie's jailers had acted a little faster, he might have lived long enough to have permanent brain damage. Instead, they assumed he was in withdrawal and ignored his convulsions too long, and he'd died at the hospital.

Someone had tried to make it very obvious that our boy had been murdered by our lawyer.

At the main entrance to the detention center, I produced the fake ID I'd created for myself when I was studying money laundering. Since I had already called ahead to get on the appointment roster, the guard had no reason to examine my credentials closely. I had even found the name of the occupant of the cell across from Reggie's —Lemuel Hackman— and arranged a visit with my "client." The success of my foray depended entirely on Hackman's cooperation. I'd done my research there, too.

This was a facility for those prisoners who hadn't yet been convicted. We're all innocent until proven guilty, right? Some of us are just more innocent than others, or have friends with bigger wallets.

Hackman had been charged with a drive-by shooting. He had priors and his bond was off the charts. Read between the lines and you see gangbanger and someone the cops want off the streets—even if he didn't commit the crime with which he was charged—under the assumption that he was undoubtedly guilty of others. That's what happens when you hang out with the wrong crowd.

The guards led me to one of those rooms with a glass wall down the middle and telephones on either side. Lemuel didn't look surprised to see me when he picked up his phone. He was even younger looking than I'd expected, although the reports said he was eighteen. He was slight, with a burgeoning goatee and a gang symbol shaved into his cropped nap. "You from the public defender?" he asked.

"No, I'm better, Mr. Hackman. I can get you bail. Convince me you're worth it."

I'd give him credit for intelligently narrowing his eyes with suspicion. "How?"

"First, if I get you out of here, what are you going to do?" I had ulterior motives on top of ulterior motives, but I wasn't letting a murderer into the street if I knew about it.

Correctly guessing that was a loaded question, he didn't pull the bluffing thug act. I gave him another point. He shrugged. "Run," he said. "The state's got evidence that points to me. I can't prove I didn't do it. And the guy who did do it will figure I squealed and kill me."

"I've been worse off," I said with a similar world-weary shrug. He looked disbelieving, but that was pure honesty and the reason I had the audacity to follow this game. "You've got nothing to lose if you trust me. I've got a lot of money to lose if you run. If you can give me the information I want, I'll bail you out, find you a safe place, and you can squeal like a pig so we can lock up the gun-toting cretin. Fair?"

"What you want?" He emanated suspicion like bad body odor.

"I need a list of everyone who visited the guy who died in the cell across from you, and I mean jailers and anyone who just looked ugly passing his cell that day." I sat back and waited. I figured my chances were fifty-fifty that he'd spill. Far less that he'd provide what I needed.

He nodded slowly. "I can do that. I'd be real happy to do that. Just get me out of here and somewhere safe."

"You're good." I smiled in approval. "But I'm the one with the money and the safe place and you're the one with incentive to run. What I'm asking costs you nothing. You either trust me now, or we have no deal."

He weighed his options. He didn't have many. "Okay, but if you don't come through, my homeys are gonna find you."

"No, they aren't, but they won't need to. I'm straight up." I took a notebook and pen out of my hand. "Spill."

He'd been bored that day, apparently. He began listing every guard who walked past their cells from the moment he woke up. This kid needed an education for that brain of his. I took notes. I tried not to flinch when he hadn't named anyone whose name I knew by the time he reached Reggie's departure to visit Oppenheimer.

Reggie had been acting as his own lawyer—a fool's job but his only alternative had been a public defender. He wasn't allowed any visitors except a lawyer on weekends. He'd agreed to see Oppenheimer on Saturday. I couldn't see how Oppenheimer could have passed anything poisonous through this glass wall, as the police report suggested, but maybe real lawyers knew the protocol. Or maybe they'd been given a private room and the report was wrong.

"When the guy got back to his cell," the kid continued, "his preacher came by to talk to him. That's the last I saw before he started screaming and throwing up and causing a racket," Hackman concluded.

His preacher! I almost smiled. "And did you catch the name of his preacher by any chance?"

Lemuel just shrugged. "He just called him Smitty."

Smitty?

I recalled Dr. Smythe of the R&P had a religious doctorate of some kind. Reggie's *preacher*?

"Tell me which bail bondsman you recommend," I said in satisfaction, "then tell me what the preacher looked like."

Sixteen

I CALLED Nick from the Detention Center and arranged for him to have one of his buddies pick up Lemuel after he was released on Monday. Our family bank account was badly hit by the kid's bondsman and would be more so after we paid one of Nick's chronic moocher friends to take Lemuel on as a roommate. But I was counting on Lemuel being a smart boy and willing to stay on the opposite end of town from his usual haunts until the real drive-by killer was caught.

I needed to see if I could find the kid an anonymous dishwashing job so he didn't take to pawning his new roomie's TV. I'm no bleeding heart. I didn't expect *anyone* to be pure of soul. But given a choice, the smart ones discovered work was simpler than a life of dodging the law and gangs.

Once I returned to my basement, I ran a quick Google on Dr. Smythe and printed out a photo. I'd show it to Lemuel for verification once he was out on bond, but Smythe fit Lemuel's description.

It was Sunday, and I didn't know how to reach Oppenheimer to relay the information of a possible killer to him. There wasn't much he—or the police—could do about Smitty anyway. The good reverend was a hugely popular advisor to politicians. I needed real evidence or the preacher had pretty much accomplished the perfect crime—as had my grandfather's killer.

When I learned Patra had taken off to pry files out of Mrs. Bloom, I wasn't too happy. But I wasn't too happy about her being a walking target for her father's enemies either, so I sucked it up. EG and Nick had done the laundry, and I owed EG a visit to the zoo.

We'd earned our afternoon off.

* * *

Patra's perspective

Patra straightened the boxy jacket that concealed her figure and nervously tried to ignore the gray cat twisting around her bare ankles. Her long, flowered skirt had been a Goodwill purchase. It was nasty enough to attract cats and small rodents.

This was her one and only chance to retrieve Bill's papers. *She would not kick a cat.*

"We are so sorry for your loss, Mrs. Bloom. With more time, I'm sure your son would have seen the error of his ways and returned to the fold. It's always tragic to see a young man cut off before he achieves his prime."

Patra didn't dare look at Sean. Last time, he'd crossed his eyes at her and stuck a finger down his throat as if he wanted to puke—juvenile behavior for a grown man. Fortunately, Mrs. Bloom couldn't see him. He stood behind their hostess, keeping an eye on the street outside.

"Bill was smart," Mrs. Bloom said with a sniff. "I'd hoped he would make something of his fancy education. But then he dropped out and fell in with the wrong crowd."

Yeah, he fell in with educated people with open minds. Patra nodded. "It happens. I understand. But Dr. Smythe fears those papers in your possession might contain anti-Christian propaganda. If you would entrust them to us, we'll see that they're shredded. And I believe a small payment has been authorized for your service to the cause."

Mrs. Bloom frowned. "I told that other nice girl that I'd call her..."

"Oh, she works for us. She's the one who told Dr. Smythe about the papers. I'll call her now if you'd like to talk to her." Patra produced her phone while frantically trying to remember if Ana had told her the name she'd used when visiting Bill's mother. Ana never used her own name.

"Oh, that's all right, then. Ken is out in the garage. He'll help you load them into your car. He was planning on burning them in the fireplace this winter, but it's probably safer if you shred them."

In relief, Patra stood up, nudging the cat away from her pump. "We'll dispose of the boxes, and you'll be receiving a small check in the mail. It's been a pleasure meeting you, Mrs. Bloom. This country needs more righteous citizens like you."

Even Patra was gagging on her own poppycock by the time they had loaded the trunk of Sean's sports car and waved farewell to Bill's surly brother. Ken had scarcely spoken a word despite her best efforts to charm. He was on the phone when they backed out and didn't even notice her wave.

"How do you plan on sending a check from the R&P?" Sean asked as they drove away.

"I don't. Let her pester the bigots for the money. Give them something to do figuring out who we are. With Riley following me around, it's only a matter of time anyway. We just need to work faster." Patra sank deeper into the classic MG's leather seat and watched the road behind them over her shoulder. "I'd rather not lead strangers back to the house, though."

"To the batcave?" he asked incredulously. "I don't think anyone short of the CIA has the know-how to get past Graham's fortress."

"They won't need to go near Graham if they catch us first. Shiny white Cadillac sedan two cars back."

Sean shot her a frown before checking his mirror. Two demerits, Patra thought, using Ana's old system of rating character. For safety, one always checked out the credibility of the warning first, not the messenger.

"What's wrong with a Cadillac?" he asked warily.

"I'm not familiar with DC, but humor me. Try going around the block and come up behind the Caddy. In this traffic, he can't get too far, and if he's heading for the freeway, he should be easy to follow."

Sean made a sharp left turn in front of oncoming traffic, floored the little car through a yellow light, made a left at the next intersection, then made two more lefts to take them back to their original route.

She couldn't see the Cadillac. "Well done, grasshopper. Those left turns should have shaken him for a while." Patra scanned the side roads they passed.

"It could have turned off anywhere," Sean argued.

"A pricey car like that does not belong in this neighborhood." She gestured at the dirty Ford Econ-o-vans and battered pickups around them. "Cadillacs would only be passing through on the way to the interstate, which is straight ahead, if I remember correctly.

Continue as if we're going home. I think darling Ken called a tail."

Patra pulled out her phone and rang Ana. She got voice mail. Nick, the same. She didn't have a message to leave. Yet.

Sean took the entrance ramp. Still slumped below the seat back, Patra studied the traffic behind them in the side-view mirror. "Convertibles make a rotten getaway car, especially if the villains start shooting. There he is, three cars back, coming up the ramp. He knew our route and waited for us to pass him."

"Not that I'm buying your family paranoia..." Sean floored the MG, passed a semi on the left, swerved back to the right lane in front of the truck, and recklessly caught the next exit ramp.

Patra almost swallowed her tongue as the semi came a hair's breadth from rear-ending them. "You're too visible. The Cadillac saw us. But nice maneuver."

Sean swore vividly as the Caddy veered right and off the ramp at the last minute. "That should screw anyone waiting for us on the usual route, at least."

"They could have picked up Bill's papers anytime, just the way we did," Patra said, brain cranking as genuine fear set in. "It's *us* they're after."

"Yeah, that was my conclusion, too. The papers were bait. They just waited to see who was interested and hooked Ana. And then they waited for her to come back for them. Or us, as it turns out. But you were the first one at the scene of Bill's apartment that night, so you're more likely who they were expecting."

"I'm not as sneaky as Ana," she admitted with a shrug. "People notice me, so I play it."

"Play it with someone else, please. I don't relish turning gray before my time." He zipped the car into a shopping center, took an alley back to the Dumpsters, bumped across a parking lot edger, over a grass divider, and into a parking lot behind an apartment house.

"You'll tear the bottom out of your pretty car," she protested, trying not to look impressed.

"My office is out here. I know the shortcuts."

Torn between wide-eyed awe at his ability to dodge garbage bins, and watching over her shoulder for the white Caddy, Patra was working on a bad case of neck strain. She almost fell over in relief when he rolled the midget car into an underground garage.

"I hate leaving my baby like this, but let's get these boxes upstairs. Maybe I can send security down." Sean jumped out and began unloading the convertible.

"Don't suppose you have any friends to help us with these?" Patra complained when she tried to balance one box too many on her stack.

"Sunday, remember? Nearly empty garage?" Arms full, he gestured with his chin at the few old clunkers occupying the enormous space.

Slamming the trunk, Patra shut up and followed him to the elevator, expecting the Cadillac to run them down any minute. She didn't breathe until the elevator doors closed. Remembering the horror of her scorched apartment, she shuddered. "Do you think they'd torch a newspaper office?"

"They can't know there's anything of interest in these boxes or they'd have destroyed them first and worried about you later."

"Theory," she argued. "Why me?"

He glared at her. "Aren't you the one who had her apartment burned? Wasn't Bloom *your* contact? Wasn't he doing some spy work for you? Why not you?"

He had a point, even if she didn't agree. Bill had only one of her father's files. These boxes contained something else.

Getting off the elevator upstairs, Sean dropped his stack on a table in a cubicle farm and punched up a land line. "Security? Keep an eye out for a white Caddy in the garage. Call the cops if it shows up."

Seventeen

Patra's perspective

SEAN led the way through an office packed with ancient desks overflowing with file folders and yellowing documents as well as aging gray computers. In comparison with BM's modern cubicle farm, this fifties-era office reeked of old cigarette smoke and Jack Daniels. She didn't know where the other employees were hidden, maybe another floor.

"Don't modernize much, do you?" she asked.

"We're small change compared to the *Post* and BM. Competitive newspapers are a losing proposition in the computer age. Our on-line edition costs more than it earns, from the way the upper echelons make it sound." Sean dumped the boxes in a cramped conference room. The table was dusty and half the chairs had disappeared. Old computers littered the floor. "Essentially, to earn market share, print papers have to appeal to the old, the barely literate, and the poor who lack technology. Or those too set in their ways to change."

"That's harsh." She unloaded her boxes on the table and began looking through them. "Basic journalism hasn't changed. People still buy papers to read about themselves and their friends. It's just harder to do in a metropolis where most of the population are strangers."

"And not profitable on a small local basis given the cost of newsprint, hence, national scandal rags like Broderick's. Gossip is internationally popular." Sean lifted one of his heavier boxes to the table and began ransacking it.

"Great minds discuss ideas. Small minds discuss people," Patra said absently, flipping through an invoice file.

"Eleanor Roosevelt, nice." He set aside the big box and opened another. "You quote Americans and don't speak with a Brit accent.

Magda's work?"

"And American teachers on military bases. We all have citizen-of-the-world accents." Ana had said she could trust Sean except on topics of Graham, so Patra continued with a shrug. "Except maybe my half-brother Tudor. His father pays for a Brit boarding school. Right chip off the old block, he is," she mimicked her younger brother's mocking imitation of his father.

She shut up to study the invoice she'd pulled.

A phone buried on the desk amid the debris of boxes began to ring. Patra didn't glance up from her reading but was aware Sean had located the source of the noise. She tuned in when his tone registered urgency.

"Call the cops. Warn anyone else in the building to go into lockdown. Lock the elevator, if that's possible. And if it's not, blast them to hell if they get near my car!"

Anticipating his next command, Patra began cramming file folders into a fold-up tote she carried for just these impromptu occasions. Running with stacks of boxes while wearing a skirt and pumps simply wasn't a smart idea.

Sean slammed the phone and began tossing a few folders he'd sorted out into one of the smaller boxes.

"Not the white sedan, but a black Escalade just pulled into the garage. No one here drives tanks like that."

"That was a black Escalade limo at Bill's apartment the night he was killed." Patra grabbed another handful of files.

"Worse yet if they've set the thugs on us." He crammed a few more folders in the box. "We've only got one guy on security, and he's eating lunch and just watching monitors. I don't know if he can lock elevators, and I don't plan to take any chances hanging around to find out." He grabbed her arm and tugged her toward a rear exit.

"I just found a file on Broderick!" she protested, digging deeper into the largest box. "They're just invoices, but where there's smoke—"

"You want to get caught in the next fire?" Realizing he couldn't budge her, he started flinging boxes beneath the table. "Shove the rest of your boxes under a desk and grab what's loose."

Patra added handfuls of folders to her tote. "Surely they wouldn't set an entire *office* on fire?" she asked, glancing at all the lovely information they were leaving behind.

Sean snatched a sheet of plastic from a stack of monitors and flung it over the desk concealing the large cartons. "We've got sprinklers and fire walls, but they won't protect cardboard, if these guys are your arsonists. C'mon, out the back way."

Carrying their loads, they ran down a hall of empty executive offices. Sean opened a door marked "maintenance only," and they dived into a concrete jungle of deteriorating metal staircases and peeling paint.

"You're like a rat with bolt holes all over," Patra said breathlessly as they raced down the stairs. She hoped sounds didn't carry as their shoes rattled the metal stairs.

"Very handy when the boss wants me to do something I don't want to do." He caught her elbow as they reached the basement level. "This last part's tricky. Careful where you step."

The dank, dark basement smelled of must and old cleaning fluids. Obviously, this portion of the building was older than it looked and once had a coal cellar. Patra could hear mechanicals rattling beyond the dividing walls, but this maintenance area had been abandoned for all practical purposes. Water dripped somewhere, and moisture seeped through her soles. *Ewww.*

"Up here," Sean said triumphantly, tackling a metal door at the top of a couple of concrete steps. "When the *Times* still owned this whole building, they used to hand the papers out to newsboys here, fresh off the old printing presses."

"They don't keep it locked?" she asked incredulously.

"Can't open it from the other side." He peered down what seemed to be an alley. "Shit." He shut the door again. "There's a suspicious suit blocking the alley. They definitely want us as much as the boxes."

"A suspicious suit?"

"He's wearing a suit coat to cover his shoulder holster. Ring bells?"

Patra already had her phone out, dialing Ana. This time, her sister answered. "We're at Sean's office. Goons to the left of us, possible arsonists to the right. How far away are you? The *zoo?*" She glanced at Sean.

He snorted. "She can't get any further away and still be on the Metro. Want to try calling Graham?"

If that's what Sean was after, he was out of luck. She'd die before she broke her vow to Ana to leave Graham out of their lives.

"Not even Graham could get here in time," she whispered, dialing 911 even though they had no real emergency to report. Yet.

* * *

I watched EG admiring the ugliest, largest bat I'd ever known existed, while listening to Patra's explanation of events. "So we have no idea who's after you? Okay, Nick is chatting up a chimp somewhere. Keep your phone on vibrate. I'll get back to you."

My protective mother radar instincts were gearing up, but they were torn in two directions. Patra was old enough to take care of herself. EG shouldn't have to live as we had. Ergo, I couldn't destroy a rare normal family outing by haring off downtown to blow up an Escalade, no matter how much I'd enjoy it.

I punched in Nick's number to drag him out of the chimp house. I didn't think it was the animals Nick was admiring.

It would take much too long to travel downtown. While I was waiting for Nick to put in an appearance, I ground my teeth with impatience and fear and contemplated my next step. I hated calling in Graham. Patra's bad guys were related to Bill. We had no evidence of a connection to BM.

But Broderick was one of Graham's targets in his Top Hat investigation. Graham was inordinately interested in Patrick Llewellyn's files. And Bill had Patrick's media manipulation file. Close enough.

I'd never willingly called Graham's number, but I'd nabbed it back when EG had been kidnapped.

He answered with gratifying promptness and a grumpy, "What?"

"Patra is trapped with Sean at the *Times* office. They were followed from Bill Bloom's house. There is apparently a man with a shoulder holster preventing them from escaping. They've not been threatened yet, but I told Patra to call 911 anyway. What are the chances this has something to do with Broderick?"

"It's as likely to have more to do with her father, but the two could be related," he admitted. "You need to finish de-coding your sister's files so we know the scoop. I'll handle the newspaper office. Send me a photo of the zoo's flying fox bat."

He clicked off. He wanted a *picture*? Of a *bat*? Did I dare ask why? Nope. I was praying he had contacts on the police force who would check out the Escalade *before* a crime happened. Or maybe Graham had his own hit men. I just wanted Patra to be safe.

I sauntered over to where EG was happily snapping her camera at a creature with wings bigger than I was. Sure enough, there on the descriptive sign was the common name, the *flying fox* bat. And yeah, judging from the sign, it kinda looked like a fox. It was too dark to tell much in the cage.

I snapped and sent a photo of both sign and bat. In my thoroughness, I went online and found a better image and sent that. I needed something to occupy my head besides worrying about what was happening back in town. Out of sheer devilment, I gave EG my phone and let her snap more pics to send Graham.

I had just let someone else handle a danger to my family. It made me uncomfortable not to be running to the rescue. Had I trusted Graham to help because he'd dared to kiss me? No, probably because I thought he was my diamond-cufflink hero. I'm not *always* rational.

Nick arrived, cheerful as ever despite my interrupting a possible tryst. "Did EG steal one of the darlings for her collection?"

EG sent him a dark look and proceeded to the next cage. I backed off where she couldn't hear us.

"I just sicced Graham on some creeps following Patra. Am I getting old and weak?"

Nick hugged my shoulders. "No, you're turning human. Maybe now you'll even get a life. Although admittedly, I'd love to see what the spider is doing right now."

So would I. I glanced at EG, who was enrapt by another flying rodent. Mammal. "We'll never keep her out of the family occupation, will we?"

"Nope. Curious minds and all that. If we tell her where Patra is, EG will want to go see, too, and she'll probably concoct stink bombs out of train trash and annihilate the enemy upon arrival. All we're doing by taking her to the zoo is feeding her more ammunition for her lethal mind." He shrugged and checked his watch. "I'm ready to ditch babysitting. Want me to go see and tell you what's happening?"

"Graham sure won't," I said in irritation, even though I was relieved that Nick offered. "But you won't arrive in time."

EG snapped one last photo and returned to us. "Okay, it's time to go now."

We stared at her in incredulity. I spoke first. "We came all the way out here just to take pictures of bats?"

"Yes." And she began marching for the exit. "I have a report to do."

"Rock, paper, scissors?" I asked Nick as we followed her out.

I held out my fist—rock. He opened his palm—paper. *Damn.* We took the Metro back to Dupont Circle. EG and I got off. Nick went downtown.

* * *

Patra's perspective

Patra paced the moldy basement, waiting for security to give an all clear signal. Sean used his cell phone to keep in touch with the guard, who was busy notifying the newspaper's offices to lock down.

Sirens sounded on the street outside. At the same time, the security guard reported the cameras shutting down in the garage.

Sean cursed, shoved his phone back on his belt, and looked from door to stairs.

"Want to go up and watch the fun, or stay here and wait for Sam to tell us the cops chased the baddies off?" He sauntered toward the stairs.

Men were so predictable. He was worried about his midget car.

"If there are no cameras, how do we know the baddies have been chased off? There could be creeps roaming all over the place."

Sean shrugged. "You stay here. I'll call if the coast is clear. Right about now, I wouldn't mind a good look at these thugs."

She really ought to let him go. It was relatively safe down here. But she didn't like basements, and she was as curious as Sean. With the police right outside, how much trouble could they get into?

"Won't the other people working up there scare them off?" she asked, following him up the stairs.

"What, after telling them to lock down, you want me to tell them to stick their heads out?" He eased open the door on the first floor and listened. He dialed up his security guard again, then put his phone back in his pocket. "Sam's not answering."

"Fifty-fifty, he's answering the door for the cops or the baddies have him at gunpoint."

"Can't leave a friend in jeopardy," Sean replied insouciantly, stepping into the hall.

The building was eerily silent. Patra looked for a weapon in the offices they passed, but there was little more than mail and copy rooms in this back hall. More sirens sounded outside. It seemed sensible to just walk out the front door.

The front door was apparently half a block away. They crept down the battered tile to the corner where the floor became polished marble. That should lead outside, according to Patra's calculations. Sean held up his hand to halt her, and keeping his back against the wall, he peered around the corner.

His muttered curse told her all she needed to know. She peered around the corner to see a man in a black suit accompanied by a slug with a gas can enter an elevator. She swallowed hard and clutched her tote of papers tighter. Sean pressed her back against the wall.

She swung around to look for another exit. A suit-coated man with an AK-47 stepped into the corridor from one of the offices. She uttered a curse of her own.

Not tall, but square, the gunman deliberately raised his weapon. "About time you turned up. We're going for a walk. Hurry it up."

"Really?" Patra asked in disbelief. "You're really going to use that line? Watch too many films, do you?"

Sean stepped in front of her, blocking her with his larger frame. "The cops are outside. You can't get anywhere. Why don't you run while you have the chance?"

"I've got a chance to make my boss happy. Move it. The boss don't like to do clean up, but you're expendable." He gestured with the assault rifle, standing aside so they could pass in front of him.

Patra had no inclination to leave the safety of the fastest route to the front door. "What do you want? Maybe we can help and then you can just leave quietly."

"I'm leaving quietly, with you. Now get your bony ass over here!"

She'd move her bony ass, all right. And then she'd smack him upside the head with… Well, all she had was the tote. That would have to work. She'd never learned martial arts.

She stalked in front of Sean, intent on eliminating one imbecile from this world.

The sirens had stopped. She hoped that was because the cops had arrived at their destination and that was out front. Before she could swing, Sean grabbed her arm and flung her into the closest office. Patra screamed in outrage. A shot rang wildly in the hall, and she ducked in terror.

Sean limped in, slamming and locking the door behind him. "Don't do this at home," he muttered, dragging her down behind a metal desk, then shoving the desk to block the door.

"You're bleeding!"

His fancy Nike was ragged and covered in red.

Another shot shattered the flimsy door lock.

Eighteen

Patra's perspective

THE OFFICE they were hiding in had no window.

Patra heard shouts outside, but they seemed in the distance. This back hall had to be half a block from the street. No one could arrive before the goon finished shooting out the door.

"No time for a smoke bomb," she murmured, glancing around the room for weapons as the shooter kicked at the barricaded door. "Why didn't you let me smack him?"

"Because that would have got us both shot." Sean dragged her back to a second metal desk, pulled her under it, and curled his body over hers.

A bullet ripped through the steel of the first barricade to dig into the back of the desk they were hiding under. Patra swallowed hard in disbelief.

"Leave now or die here!" the goon shouted.

He finally smashed through the door, shoving the first desk back enough to point the AK47 into the room.

"Will you tell us what the devil we're dying for?" Patra shouted back, although she calculated the idiot stood only a few yards away. If he could shout, so could she.

"Because I don't like bleeding liberals," the goon said snarkily, leveraging the door with his shoulder until he had a full view of the room.

Sean was bleeding, because of her. Fury simply made Patra think faster. Sean tried to hold her down, but she shook him off. She'd had training in what to do if gunmen invaded.

Popping up from behind the desk, she grabbed a stapler and flung it at the thug's head. She hadn't practiced in a while, but she'd always been good at rock slinging.

The large stapler hit their assailant smack in the nose. He cried out, falling back and pulling the trigger in his surprise. This time, the bullet ripped through the ceiling.

The shouts outside were closer.

Sean caught her waist and tugged her back to the ground again. "You're crazy. That bullet could have hit you."

"I'll die fighting." She grabbed a tape dispenser from the desk behind her. Without a hitch in her movement, she shrugged off Sean, popped above the desk long enough to take aim, and flung as hard as she could.

The roll of tape smacked the gunman between the eyes. The dispenser bounced off his jaw just as he shot again. This time, the bullet thudded uncomfortably close into the floor on the side of the desk where they hid. The smell of scorched carpet joined the stink of gunfire.

Losing his temper, the badgered gunman scatter-shot wildly. Sean slammed Patra flat to the floor and weighed her down with his body before she could locate more weapons.

A solid wave of water hit the desk and keeled it over on them.

The would-be killer screamed, and knocked flat by the torrent, slid across the room.

"What the f—" Sean muttered.

The water stopped as abruptly as it had hit.

Sean pushed the desk off and slid it between them and the gunman. Shakily, Patra pushed wet hair out of her eyes. Peering around their shelter, she located a fireman in rubber suit and protective headgear in the doorway, holding a hose.

"Where's the fire?" the rubber-suited newcomer asked, turning off the nozzle while another entered in full gear, carrying an ax.

"Fire?" Which was when Patra smelled smoke a little stronger than scorched carpet.

"Oh, shit," Sean muttered, apparently smelling it at the same time.

Glancing over her shoulder, Patra saw the saturated goon hunting for his gun. She dived for the weapon first and handed it to Sean. She had to help him stand on his injured foot. Together, they stumbled into the hall. Their guardian angel was already hauling his hose up the stairs. Sean flung the weapon into the nearest file cabinet.

Patra didn't bother looking back to see if their assailant had escaped. She clutched the tote that had almost cost them their lives. Sean held his soaked box and limped after her. Now that the moment was over, full panic mode kicked in. She wanted out of the building—with the man who had taken a bullet for her.

Down the main corridor, they could see ladder trucks through the front windows.

"Run ahead and find a policeman," Sean ordered.

"Bullshit." She grabbed his arm, hauled it over her shoulder, and kept marching. "I'm not leaving you, and I'm not sending anyone into a burning building."

"Your whole entire family is nuts, aren't they?" he asked as he hopped beside her.

"My father worked in war zones for a living and loved it, so yeah, it isn't just Magda."

"Adrenaline junkies," he said as they stumbled out the front door.

Patra winced at the sight of a tall, broad-shouldered man in a dark suit near the front door, gesturing to uniformed officers. She steered Sean in a different direction, while the man distracted a policeman and a fire captain by pointing out a window in the front facade. She hoped he was a newspaper exec explaining the building's layout.

One of the policemen holding back the crowd broke off to head their way. Another fire truck arrived, and the crowd surged. The cop had to turn around and drive them back. Accustomed to slipping into mobs and hiding in plain sight, Patra nudged Sean away from the action.

"Patra!"

Wearily, she glanced up to see Nick behind a police barricade. Handsome as always, he didn't do anything so crass as to jump up and down to catch their attention. He merely held his hand up so the sun caught his gold watchband and snapped his fingers.

He had a medic pointed their way before they reached the yellow tape.

"Thank you," she murmured to Sean, kissing his cheek and appropriating the soaked box in his arms. "And here's where I must say good-bye. Don't mention my name if you can help it."

That was family habit—slip away unnoticed, unnamed, and uninvolved.

"Hell..." Sean started to protest, but the medic hauled him to a stretcher.

With more cops heading her way, Patra merged with the crowd gathering around Nick.

"Can't leave you alone for a minute," Nick said cheerfully, pushing her back through the mob. He draped his blazer over her soaked shirt and took Sean's box. "Do we need to follow the ambulance?"

"No, we need to dry out these papers. From what I glimpsed, I think Bill was working for the Righteous and Proud a few years back."

"I have no idea what that means," Nick admitted, "but to the Metro we go, then."

A shout rose from the crowd behind them, and Patra checked over her shoulder.

A spotlight projecting a fanged bat image had distracted every eye on the block.

The spotlight illuminated a second story window through thick clouds of black smoke. Framed in the light was a fireman dragging a coughing shrimp over the sill and onto the ladder.

"What the devil is that bat doing up there?" Patra asked in awe.

Nick nearly doubled over in laughter, then patted her shoulder. "You catch the Metro. I'll go collar a thug. Batman is apparently bored and has left his batcave."

* * *

Back in my cellar office, I followed the news on Graham's network of legitimate news feeds, plus individual postings from smart phones, and twitter accounts. The Internet is normally a faceless wave of information impossible to comprehend. Graham's genius was to filter out the useless flood and catch the flakes of gold.

I sighed in relief when I saw Patra emerge from the building with Sean. They were both soaked to the skin, and Sean seemed injured, but they were alive.

The image of the bat signal made me sigh in exasperation. I hit the intercom. "Why come out of the cave now?" I shouted at the faceless machine.

No reply, naturally. I'd sent Graham into the fray, and he'd probably gone. There was no other interpretation of the bat images.

I didn't care *how* he did it. I wanted to know *why*.

I paced restlessly until Patra arrived. I knew she'd arrived because I could hear EG break into excited chatter in the foyer above. I was ready to fly into a million jagged pieces, but I couldn't let my siblings see that.

Taking a deep breath, I hastened up the stairs before Patra could escape to her room. I needed to know she was really okay before I could breathe normally.

Patra's eyes lit as soon as I appeared. "Ana, can we dry these out?" She held out a mangled wad of *papier-mâché*.

"Looks like a task for Mallard. EG, will you run that mess down to the kitchen?" I assumed Patra had risked her life for that trash, but I would not judge. Repeat fifty times. *I will not judge.*

"Where's Nick?" I asked the instant EG ran off.

"A fireman carried out a guy who might have been the arsonist. Nick took off after him. What the devil was that bat signal about? Nick almost died laughing."

"Inside joke. I don't suppose we have any names or explanations for this incident?"

"I tried, but it's hard talking to men with guns," Patra said, shoving her wet hair from her eyes. "But they didn't just want Bill's papers. They wanted *us*. I don't know anything. Why would anyone think I would?"

I held up my hand and began ticking off fingers. "If it really is you they're after, let me count the ways. Because you had your father's papers. Because you came here. Because you talked to Bill Bloom—"

Patra interrupted. "Bill was mixed up in more than my business. That's what I want to dig out of those files. There are invoices to Dr. Smythe in Bill's files. I don't know what Sean found but he pulled a bunch of folders, too. What if Bill wasn't killed because of me?" she asked with a hint of desperation. "What if he was killed because of what he knew about someone else?"

"Then you'd better figure out what you know that someone nasty would want to talk to *you*. Until that time, we need to put you on a plane back to London."

Patra ignored my sage advice. "You said some of my father's papers are coded. Have you had any success in de-coding them?"

"I've decoded a few lists of times and days but I haven't

matched them to anything yet. You brought us decades of files to sort through. It takes time. Why don't you go visit Magda while we work on it?"

"I've got an interview with Rhianna to do yet and a job to start tomorrow! Going to take a shower now." Patra ran off.

"Would you have gone to London?" the hall lamp asked. "Leave your adult siblings alone."

Graham was back. And he was right, but I used to change her *diapers,* even if I hadn't been as old as EG at the time. It was hard to ignore the maternal instinct.

"One of you will have to find out what Sean is telling the police. Or get to him before the police and tell him what to say if you wish to keep Patra uninvolved," Graham continued.

We really didn't need Patra's name involved. Or any of us, if it could be avoided. Like Graham, or any good spy, we'd learned to live in the shadows. I liked it there. I could accomplish much more if people didn't notice me.

Patra had chosen a different path, but I respected Graham's desire to be overlooked. Although that bat signal may have been a sign that Graham had become more concerned than usual.

"Hold the fort while I'm out," I agreed. "Don't bomb any small countries while I'm gone."

Me and Graham working in tandem—what a concept. Gave me goose bumps, I admit.

* * *

I called Nick and located the hospital where Sean and the potential arsonist had been taken. That someone had twice tried to burn papers in Patra's possession wasn't exactly a pattern. Yet. They weren't the same papers. The incidents had happened an ocean apart, and fire is the obvious means of destroying paper. But it established a pattern of violence. Paper shredders were far less dangerous.

Since Nick had said he was in the emergency room, looking for a chance to get at the thug with smoke inhalation, I went in search of Sean through normal measures. I asked at the information desk.

He'd been admitted for observation. When I reached his room, Sean was already dressed and trying to figure out how to cover up his bandage and escape.

"If the police ask who was with you, tell them it was this person," I said by way of greeting, handing him my Linda Lane alter ego card. "And thank you for looking after my idiot sister."

"I think I'm asking for a job transfer," he muttered. "Do you know she flung a *stapler* at a brute with a *gun*? Who does that?"

I opened a drawer and found paper booties to protect his bandage. "We do. Any weapon at hand rather than be held hostage. Family motto and sound tactical strategy. Even the police recommend that teachers fling books or anything at hand if a gunman threatens. I'll pay for a taxi to take you back to your car. Can you drive with that foot?"

"I'm afraid to look at my car," he grumbled. "What's with the bat signal?"

I was getting tired of being asked that, probably because I didn't have a good answer. I just kept making them up. "Batman apparently wanted us to know which thug was our arsonist."

"The guy with a gas can that we saw wasn't wearing a suit like the gunmen," Sean said, pulling on his booty. "Neither was the man they hauled from the window."

Duly noted—gunmen wore suits to hide their holsters. Arsonists wore inflammables? "Nick's down there looking for him now," I told him. "If you want to be in on the fun, I'll help you down there."

He actually looked interested in hunting an arsonist. His dark curls were starting to dry without benefit of whatever he usually used to control them. His cheap shirt looked a little the worse for its drenching, and his jeans were still wet. He had to be uncomfortable, and he still wanted the story. I appreciated perseverance in a man.

"I've got to hobble downstairs anyway, why not?" he asked, standing.

"I hope they gave you a lot of good painkillers," I muttered. "I'm not tall like Patra, and I make a very bad walking stick."

"It's just my toe. I can walk on my heel. How are you planning on getting through the emergency room?"

I smiled, and he actually had the sense to back off a step.

I'm devious, and he knew it.

Nineteen

NICK was chatting up an intern when we reached the emergency waiting room. He didn't even lift an eyebrow when he saw my surgical cap and scrubs. With my long black braid pinned inside, I was next to invisible.

Carrying a clipboard I'd appropriated, I nodded greeting. "Mr. Nicholas, your friend will need some help. If you'll come this way, please." Leading Sean on his booty, I headed straight down the hall as if I belonged there. I didn't bother to see if Nick followed. I knew he would.

If he'd been setting up a date, he was probably scowling, but I was into authority mode and marched on without checking. I waited until I found an empty corridor before halting to let them catch up. "Where's our arsonist?"

Sean leaned against the wall to rest his foot, still regarding my baggy green disguise with distaste. More accustomed to my methods, Nick merely nodded to the next intersection. "A cop just arrived to ask questions. Admissions has already been in, but from what I can tell, he was too groggy to give information. I think they've rifled his wallet for next of kin and insurance, but they'll be back shortly with paperwork."

"Okay, come along and show me the room and just follow my lead." This was a decent hospital, with private examining rooms instead of open beds. I spotted the cop as soon as we turned the corner.

"I'll be right with you, Mr. Nicholas, just as soon as I check on this patient," I said loudly enough that the cop could hear us chatting. "Why don't you and your friend go get some coffee?"

I nodded at the cop and opened the door of the examining room without consulting him. Behind me, Nick was asking the officer if he'd like some coffee, too. Knowing Nick, he'd already determined the fellow's preference in milk and sugar and all three would investigate the cafeteria. I couldn't count on being left undisturbed for long, though.

The patient didn't look big enough to be a thug. He was wiry and short with a receding hairline and a big nose. He was faking sleep. Deal with half a dozen sneaky kids and you learn the difference. I'd intended to be polite and pretend I was actually an admitting nurse, but if he was going to be stupid...

I found his clothes and began searching his pockets. Why ask when I could see for myself? His wallet was good leather and had protected the contents from the deluge of sprinklers and hoses. A driver's license to one Don Toreador, a fake name if I'd ever heard one. I photoed the address and the rest of his cards. A prescription for Viagra. Cute. A cheap photo of a half naked woman with *Call me* on the back. Real sleaze we had here.

He had a Blue Cross insurance card—bingo! R&P Inc was listed as the employer.

"Dr. Smythe has been in to check on you, Mr. Toreador," I lied blithely. "We told him we'd let him know when you're awake. Are you awake yet?"

"He gonna get me out of here?" the beanbrain growled, not bothering to open his eyes.

"I don't think that's up to him. I just told him I'd let you know. I can send the policeman out to talk to him, if you like."

That got him opening his eyes. I liked them better closed, but I had my mask on.

"Who the devil are you?" he demanded.

I laid his wallet on the table. "Got it in one. I'm the devil, and I suggest you take a long sabbatical and rethink your occupation. I can give you the names of people who will be happy to question you about Smitty and your involvement in Bill Bloom's death should you care to ease your conscience and make a clean getaway."

"Why should I?" he growled, looking justifiably wary.

"Because I'm about to identify you as the arsonist who set fire to the office and attempted to murder two reporters. And then I'll tell Smitty you sang like a canary. But if you'd rather I didn't, you could tell me what you know, and I'll never be heard from again."

"Bullshit." But he looked worried.

And I'd just confirmed his guilt and possible connection to R&P. "I calculate we may have three minutes before someone comes in. Talk or I go my merry way."

"I don't know nothing. I get orders and follow them." He tugged at the IV, then coughed as he breathed too hard on his oxygen.

"And your orders today were?"

"Same as every day since the Bloom guy died. Follow anyone who came for the boxes, destroy the papers, bring the person in for questioning. That's all I know. Give me my wallet."

"One of your buddies shot at the person you followed. Was that order 'Bring them in, dead or alive?'"

"Don't think so. Harry's got a temper. But I'm just the paper guy. We were supposed to find the papers and computers in Bloom's apartment but we got run out before we could do more than scarf the computer."

In other words, we didn't have Bill's killer here, just a low-level thief.

"And who did you give the computer to?"

"Harry took care of that," he said, still fiddling with the tubes keeping him tied to the bed.

"Is Smitty your main employer or are there others?"

He was starting to look kind of pale under his weathered tan. "Look, people disappear who work for my employer. Smitty's just a friend of my employer. He helps us, we help him. Ain't nuttin' illegal in that."

"Pull another one," I said with an undignified snort. I heard voices in the hall. My time here was done. I wished I knew more about interrogation, but I was better at running away. "You have any names for your employer?"

"I get paid cash, okay? Give me my wallet." He apparently heard the voices too. "I got kids. I gotta feed them somehow. Papers ain't special. There's a lot of us. They call us corporate spies. We don't hurt nobody."

"Oh, cripes, and you believe in Santa Claus, don't you? It says R&P on your insurance card. How did you get that?"

"We all got 'em. Smitty's company helps the indigent like me."

I really wanted to hit him, but for all I knew, he actually believed that. I didn't have time to question more and didn't want to go to jail for low level scum. "Look, here's a number to call when the walls start closing in." I gave him my Linda card with the voice mail number. "You're working with a dangerous crowd. They killed their own lawyer. They'll kill you, too. Call me and I'll find a way to get you out when you're ready. Your kids would rather have you alive and unemployed, I assure you."

He looked pretty nervous when I left. He had a right to be. I was beginning to suspect that half this town was controlled by Top Hat, and that included the R&P. I just couldn't prove anything. Conspiracies were so very last century. I wanted to be wrong.

But it didn't hurt to use Top Hat's example to terrorize the jerk after he and his kind had terrorized Patra. *Harry.* I'd have to remember that name. Bullies with guns were fair game in my book.

Nick was chatting up a stern administrator type with a clipboard when I emerged. Sean and the policeman were sipping coffee. I nodded at the administrator. "Mr. Toreador is awake now. You can go in."

Then I sauntered off as if I worked there.

I could blend in almost anywhere. I just never really belonged.

* * *

I gave Sean just enough information to persuade him to leave in a taxi and do his own digging. Nick and I took the Metro home.

We found Patra and Mallard in the cellar kitchen, drying paper on a clothesline strung just under the low ceiling. They were ironing the more interesting bits.

"Look!" Patra cried as soon as we entered. "Invoices to R&P for services rendered three years ago regarding Broderick Media! And here's Bill's index number referencing his files—from his computer, maybe? Didn't some of his CD's have numbers like these?" She gestured at one of the papers.

"We can look. But we have to remain objective and not rush to conclusions. As far as we are aware, Bill was running a legitimate business analyzing speech patterns, not a spy agency. R&P could have just been testing someone's speech-making talents. Without Bill's computer, we're up a creek." I helped myself to one of the lovely canapés Mallard had been preparing, probably for Graham. "Ummm, mango and salmon, well done."

Mallard glowered instead of beaming. He produced another paper and waved it in my face as I licked my fingers.

My eyes widened. I grabbed a napkin and used it to hold the paper.

Nick peered over my shoulder. He whistled.

It was a print-out of a series of emails between Bill and someone at R&P with the email address CS1%@RP.org. Bill liked his back-ups. Ironic that it was old-fashioned paper that had survived. RP.org? Righteous and Proud?

The contents of the audio you provided contains politically sensitive material, Bill had carefully noted. *I am returning it in its entirety. You will not be charged for my examination.*

The reply time had been within minutes of Bill's refusal. *For the sake of your country, we must have the identity of the speakers. If we cannot trust you, who can we trust?*

Bill's reply was almost twenty-four hours later, to the minute. I was beginning to recognize the caution. Had he called his mother? Started asking questions about CS1%? Talked to some of his liberal friends in the media?

From my research, I knew Bill had dropped out of college and set up his own business four years ago. These emails had been from over five years ago, before he'd moved out, when he had been living with his mother, the flag-waving upholder of the Righteous and Proud. I supposed the R&P had had reason to believe he was one of them.

It was pretty arrogant for the writer to associate himself with the 1% that his crowd theoretically didn't belong to, but I didn't own a corner on the irony market.

I have copied enough of the voices to begin an analysis, Bill's return mail replied. *I do not wish to have the rest of the material in my office. I am deleting the full audio file.*

There were a few more brief emails negotiating the deal. And then the final email from Bill: *The voices on this recording match that of the VP of the US, Senator Paul Rose, and Sir Archibald Broderick. A fourth person as yet unidentified appears to be on a speaker phone and not present. His voice is not matched in any of my files.*

In Bill's handwriting at the bottom of the page: "#1143 manipulation of media." He added no further comment on the content of the discussion that had him deleting the file.

Paul Rose and Broderick. Rose was the conservative candidate running for president, the apparent brains behind Top Hat, the wealthy shadow group who had almost certainly prodded Reggie into killing our grandfather. Rose and Broderick— speaking to the vice president of the United States.

Damn, I needed to know what had been on that recording.

Poor Bill had been seriously in over his head. If Broderick or Rose knew he'd heard that conversation, he'd been in serious danger from day one. And now I had to wonder about the morals of a VP of the US—as soon as we figured out when this was and which VP. The emails were five years ago. That didn't mean the audio file was.

"How much do you want to wager that Bill didn't delete the audio file?" I asked the room at large.

Patra was running for my office before I finished speaking.

Before I could follow, the food processor spoke.

"I expect my dinner on time despite this fascinating digression into a topic everyone already knows about."

"Of course, *mein Führe*r." I patted the processor. "And when we find Bill's killer, you can say you knew that, too, just the way EG does."

I didn't linger for a response. Graham knew how to find me if he wanted. I think our game was as much sexual frustration as psychological warfare.

I shrugged at Mallard in regret. "Thanks for the help. We'll get out of the way and let you know what we find."

Our stuffed penguin of a butler almost smiled.

When I reached my office, Patra was flipping through the stacks of disks she'd rescued, organizing them in numerical order.

"Assuming Dr. Charles Smythe of the R&P is a sarcastic bastard using the name CS1%, why would he need to analyze audio files of Broderick and Rose discussing media manipulation?" I asked, pulling out our earlier files stolen from Bill's apartment and handing half to Nick. "Better yet, why would he poison Reggie?"

Patra dropped a disk and stared. She hadn't been around when Nick and I had discussed this. "The religious leader of the Righteous & Proud killed our grandfather's thieving lawyer?" she asked.

"That's our theory, and we have a witness. Story at ten," I said, flipping through files.

"Smythe worked for the VP's office a *decade* ago," Nick reminded us. "Is there any chance that he was the undetected voice on the tape? Maybe he was testing Bill."

"Number 1143 isn't in here," Patra said in disappointment, restarting her search of the disks.

"You saved what, a few dozen CDs? And if he was already at 1143 years ago, he must have had thousands we didn't save," I said. "We really need his computer."

"There weren't any more CDs on his desk," Patra said. "He had no filing system for his disks. I looked. Maybe he cleaned and reused them when he was done?"

"Not if there was any liability attached to his work," Nick argued. "He'd either store them on external drives or keep a vault for the CDs or both."

"It was a crappy little one hole apartment. No vaults. And any drives went with the thieves," Patra said, sounding depressed. "I hate this."

My overactive brain cells were dancing with ideas. "We're pursuing too many balls at once," I told them. "Nick, you follow up with our lawyer and Lemuel on Reggie's death. Patra, stick with Broderick and following anything you can find out about your father. I'll keep digging into Bill. But we have Smitty connected to Reggie and Bill, so he's fair game all the way around. Make sense?"

"And Broderick, since Smitty requested analysis of that tape with him on it," Patra added. "I need to get into BM's computer files."

I was thinking that was a really bad, very Magda idea.

Twenty

I STAYED up all night decoding Patrick Llewellyn's paranoid notes. He must have known there were people like Graham around who could disentangle his cryptograms. Even after I decoded his stupid laundry lists, he'd made his notes meaningless to anyone but him.

I had what I assumed were times and dates and initials that might represent people or places or both. I was leaning toward the latter. I set up a spreadsheet to look for a pattern.

My expertise is research, not field work. I really hated leaving my basement and the lovely puzzle for anything less than an emergency or a family outing.

But I'd end up like Graham if I didn't force myself to interact with the rest of the world. I didn't want to be the spider in the cellar, so I spent equal time designing a task to get out of the house.

While the computer ran code programs over the weekend, I'd had time to poke around more in Bill's bank account. I'd only recently learned how to perpetrate this illegal act through the internet money-laundering class I'd taken.

So far, the college course on literature hadn't taught me anything as useful.

Sunday night, while the others were off on their own expeditions, I dug into the information I'd gathered. Bill had an on-line bank account. I figured out his email password from a list he'd kept in the files Patra had retrieved. The girl had a good eye for damaging goods.

As a result of my research, I would have to make a foray into the real world.

* * *

Monday morning, I showered and changed while Nick and Patra slept. I left Nick a note reminding him to keep in touch with

Lemuel's bail bondsman so he could escort our stool pigeon to his new abode. Then I walked EG to the Metro where she caught the train to her private school. She was worried her bat report wouldn't be sufficiently detailed. In my opinion, it would have passed for a PhD, but what did I know? I just had a GED.

I caught the next train down to the city neighborhood where Bill had lived, and I was waiting at the door when his local tech store opened. Really, if I hadn't been so busy, I could have figured this out on my own without plundering his bank account to see who he'd made the checks out to.

I asked for the store manager, flashed my fake ID, and handed him my fake Linda business card. "I'm William Bloom's attorney and executor for his estate. I've come to clear out the disks he stored here."

I was fishing and hoping that Bill liked hard back up as well as cloud back up, which I hadn't located yet. I played nonchalant while the store manager looked at my card.

"He had an honest-to-God lawyer?" the tattooed manager asked. "I didn't think he owned his own socks."

"Family lawyer," I said with a shrug. "He made arrangements for passing on his business assets, and that includes the CDs. I assume they're not just music."

"He just kept a lock box here." The manager couldn't have been more than college age. He sauntered down the aisle to the employee entrance.

Oh, hell, he could have kept old comic books in this place. And here I thought I'd been so smart.

He led me into their storage area. Metal shelves with labels filled the space. We had to go all the way to a dark back corner where the manager dragged one of those heavy asbestos fire-proof security boxes from beneath a bin. Big enough to hold a file drawer, it had to weigh over fifty pounds.

"Bill used to work here. He asked if he could store this. He paid the store fair and square, so the boss said it was fine. Can't imagine why he kept it here." The guy looked expectant as he handed over the awkward box.

"Backup in case of fire," I said with a straight face, not accepting the burden. I didn't know how I'd get the box out the door without a forklift. "I'll need a taxi. Would you carry that to the door for me while I call one?"

Reminded he was big and strong and manly, he shrugged and did as asked. I didn't even have to resort to Magda-flapping eyelashes. Good thing, because I was in my lawyerly khaki and not very vamp like.

I grimaced in annoyance when I checked out the plate glass window for my taxi and noticed Leonard Riley hanging out on a street corner. Now really, did I look like Patra? Patra should be dutifully reporting to Broderick Media shortly. What was the point in his spying on me? Pure meanness would be my supposition, but I wasn't taking chances.

If I'd been in Marrakech, I would have simply walked out and kicked his balls until he cried. But this side of the pond pretended to be more civilized, and I'd be arrested for assault if I tried that. Redirecting a taxi isn't easy. So I just let the boy hand the vault into the taxi's back seat, waved at Riley, and climbed in. Lesson #2 in city living. It's hard to follow a cab unless you have a car of your own.

As a safety precaution, I had the cab let me out at Sean's newspaper office rather than endanger the family by taking it home. Besides, I didn't have enough manpower to handle a few thousand audio disks, if that's what was in here.

I lugged the fireproof vault—I do love irony—into the lobby and dropped it on the floor. The building stunk of wet charred wood and plastic. Anyone who has ever burned a Barbie would recognize the stench.

Maintenance men were all over, cleaning up the mess. Huge fans were running to dry the place out. I hoped Sean got to keep his job. Maybe the vault would work toward that end. I liked paying my debts.

I didn't know if Sean would remember my fake persona, but I gave the security guard my Linda Lane name, along with a request for an appliance dolly. That got their attention. Two helpful gentlemen in rumpled suits arrived in record time.

They eyed the vault with appreciation and interest. "Gold, diamonds, or jewels?" one asked.

"Sean's not getting around so hot right now," the stouter of the two said. "He said you'd understand."

"I do understand, gentlemen, thank you. This is my gift of gratitude for his quick thinking yesterday. He's a hero, and once this story breaks, the city will know it." Yeah, I learned to lie in my cradle.

They lifted the vault to a dolly and rolled it into the elevator, which was fortunately still operating. Upstairs, the cubicle farm had been dismantled while the fire clean-up people did their thing. It looked like the worst of the damage had been done to the conference room. Maybe Patra had done them a favor and insurance would buy them new computers.

Work had apparently been moved to the unscathed executive offices. Salvaged metal desks were crammed into carpeted offices beside polished mahogany ones. It made for a claustrophobic anthill, but the inhabitants seemed to be enjoying the heck out of it.

One of the exec desks was covered in coffee makers and donuts.

People watched with curiosity—these were reporters, after all—as the vault was wheeled to a tight corner where Sean sat, his bandaged foot propped on a drawer pulled out from a nearby desk.

"You'll excuse me if I don't stand," he said without sarcasm, for a change.

I don't like spies, but he'd been on our side often enough that I tolerated him. And he had prevented Patra from getting her head blown off. That was worth something. "Got a screwdriver?"

Not even raising my voice, I had everyone in the room hunting drawers for tools. Definitely not the time or place for trading secrets. But I had a more evil idea in mind—provided, of course, there was more than comic books in there.

"If those are Bill's files," I pointed at the box as a screwdriver was passed across the room, "I need #1143. I give you free rein to access all the rest. The name of the people who set the fire could be on one of them."

Sean's eyes widened in appreciation. I'd just set some of the world's best investigative reporters into hunting through audio files for revenge. I only knew that one of Bill's clients was Smitty, and that was the CD I wanted. I didn't have time to listen to all the files to find other relevant ones. But a roomful of reporters...

Popping the lock was a piece of cake with the screwdriver. Once upon a time I'd amused myself by placing childish scribbling in one of these and leaving it locked in a closet to see which of the servants couldn't be trusted. The answer—most of them. Vaults simply summon visions of glimmering jewels and gold for some reason.

Bill's stacks of CDs, USBs, and a few external drives brought crestfallen expressions once I had the box open. Even experienced reporters fell for the exciting prospect of Aladdin's treasure. But they quickly returned to business, understanding that I'd brought them information—the next best thing to gold.

Sean passed out stacks of CDs while searching through the neat labels. He produced #1143 and handed it over.

"Will you tell me what's on it later?"

"If I can. It may be of national security importance, so I make no promises. I'll ask the same of you." At his agreement, I left a room full of slavering reporters happily dividing the stacks.

I didn't see Leonard anywhere outside when I headed for the Metro, but I made sure to check over my shoulder when I got off. He knew where I lived, so the precaution was simply to determine how successful I'd been with the taxi trick.

I didn't see him anywhere, but I entered the house through the back alley and the kitchen anyway. Of course, Graham knew the instant I returned.

* * *

Patra's perspective

Reporting to Broderick's Human Resources office promptly at nine, Patra wondered if any of the people watching her knew she'd been in the competition's office the day before. With Riley spying on her, she felt as if her every move was observed. Wearing her highest heels, she gave them lots of hip-swaying motion to follow. Her office attire today was a red pencil skirt cut above her knees, a matching bolero jacket that barely skimmed her waist, and a tank top that showed cleavage.

The dragon lady in HR scowled at Patra's attire. The tall, portly, gray-haired gentleman reading through a file showed far more approval. "The new hire?" he asked, indicating Patra with a tilt of his head.

She hated being dismissed as an object. Donning a brilliant smile, she held out her hand. "Patra Llewellyn, sir. May I have the pleasure?"

He barely gripped her fingers and gave a single handshake

hinting of disapproval at her brashness. "Archibald Broderick. You'll be working in entertainment?"

Oh, rats, she should have had her tape recorder turned on to capture his voice for analysis.

"*Sir* Archibald Broderick," dragon lady inserted with an air of importance.

"Oh my, sir, a true pleasure." Patra would have bobbed a curtsy if her skirt allowed. His attitude seemed to demand it, but mostly, she wanted more time to study this man her father had despised. He appeared distinguished, impatient, and wealthy, like hundreds of men she'd met in her mother's company. "Yes, Mr. Smedbetter just hired me for entertainment news. I have a few useful connections."

"Excellent, excellent. Our company supports loyal, hardworking employees. I look forward to seeing your work." He walked out, a busy man who should never have been in HR at all. Strange.

Dragon lady dismissed Patra with a packet of material. An intern led Patra to her desk in the cubicle farm.

Apparently, access to the computer network wasn't immediately granted. Patra had to read the packet of material to determine what it would take to enter BM's precious archives—*seniority and a security pass*. Damn. She needed Ana's hacking expertise. Or maybe she could fly in their little brother, Tudor, the computer genius.

How the devil could she upload her interview with Rhianna if she couldn't insert a USB? Of all the paranoid...

She rolled her eyes. Of course, this was Broderick Media, supporter of the Party of the Paranoid, who hired generals instead of journalists. If one believed their stories, they feared everything from communists to alien invasion. Straightening her short skirt, she approached the senior manager.

In his thirties and wearing a wedding ring, he still ogled her legs before he straightened his glasses and found her face. "Miss Llewellyn, what can I do for you?"

"Give me permission to upload my interview with Rhianna? I don't see how I can work the late hours required for the international news if I can only access the computers during office hours." She confiscated a spare chair and wiggled her hips into it, bringing his gaze to breast level. She hoped he wouldn't drool.

"Rhianna?" She'd startled him into actually looking at her. "You have an interview with Rhianna? She never gives interviews!"

Patra smiled sweetly and held up the USB. "She does to old friends."

She loved watching him swallow his tongue. Without another word, he plugged in the USB, uploaded her files—she had only the interview on there because she wasn't dumb—and opened the document.

"You can access it now," he informed her, skimming the interview to verify the contents. "Just bring any files you work on at home to me, and I'll load them for you."

What a pain. Instead of expressing her disdain, she smiled again, took the USB back, and gave him another wriggle as she rose and thanked him. "Do I have access to an email account? I'll have to communicate with my Hollywood list somehow, since most of them are sleeping at this hour."

His eyes widened in appreciation. "I'll arrange an email account and access to the Internet. Don't use them for personal reasons. Everything goes through a secured server and is monitored."

"I used to work for the BBC. I understand that," she said gently, humoring him, even though she was lying. The BBC had never paid a bit of attention to whom she was talking.

She swayed off to purportedly play with the interview, which was already as good as it was going to get. She needed to be able to email Ana or Tudor for advice in hacking the archives, but how could she do that without being caught?

She sent off a batch of legitimate queries to the people Rhianna had recommended. Entertainment news was easy with the right connections.

Investigating media corruption was a whole other problem.

Before she could figure out anything, an email arrived in her brand new box.

Don't look now but Big Daddy's watching you was all it said. The sender was one SAdams@bm.com.

She didn't have to look. She'd already noted the two-way mirror near the ceiling on the far wall. When had distrust begun ruling the workplace? Maybe she could write a psychological study on the debilitating effects of fear.

If SAdams didn't fear his email would be read, he must be one of the IT guys reading it. Cool.

Twenty-one

WHEN I returned from dumping the workload of Bill's vault on Sean, I found an email summons from Graham. I ignored it. Graham was probably steaming that I'd given all that material to reporters, but the truth just wants to be free. Graham is stingy.

I knew I was daring the lion, but speed was of the essence. I didn't even have time for a horizontal tango if he'd offered. My family was in danger, and nothing came between me and them.

First thing I did when I was back in my office was call Oppenheimer. He hadn't liked my earlier threat and refused to come to the phone. "Look," I told the receptionist, "I have a witness who might be able to identify Reggie's murderer. I can call the cops, or your boss can talk to him first. Ask him which he prefers."

Oppenheimer picked up the line. We had a polite discussion about Lemuel. Rather than reveal his location, I set up a meeting so everyone could have a nice chat in a safe place. I was hoping a lawyer could arrange Smythe's arrest without having to involve me. I preferred Graham's obscurity to notoriety for lots of reasons, but security is a major one. Oppenheimer was welcome to the credit.

In exchange for my information, our lawyer generously revealed that we might have a chance of getting some of the yacht insurance in a few months—after the court debated which of Reggie's debtors ranked highest on a long list. At least a court wouldn't consider claims from his drug dealers.

The odds of reclaiming our half million still didn't look good from my perspective. We needed to find out who blew up the yacht and sue them. Not sounding much better. If it was Reggie's pals, they wouldn't have visible assets.

Family business completed, I finally inserted Bill's CD #1143 into the DVD slot of the Whiz. Graham could snoop if he liked. I'd give him that much.

I listened carefully, but if these were the voices referred to in Bill's memo, I couldn't identify two of them. I wouldn't recognize the voice of the *current* vice president. I certainly didn't recognize one from years back when I'd been in Timbuktu or buried in my Atlanta basement. I recognized a reluctant respect from others on the tape who spoke to Voice #1. Assuming Bill's email analysis applied to this recording, I assigned Voice #1 to the vice president. The date on the digital file was five years ago, but if this was a copy of a tape recording, I didn't know if that was when it had been originally recorded.

Bill's email analysis had simply named the VP, Broderick, Senator Paul Rose and possibly a voice on a speaker phone. I recognized Rose. He was all over the media these days. And I recognized the "speaker phone." *Graham.* How could I not have guessed?

I checked my time-line files. Graham had been dismissed from his cushy government job in early 2002, a victim of PTSD from the terrorist explosions of 9/11/01, according to rumor. Some months later, Dr. Smythe had left his advisory job with the Veep to create the R&P. And Riley had been charged for tapping the Veep's phone line.

I did a quick Google search on some of the names and events being discussed on the tape. The al-Askari Mosque had been bombed in early 2006. The Hay al Jihad massacre occurred in July. So the file was from after that time period—like about the same time as Patrick Llewellyn's death. He had died in the Mideast a little over *five* years ago. My pulse beat a little faster.

So Smitty—no longer in the veep's office but head of R&P— had consulted Bill Bloom for scientific verification of speakers on a recording he probably shouldn't have had. How had he obtained it and why? And how did Patra's father work into any of this—besides dying in that war zone.

Not all of the conversation on the tape was clear. Some of it was decidedly angry—especially the voice I had to assume was Broderick. Accusations of political dirty tricks flew. Hardly anything new. I perked up when Graham accused Broderick of using the media to promote war for the sake of the defense industry and oil companies. That was kind of old news now, except Graham punched them with facts instead of just making baseless accusations. Very nice.

And then Paul Rose said Broderick was working in the interest of national security and Unnamed Speaker Phone would be tried for treason if he released data only accessible by the military.

"Since no one in the presidential office or media would listen, I gave that data to Patrick Llewellyn," my desk lamp said, interrupting my concentration. "He took it and added it to the files he was working on the Brit end of the manipulation. And then he died, along with thousands of soldiers and innocent civilians."

I didn't hear regret in his voice, but he was talking through wires. Graham didn't do personal well.

I rocked in my chair a little after the line went dead and decided that wasn't sufficient information. Patra's father had *died* for this data? And that's all Graham could tell me?

I put one foot in front of the other and climbed stairs from basement to attic to beard the lion in his den. Graham's door was open. He was in his chair when I entered. He was monitoring street scenes outside both Sean's office and Patra's—two media centers.

"You had clear-cut evidence that this country went to war, spent gazillions of dollars and thousands of lives, nearly bankrupted the poor and destroyed the economy, f*or the sake of corporate greed*, and you didn't give that evidence to the world?" I asked in a deceptively calm tone. "And because of that, Patra's father *died*?"

"Five years ago, I didn't exist," he said without looking up. "No one believed me when I left office, and they wouldn't believe me after I'd been off the map for so long. Your grandfather told me to have a more objective, more respectable third party look at the data. Llewellyn was as objective and respectable as it got. He was right there in the field."

"And he *died*. You think Broderick and Senator Rose killed him to keep him from reporting their greedy operation?"

"Nothing's that simple," he said scornfully, still focused on his monitors and keyboard and not me. "You know that. There won't be a single trace back to them. The entire United States Congress voted for war. Do you think they'd admit they were manipulated?"

I hated politics. I didn't bother voting because I thought all politicians were self-serving crooks. But I'd known some of those soldiers who had died in Iraq. I'd been in some of the embassies that had burned in the Mideast. And that had been Patra's charming, intelligent, handsome Brit father who had been murdered by *our side*.

"The voices on Llewellyn's recording are not Rose or Broderick but probably their minions," Graham said. "Llewellyn could have been killed for stealing someone else's story for all we know. Maybe an angry husband killed him. Just because he knew too much doesn't mean he was killed for that knowledge."

"I'm taking Broderick down," I warned. "No man should have that much power. You must have still been around when Dr. Smythe left the VP's office to help found the Righteous and Proud. Five years ago, he was the man who paid Bill to analyze a private conversation with a different VP. Why would he do that?"

"If you don't understand politics well enough to know that, then stay out of this, Ana. Keep your sister out of it. And keep that damned pest O'Herlihy out of it or Llewellyn won't be the only one who sacrificed his life in vain."

Graham infuriated me on a hormonal level as well as intellectual. I wanted to pound his head for the sheer relief of releasing my pent-up frustration. But here's the thing... I would defend my family with my dying breath—and take his head off if he threatened them—but in this case, I agreed with the damned man. I didn't want friends or family hurt for politics. Talk about frustrating!

"Knowledge is power," I threw at him. "And murderers go to jail. You've been in the spy business too long."

He donned his earphones and tuned me out. I was officially dismissed.

I walked out. Reluctantly, I admit. But we weren't going to get physical in a computer room, so there was no point in my staying. Every cell in my body screamed in protest as I raced back to my mouse hole. But I'd had a lot of practice in controlling myself. Graham would know it when I decided to let go.

I didn't like coincidences but the whole case lacked good motivation.

Remembering the partial license plate Patra had got off the limo that had been at Bill's apartment, I pulled that up on the screen. Graham had apparently already run the partial and matched it against DMV records. D.C. was overrun with vehicles that could pass for black SUV limos but only three had the combination of numbers that Patra had caught on her phone. Out of those three, one was registered to an embassy, another to a local businessman, and the third to a limo service owned by Salvador DeLuca.

My resources were limited. I was going to profile this one and start with DeLuca. He'd been mentioned in the papers as a suspected crime boss. Thugs who broke into apartments struck me as more likely to come from the old-fashioned gangster school than an embassy.

If I'd been a cop, I'd have brought Smythe, this DeLuca person, and Toreador, the arsonist, down to the precinct and put them in the same room for questioning. I think that would have been a lot of fun. Instead, I had to start running searches on DeLuca and Toreador to find connections. I wanted gunman Harry's last name so I could draw him into this too, but all I could do was keep an eye out for any stray "Harry" in my search. Unfortunately, Google couldn't turn up a list of gunmen in the D.C. area and gangsters are real sloppy about not having websites. My virtual research unfortunately has limitations.

I called up the video Graham had copied of the street interception that had allowed the stolen car to hit Bill. The Hummer had muddy plates and the angle was all wrong for the camera to catch any numbers. But I could tell it was a D.C. plate, which narrowed the search, if I could hack the DMV for car titles. I could see the advantages of being a cop, except for the abide-by-the-rules part. After wasting an hour attempting every back door I knew, I still couldn't get through to the DMV.

I had the fingerprints Patra had snatched from Riley and his goon. I added those and the Hummer search to a file Graham could access and hoped for the best. Fingerprint searches were not the easy magic seen on TV.

The biggest, fattest detail in my notebook was Dr. Smythe of the Righteous and Proud. Why would he kill Max's lawyer? I wanted it to be because Reggie knew Top Hat secrets, but what would Top Hat have to do with the R&P?

The rich execs and power brokers in Top Hat didn't know people like Bill's mother existed.

I reminded myself to keep an open mind. Smitty could have hated Reggie for personal reasons. A crooked lawyer who did drugs wouldn't be high on the Most Liked list of righteous people.

I needed to focus on Bill's murder and not toplofty tales of political intrigue. One baby step at a time. I had to wait on others for the analysis of Llewellyn's recording and a list of what was in Bill's CD vault.

So I decided to research local gangsters, starting with Toreador and DeLuca. If I couldn't find websites, then I'd have to make a few personal visits.

* * *

Patra's perspective

Patra finished up her article and video of Rhianna, posted it off to her boss, and began lining up her next story. An email flashed in her box from SAdams. She'd yet to meet her anonymous correspondent, but she opened it out of curiosity.

A photo of her and Sean outside his newspaper office appeared on her screen. Rats. Broderick really did have spies everywhere, although she blamed this shot on Riley the termite.

She tapped in a reply merely reading YEAH, AND? And sent it back. One did not survive high school without a meaningless retort.

She was packing up at the end of the day when SAdams replied: WE MEET IN THE BAR DOWNSTAIRS.

With a pick-up line like that, this was one seriously unsophisticated nerd, pretty much confirming her suspicions of IT geek. Who else would have access to his information?

Just in case she was wrong, she took her time leaving her cubicle and primping in the restroom until a crowd had time to gather in the bar. Using family tactics, she didn't take the elevator all the way down. Instead, on the second floor, she found the stairs, and came out behind the crowded downstairs lobby where the elevator emptied. Unobserved, she located the staff entrance to the bar down a side hall and entered as if she owned the place.

Kitchen staff glanced up, but no one stopped her. She could be new management for all they knew. That ploy won her a view to the bar from a doorway customers wouldn't notice.

Sure enough, there were the usual singletons hanging out around a semi-sophisticated glass bar wearing their conservative office suits and letting down their hair, pretending they were God's gift to womankind, repeating uproarious stories of one-upmanship. If they'd been the only ones down here, she would have turned around and walked out.

But there, at the end of the bar sipping a beer, was a

bespectacled nerd in narrow tie, white shirt, and no suit jacket.

She wanted the guy with the information, not the ones with ego. Ego and two bucks wouldn't even score her a Starbucks. But there was no way of approaching the nerd without passing the herd of buffalo. Oh well.

She flashed her red suit into the room, deliberately stalking past the watering hole without a glance. If stools swiveled, she didn't notice. A shout of "Hey, New Girl," went unheeded. Crass, that. With satisfaction, she took the empty chair on the far side of the nerd from the pack.

"Sam?" she asked, signaling the bartender.

The nerd spluttered in his beer. He turned his horn-rimmed spectacles in her direction and actually studied her face, not her cleavage. "How did you know?"

"Process of elimination. Patra Llewellyn." She stuck out her hand. "Are you really Sam Adams or is that your nom de plume?"

He wiped his hand on a napkin and shook hers quickly, as if she might be too hot. "Samuel Adams. My mother was a history nut. Your father was my hero."

"Then I can count on one ally in the cubicle wars?" she asked as she ordered a pink martini.

"You know they're out to crucify you?" He tipped his head in the direction of the buffalo herd.

"They want to screw me first. Tell me more, and let's see if we can work together."

His eyes widened behind the thick lenses at her bluntness. But then he started to talk, and Patra drank her martini and bought him another.

Twenty-two

NICK tapped his spoon on his poached egg as we gathered around our morning buffet on Tuesday. "I'm interviewing with the British embassy this afternoon. Any last requests of the senator's office, should I hand in my resignation this week?"

"That's overconfidence," Patra grumbled, looking hungover.

"That's a rat deserting my dad," EG pointed out, although she didn't sound particularly upset as she scanned the morning comics on her iPad.

I swatted both their heads with my newspaper as I passed by. "That's an opportunity. Pay attention and be appreciative." I took my place at the end of the table, opened my newspaper, and sipped my coffee.

"What, no requests for the address books of D.C.'s rich and powerful?" Nick asked, sipping his tea and lifting his expressive blond eyebrows.

"Unless the senator has an address book of D.C. gangsters or Top Hat, I'm good," I said. "I doubt that Tex has enough influence left to get his bar tab picked up, much less help us get our money back. Good luck at the embassy."

"Tex isn't without his resources," Nick said, buttering his toast. "Gangsters may be beyond his scope, but I'll see what I can do. I'll truly miss his files."

"Does he have one on Broderick?" Patra asked, finally understanding the extent of Nick's invitation.

"I do," I said. "And no, there's nothing you can use or I would have told you. Tex is good for the connections behind the connections. If you want to know what lobbies Broderick hid behind to finance Tex's campaign, Nick's your boy." I pondered that half a second. "Maybe we could use Tex's entire campaign finance file. One never knows where the names might take us someday."

"I have that," the candelabra said dryly. "Miss Llewellyn, you have a Samuel Adams attempting to access your email password.

I've sent him a highly sophisticated virus that will no doubt destroy his computer within ten minutes if he does not desist."

I snorted orange juice. Patra swore and ran for her room looking like the Wicked Witch of the West in her shabby robe, with her hair still down.

"That wasn't very nice, Mr. Graham," I said in the same tone he'd used. "You may have unleashed a deadly new virus upon the world if Mr. Adams is a techie."

"I know who Samuel Adams is and the virus will self-destruct before he knows what hit him. Your sister has entertaining friends." The candelabra clicked off.

I used to be annoyed by our morning interruption, but I insanely wanted to giggle today. I was starting to understand Graham's dry humor better. Or maybe that hot kiss had deranged my suspicion-ometer.

"What?" I asked innocently as both Nick and EG stared at me.

"You didn't punch the silver," EG explained. "Does this mean Adams is friend or foe?"

"I haven't the foggiest notion who Adams is. I want that virus. I have a whole roster of people I'd like to set it loose on." I was happily making lists in my head when Patra returned, still talking into her phone. She didn't look any less green than earlier, but animation had returned.

"Sam was only trying to verify the safety of my password," Patra said, clicking off and returning to her seat. "Will you please call off your pet vulture?"

"Graham has moved on to more interesting entertainment. If your friend quit his quest, he'll be all right," I promised. "As long as you're wired into our network, you don't have to worry about having a watchdog. You'd best tell your friend to cease and desist or *I'll* sic a virus on him. Hacking is a nasty bad habit," I added virtuously.

Patra narrowed her eyes at me but refrained from commenting in front of EG. Nice. She'd grown up and learned manners.

"Does Sam have an apartment big enough for you to move into?" Nick asked with devious motivation.

"I'll look into that," Patra grumbled. "I don't know how you endure this prison. Can I even think without being overheard?"

"Presupposing you can think..." EG started to say. I pointed a knife at her. She caught on quickly and returned to her comics.

"Think of this as our hive," I said. "No, you cannot think without being overheard. Given our talents, that's a good thing. It means if you're out with Sam Adams and he tries to murder you, we'll have some idea of where to find your body. Who is Mr. Adams and why is he playing your watchdog?" I asked.

Patra gulped her black coffee and swallowed a piece of dry toast with a look of distaste. I pretended the look was for her breakfast and not my analysis of life with Graham.

"He's an IT person at Poo Manor and sees all the good gossip. He idolizes my father, despises Broderick, and is willing to share. Believe it or not, I have a few enemies in the cubicles already."

I bit back a grin at her creative appellation for BM. "Any person of intelligence has enemies. Practice basic Machiavelli." I processed her news while I added fresh blackberry jam from a local farm to my toast, far more appreciative of Mallard's repast than our resident journalist. "Is Sam helping you hack Broderick's archives?"

Finally, Patra grinned. "Yep."

We all punched our fists into the air.

* * *

I had more of Patrick's decoded notes loaded into my spreadsheet, and I was starting to discern the pattern of dates, places, initials, and odd numbers. The dates started nearly ten years ago—before Graham had given him information— and continued up to the time Patrick was killed—not too long after Graham's interference. The first date was a month after the September terrorist attacks and about the time of Graham's spectacular descent into hell.

If the pattern represented meetings, I hadn't found the decoder for any of the initials that I assumed would tell me who attended, although I was fascinated to note that a *PR* was included in many of the old ones. I had a grudge against Paul Rose, the conservative presidential candidate.

I did a quick search and lo and behold, *Rose had been serving in the army nine years ago*—early in the war, when a horrific American military atrocity in Iraq had left the nation stunned.

It was before my arrival in Atlanta, so I couldn't say I'd experienced a horrified nation first hand. But I did remember the ugly mood all over Europe at the time. The guys in the white hats weren't supposed to kill civilians and blow up religious edifices, even in wartime.

Scanning through the news files, I could tell the story had disappeared quickly, buried under stories of a crazed gunman running amuck in a mall. There were private websites dedicated to war atrocities, but the mainstream media dropped the military story like a hot potato. My paranoia radar detected media manipulation, but conspiracy theories are a dime a dozen.

More recent dates in Patrick's files corresponded with different initials: DS, EB, and LR stood out, but I'd have to do a lot more research to determine if Broderick exec David Smedbetter or Leonard Riley might have been in a war zone back then. The only EB I knew of in this case was Bill's dad.

I couldn't explain the coded numbers yet, although my bet was that they referred to topics discussed. Or like Bill, had Llewellyn kept numbered disks? I left the file where Graham could get at it.

Just as I was debating contacting the Seattle speech analyst and asking how far they'd gone with Patrick's recording, Sean called.

"We've sorted the material in Bill's vault. Given what's on these files, the little worm was in a nice position to blackmail a few powerful folks. Any number of people might have wanted him dead if they knew he had these files. What we want to know is who was making the recordings and giving them to him?"

"I don't think Bill was in a position to record powerful people," I reminded him. "He was just a dumb schmuck who was starting to learn about the real world. From the memos we've read, I'd have to say his clients made the recordings and gave them to him."

Sean growled almost as nastily as Graham. "We don't need speech analysis to identify half a dozen conservative senators and even more representatives on these recordings. His clients must have wanted to identify the lesser known quantities to whom they're speaking. I need an index to Bill's files, but most of them aren't here. They probably went up in the fire or were stolen with his computers."

"Judging by the recording we're working on," I told him, "I'd say the R&P trusted Bill, and that the unknown voices belong to some of their members. Do your recordings sound like interviews or arguments or what?"

He took a second to access a computer file. "We have a lot of promises being made, so those are probably your R&P people lobbying for legislation in return for campaign financing. One of these congressional idiots actually promised to shut down a local CBS station that had irritated a local millionaire, in exchange for a substantial contribution. Not sure which side of that conversation was stupider, but given the current political situation in that state, they'd both pay money not to have that little meeting revealed."

"Interesting." I was pulling up Bill's bank account information and studying deposits. "Unless Bill was stashing cash elsewhere, I'm not seeing riches. From everything I've learned so far, I'd bet that the killers took out the last honest man in town. Bill kept everyone's secrets. Personality-wise, I'd say he hoarded them just for the pleasure of possession."

"What, you're a psychiatrist now?" Sean asked incredulously.

"Just finished an on-line course on psychology," I told him with smug satisfaction. "Piece of cake. I've been studying people all my life, mostly so I can avoid them. Bill's choice of a reclusive occupation and lack of friends was a classic trait of borderline personality disorder, and hoarding is a symptom. Did you hear any journalists conducting interviews in those files?"

"Journalists?" he asked warily.

"I would think you'd at least recognize a professional questioning technique. Unless you're recognizing anyone from the nightly news, the journalists would be the voices you can't identify," I said. "I'm looking for a connection to BM, unless R&P has their own media."

"The R&P subsidizes a lot of right-wing media. Where do you think BM gets their shit?" he said with journalistic cynicism. "There are several files labeled 'interview.' Maybe I should listen to them."

"Sounds like a good way to put yourself to sleep, but it would be nice to know if BM was involved," I agreed, only because knowledge is power. I certainly didn't see the connections. Yet. "What have the police found out from the arsonist they caught?"

"That Toreador is a small time thug with connections to the DeLuca crime syndicate. They got him out on bail," he said dismissively, as if he hadn't just handed me a huge puzzle piece. "And what the hell am I looking for if I listen to these files?"

"For who killed Bill, of course. So far, I can't tell that he stirred any particular nests on the day he died. Although…" I tapped my pencil against my desk. He'd called his mother three times that day. And they weren't exactly friends, as I'd originally thought. I needed to look closer into EB—Ernest Bloom?

"Ana?" Sean called through the line. "Are you still there? What was that 'although'?"

"Families are complex structures," I told him. "Maybe Machiavelli should have said keep your enemies close but your families closer. Certainly would have been smart in his case. Thanks, friend, I owe you." I hung up.

The phone rang again but I switched it off and dived into the life and crimes of Carol Bloom and family.

* * *

Patra's perspective

Later that morning, sitting in her cubicle, Patra concluded that Ana got lost in the details and ignored the big picture. Ana thought ferreting out Bill's killer would lead her to Patrick Llewellyn's death and wanted all the pieces to fit neatly together.

Bill's death was puzzling but not necessarily related to the world at large. But Broderick…there was the big picture, she decided while merrily working her way deeper into BM's archives, courtesy of Sam's passwords. Sam had promised to hide her activity if she just worked when he was available, like now.

Broderick's worldwide media conglomerate had the power to buy and sell entire countries and probably had. The conversation on her father's tape had to be Broderick operatives. If so, his media outlets had started wars. Voila, BM had to have killed her father for the exposé he had no doubt been planning. She simply needed to go straight to the source and skip the baby steps.

The problem, of course, was that the names of murderers didn't generally get recorded. But she had the date and location of her father's death, and now she could see which of BM's henchmen might have been in the area at the time.

The access to BM's archives was nothing short of miraculous—well worth the office jerkwads. As long as Sam was at the IT desk, she should be good.

The name *Smedbetter* leaped out at her from a special report by

Broderick Media at the time of her father's death. She skimmed the article. *Ernest Bloom* had been a Broderick embed in Iraq who had obtained an interview with *General* Smedbetter through the offices of a PR flack by the name of Charles Whitehead.

Well, shite, maybe Ana was on the right trail after all.

She did a quick search. Yup, Bill's dad, Ernest Bloom, had worked for Broderick. The PR flack Whitehead wasn't on the BM roster, but *David* Smedbetter was the fat cat who'd interviewed her. Had he been a general? Puzzles within puzzles.

Whistling, Patra used her private cell phone to put in a call to Magda. Her mother had connections everywhere. Ana might have a problem asking for help from their parent, but Patra used her as the best gossip source in the world. She got voice mail, of course, but she left queries about Smedbetter and Whitehead and threw in one about Bloom, too. Magda was more likely to know generals than minor journalists, but one never knew.

The office manager prowled by, and Patra hastily scrolled up her next piece on a new rock star that Rhianna had mentioned could use some publicity. Reading the press releases was like wading through dog poo. She gagged, typed, and challenged herself to write the article with one hand. Awkward, but amusing as she used her free hand to call one of the other women she'd met here and ask what was on for lunch.

At lunchtime, she cleared her computer history and caches and left the rock star article up and running so any spare corporate spies could see she was diligently working.

Back at her desk after lunch, she uncovered a whole file of interviews from Iraq by Ernest Bloom— when some clown shouted across the cubicle farm *"Zombie run! To arms!"*

Everyone shoved back chairs and began talking excitedly, as if this were a welcome party break. Patra ignored them and opened the first of Bloom's interviews to skim over it. Dear, dear Ernest was a military geek who fawned all over the officer he was interviewing— Good ol' General Smedbetter. Interesting. The piece was entirely PR flak and showed off Bloom's knowledge of ammunition and weapons more than posing any in-depth questions about the status of the war.

"C'mon, New Girl." A jerkwad in navy blazer yanked her chair back. "We all go."

Patra hastily sent the interview to Ana's anonymous email address and closed the file before Jerkwad could read it. "I'm working. I don't play games," she told him, opening a new file and picking up her phone.

"I said, we *all* go." Jerkwad grabbed her arm and dragged her out of the chair.

She wished she'd learned martial arts. Not a soul noticed that she was being manhandled. She jammed her high heel into his instep, but he was wearing combat boots.

This couldn't be good.

The sheep hurried into the hall as if given a call to recess.

Patra regarded tall, dark, and stupid with pretend interest as he dragged her after the herd. "Hi, I'm Patra. And you are?"

"Public Enemy Number One. You aren't really interviewing Rhianna, are you?" Jerkwad's tone reflected suspicion.

She couldn't fight his grip without getting her arm broken. She reluctantly joined the excited crowd in the elevator.

"My article will be in Sunday's entertainment section. I'm sure she'd sue if I made it up," Patra said in her best posh Brit accent, trying to determine what the real game was here. "Do I call you Number One or just Pee? Perhaps Wee-wee?"

She thought Pee might murder her on the spot, but the plummy tone always put them off.

"Profound, Lady Jane," he said stiffly. "We don't use our names in the games."

"Lady Jane was a wuss." Who got executed, but Patra didn't show off her knowledge. She studied the young crowd in the elevator—none of the seniors seemed to be involved. "If I get to be a zombie, I want to be Boudicca."

"Booty it is," he agreed.

"Who's the challenger, PE?" someone crowded into the corner called.

"The R&P!" Pee called back. "I think they've hired a ringer to get us back."

Oh goody, Patra thought in gloom. Journalists versus preachers. How did zombies work into that scenario? The R&P was out to bury them?

Twenty-three

PATRA'S email attachment intruded upon my search into Carol and Ernest Bloom and sent me down a whole new set of bunny trails. Ernest as a militaristic BM correspondent opened an entire world of options. And this David Smedbetter not only had initials matching those in Patrick's files, but he'd been promoted to general not too long after friendly fire had blown up a mosque in Iraq and outraged the world.

I wasn't happy with where the bunny trails led.

Unless I wanted to believe in coincidences, I was thinking Patra had been set up when she'd found Bill, and conspiracy theories might not be paranoid, after all.

Ernest Bloom—a BM employee and Bill's father—had died in the Mideast just like Patrick Llewellyn, and not too long after Patrick's death. No one had done an autopsy, and heart attack had been listed as cause of death.

Mallard's voice through the intercom interrupted my muttering. "There is a journalist at the door, Miss Devlin," Mallard said in a tone that indicated *journalist* was synonymous with *big fat dirty turdy*. "He wishes to interview you regarding the death of Reginald Brashton."

"If wishes were horses, beggars would ride." I opened another file. "Tell him to bugger off."

"Yes, miss," he intoned dryly. Mallard was a fantastic butler. He just didn't like being ordered around by anyone other than Graham. I could scarcely blame him.

I had Bill Bloom's family tree and a life line of events for his immediate family arranged across the Whiz's three monitors when the intercom buzzed again. EG had my cell number and could call me directly, but one never knew when the cops or immigration or Magda might arrive at the door. I tried to keep lines of communication open.

"A gentleman from the *Post* and one from NBC are now camped on the doorstep," Mallard said with impressive dignity.

"Did someone shoot Reggie again?" I asked snidely. "Or did they take out Oppenheimer?" My eyes widened at that horrible thought, and I hastily switched all three monitors to different news outlets.

Dr. Smythe had been arrested for Reggie's murder!

Oh, fun. I'd given Oppenheimer my information on the witness. He hadn't wasted any time in checking it out and calling the police.

Why hadn't he called *me*?

I called him. His receptionist said he was out and took my number. What the devil was Oppenheimer up to?

"The reporters have not revealed the mysteries of the universe to me," Mallard replied as I logged into police scanner calls and scrolled through the most recent news reports.

I was turning into Graham. Crikey. With a sigh, I used Oppenheimer's tactic. "Tell them I've just stepped out and you don't know when I'll return, that you're not my babysitter."

"With pleasure," he said in what sounded like gratification. Nice that I could make someone happy.

"NBC News?" the intercom asked next. Graham. Did I hear just the faintest hint of amusement or was that my imagination? "Your mother would be wearing Dior and inviting them in."

"You may have noticed—I am not Magda," I growled with irritation. I *hated* that comparison. "What's the story here? Reggie isn't that important."

"Dr. Smythe is. That's quite a coup, and you should have thought twice before giving up Smythe to your tame tiger lawyer. Smythe has connections to every conservative politician in the country through R&P. You really need to learn the game if you wish to live a long life. Get rid of the news vans. They're interfering with reception."

I heard the speaker snap off as if some more interesting topic had caught his attention.

I called up a local news video under the *Dr. Charles Smythe Arrested* banner. Oppenheimer stood next to Lemuel, our star witness. Crap. Our lawyer was grandstanding. He was getting even with the media for blaming him for Reggie's murder. Fair enough—we'd hired him because he got in people's faces. But I knew this wouldn't be good.

Sure enough, Lemuel happily described how a Miss Lane had interviewed him in jail and then bonded him out and found him a job. That was bad enough. It made it sound as if I'd bribed him to pin the blame on Smythe. But Miss Lane didn't exist, so no one could ask me—which worked out just fine.

Unfortunately, Oppenheimer swung the cameras away from himself and right back at the notorious Maximillian family, the disgruntled—and increasingly notorious—heirs whose grandfather had possibly been *murdered* by Reggie. The shyster should have been a screenwriter. He'd practically scripted the next day's news reports.

Curse words sap the vocabulary and turn people into blithering idiots. I'd encouraged my siblings to be creative in their epithets, but I *thought* a lot of four letter blasphemies as I scrolled through the news.

Nick called. He was not happy. "I'm due at the embassy in an hour. What should I tell them when they ask if my sister bribed a gangbanger to pin a murder rap on a highly respected US citizen?"

"That you found said gangbanger a job and an apartment?" I asked with fake cheer. "Tell them that the truth will set them free? Lie through your pretty white teeth, lad. You learned from the best of them. Lie, evade, and ask if they need any publicity because you have national news on your doorstep."

"I... wait...what?"

I hung up while he was still spluttering. Nick just wanted to vent his rage. He knew better than I did what to do. He roamed political circles and knew where half the bodies were buried. He'd figure out the rest in another year or two. Not me. I just wanted to kill politicians *before* they got buried. Or Oppenheimer. I'd known he was a bloated parcel of hot air with a brain. I'd hoped he'd use that sharp mind on our enemies, not us.

I could ask What Would My Lawyer Do? Alternatively, I could ask what Magda or Graham would do. They were all authorities on evasion.

Personally, I preferred hiding and letting Mallard act as guard dog. But I was trying to learn assertiveness and action rather than reaction. Personal growth came from pushing boundaries, not just college courses.

So, my goal was to remove news vans before Graham blew a

gasket, then screw the lid down tight on Smitty so they couldn't say I bribed a witness. I am nothing if not focused.

I was feeding the list of prison visitors from the day Reggie was murdered into the back door Graham had opened into police files when I received an IM from sadams. I was not amused. I detest instant messages and never give out my ID. And *sadams* sounded more like a terrorist than the person I assumed had actually hacked into my program—Sam Adams. Jerk.

"I want that virus file," I told the intercom. It didn't answer.

I warily read the message, vowing to install two firewalls. *Problem,* it read, as if words were at a premium. I wanted to shake the computer. Or Sam Adams. Instead, I typed *With?*

Great Falls.

Getting a little nervous, I Googled Great Falls and replied *How?* to the IM.

Google revealed an area less than half an hour away with waterfalls, gorges, a swift river, and big rocks—not the kind of place my very civilized, city-dwelling family would appreciate.

These cryptic messages were taking caution to whole new levels. Patra knew Sam Adams. Patra should be at work in Broderick's cubicle farm. If she was merrily rooting out data on BM versus her father, with side roads into Blooms, Sadams had no reason to IM me. What the hell did waterfalls have to do with anything?

Danger was all I got in return.

I hit the intercom. "Track this twerp and smash him into atoms," I yelled, hoping to get our attic spider's attention. At the same time, I was typing *Who? What? Where? When?*

The IM screen disappeared. My phone rang.

Patra's caller ID appeared on my screen with the text message 911.

* * *

Patra's perspective

Wearing the red shirt and old overalls she'd been given as part of the "race," Patra scrambled up a bush-covered hill, keeping her head down. Covered in mud and burrs, she collapsed under a thorny shrub and gasped to catch her breath. Until now, she'd been playing along, dodging maniacal zombies.

Not to be paranoid or anything, but she was pretty damned certain a contingent of those zombies had singled *her* out for a purpose. They'd not only taken most of her red flags, but chased her off the marked route in the process. She'd been herded in the same way lions cut baby elephants from the pack. Ana had taught her the tactic when they were all just kids and needed to re-arrange a bully's thinking.

And if she needed any reinforcement in her belief that Broderick Media and the Righteous and Proud worked hand-in-glove, Patra's team had not only abandoned her, but joined the R&P zombies. Those were some of her red-shirted teammates surrounding this remote outpost, preventing anyone from coming to her rescue.

She texted Sam and Ana while she scanned the shedding forest below. Late October and many of the trees had lost their leaves, so she could see the trails between them. The thunder of the waterfall in the gorge was not too far in the distance. She didn't know what Ana or Sam could do, but at least Sam might know where to look for her body, just as Ana had predicted with her stupid hive mind theory. She had to remember that Ana wasn't stupid.

Neither was she. Patra spotted the red T-shirts of two of her fellow employees, and three wearing R&P's zombie rags, creeping down the trails through the trees below. They weren't chasing each other—kind of a dead giveaway.

She didn't like this game, and she didn't like being herded. Where were they trying to push her, anyway? It was a damned state park. There were probably Mounties or some such riding all over. Not that she could see any in the immediate vicinity, and it was starting to get dark. That was a bit scary. She was already pretty chilly.

The rapids were just on the other side of the hill from the sounds of it, but this wasn't Africa. The pathetic rocks and falls here looked like a Disney stage set and not a life-threatening environment. There were kids laughing and shouting not too far away. Only a suspicious mind or a guilty conscience would see anything ominous in a game of tag. Guilty on both counts.

Her bright red T-shirt made her an easy target among fading greenery. Damn, she wished she'd had time to prepare, but it had all happened too fast. She'd been shoved onto a bus, handed this horrid costume, and dumped out here without much of an alternative except to hope it really was a game.

She wiggled the red shirt off from under the overalls and tied it to the bush. She was going to freeze to death in her overalls and athletic bra if she didn't find a way out.

One of the zombies shouted and pointed up the hill. Oh, *copulation*.

She edged over the crest of the rocky hill. On the other side, she saw only the nearly perpendicular bluff to the river. She could jump or climb down and pray she'd find a crevasse in the bluff where they couldn't find her, or her skeletal remains. Zombie race! Someone had a macabre mind.

She'd be in real trouble if they had bullets. As it was, she just needed to keep her head, find a place they couldn't reach her, and outwait them. Gazing down the steep, rock-strewn bluff to the gorge below, she finally understood why she'd been herded in this direction. She'd have to be a mountain goat to escape that way. Or turn into one of EG's bats, vampiric preferably, so she could suck those zombies dry.

She punched her phone again, but the reception on this side of the hill was gone. Inventing more pithy epithets, she grabbed a sturdy bush and eased her way to the nearest ledge.

* * *

I sicced Graham's nifty GPS phone tracker on Patra's call—it came from Great Falls, Virginia. Crap, Sam Adams had been right. What the devil was she doing playing in a park? Patra hadn't trusted the neat hedgerows of Hyde Park when we'd been in London.

Graham wasn't responding to my intercom. For all I knew, he was steering Air Force One out of danger. Or fomenting revolution in Belize. I was on my own.

I didn't own a car. Mallard had access to a Bentley which was too huge to zip through DC rush hour traffic. How the devil did I find Patra in a park even if I could miraculously fly there?

I called Nick but got his voice mail. He must still be interviewing. Desperate, I called Sean. He had an old MG he raced through traffic as if he were on a NASCAR track. I'd vowed never to ride with him again, but I was out of my comfort zone. No phone, no internet, and a sibling sending distress signals stressed my mother hen instincts. And yeah, I'm sure there's a personality disorder in there. Stupid psychiatrists just hadn't diagnosed it yet.

Sean answered warily. I couldn't blame the man. We'd already got him shot once this week.

"Patra is sending distress calls. An IT nerd at BM is telling me she's in danger. I don't know what the hell is going on but she's in Great Falls. How do I get there fast?"

"I'm at the pub. Meet me on your curb in five minutes. If you've got tracking devices, bring them. There's a damned big state park out there."

"No can do. News vans all over the street. I'll meet you at the pub."

I hoped he hadn't been drinking for long. I grabbed my phone, told Mallard to watch out for EG when she got home, and dug out my army coat.

I took the kitchen steps to the backyard. I peered over the wall at the piece of street I could see—the local NBC news truck in front, and across the street, a red van in a no-parking zone. Where were the police when you needed them?

I slipped out the back gate into the concrete yard of the building on the street behind us. A smart reporter would cover this escape route. I looked around but didn't see any. We weren't a real story yet.

I ran down the street to the Irish pub on the corner. Sean was parked right outside, waiting in his nifty two-seater. He threw open the door so I could climb in. I winced as he hit the gas with his bandaged foot and spun into the Circle. Shot toes didn't seem to slow him down.

"You own a proper coat, don't you?" he asked mockingly. "Most women go for leather or wool."

He referred to the ratty old army jacket I'd pilfered from one of Magda's boyfriends. I patted the pockets now to be certain all my supplies were still there. "This *is* a coat. You'll remember I don't have to leave the house to work."

He snorted, steered the car in between two delivery trucks, floored the gas pedal at an intersection, and hit the highway already cruising faster than the rest of the traffic. I held my breath and closed my eyes as horns blew.

"We have to arrive alive to be of any help," I reminded him.

He tossed me his phone. "Call Morales. Tell him to give you the lowdown on BM's zombie games."

"Who's Morales?" I asked in suspicion, searching through his address book.

"A damned good reporter on our side now. He once worked with BM and can tell you the tales. Broderick likes his employees to be lean, mean, and nasty. The zombie game is just a fun warm-up to cull the herd. He has more intriguing competition for older employees, usually involving war zones and real terrorists."

Had Ernest Bloom been one of the employees "culled"? And dead.

Hand shaking, I found "Morales" in his address book and hit the number.

"Yo, O'Herlihy, you owe me," was the reply. "I want the scoop on the Maximillian chick."

I raised my eyebrows at Sean, but he wasn't paying attention. Not in the mood for games, I replied a little nastily. "My name is Devlin, the only Maximillian chick is nine-years old, and the scoop is in Great Falls and Broderick Media and not my front door."

I gave him a minute to absorb all that ripe information. At his muttered *shit,* I gathered he'd put pieces together, and I continued, "O'Herlihy tells me you have the scoop on Broderick's zombie games. Want to trade?"

"Shit, yeah," was the low-throated reply. "Give me a second to pull up my stuff. I was just on my way out the door. Sean with you?"

"He's become one with the wheel right now. We're heading for Great Falls. How much trouble is my sister in?"

"Last guy they culled went into the gorge, broke his leg in three places, but didn't hit the river. One before that drowned. The police called them tragic accidents. You know for certain they're culling your sister?"

I think I had a heart attack.

Twenty-four

BY THE time Morales and I had finished exchanging pleasantries, Sean was swerving into the parking lot. I was pretty certain I was gray-haired by now. I checked my braid to see. Still black. My parents obviously had strong genes.

I was beyond terrified and wanted an AK-47.

There weren't many cars left at this hour. The park would be closing shortly. I took photos of all the license plates and sent them to Graham. A few zombies were laughing and waving their flags as they shared a flask near a flashy dual-cab pickup. I growled and reached for the MG's door.

Sean caught the back of my neck, freezing me. "Those are the ones *not* chasing your sister. Go easy on them," he warned.

I'm a sneak—hence the protective coloration of army coat and hippy braid. I'm small and not dangerous-looking enough to intimidate self-confident clowns. But it was irrationally satisfying to know that Sean thought I could.

I strolled up and snapped a photo of the group. As expected, that brought them down off their happy cloud.

"Hey, who do you think you are?" Zombie #1 asked, wiping mud off his face with one of his rags.

"Your worst nightmare," I said sweetly. "I grew up playing with real terrorists, not fake ones. My sister had better be in one piece when I find her or Broderick will be the subject of the next congressional investigation. And oops, looks like the lot of you will be first on the witness stand. Want to help me get my sister back safely?" There, I'd been as polite as I knew how.

Sean leaned against his car door, crossed his arms, and just watched, reserving his injured foot for back-up, I had to assume.

Zombie #2, a big, square brute who apparently enjoyed throwing his defensive tackle weight around, loomed over me. "I want to make pizza pie out of you."

This game was more fun with Nick to laugh and wallop the

brute's skull with a blackjack. Sean wouldn't appreciate my nefarious talents. Oh well.

"You and who else?" I asked without an ounce of menace—as I rammed my brass knuckles into his nuts. I saved that particular trick for times I'm dealing with bullies a foot taller than me. The angle is good.

He went down hard, holding his junk. Since brass knuckles are just a shade illegal, I slid my weaponry into my capacious pocket and smiled at the rest of the zombies.

Sean snapped photos and pretended he hadn't seen what I'd just done.

"I repeat, I grew up with real terrorists." My heart was pounding, and I wanted to scream and kick shins, but I had plenty of experience in getting a message across with a barely sane composure. "Your friends may be out there attempting to push my sister over a ledge. Either you help us bring her back alive, or you'll end up in war zones you don't even know exist yet. Right now, I'm asking nicely to help me find my sister. The invitation will not be extended again."

"Most of us have tagged out. There are only a few stragglers still racing," Zombie #3 said with some puzzlement, gazing down at his groaning compadre. "They could be anywhere."

Since he was being reasonable, I focused on him. "Where is the most dangerous area of the park?"

"The gorge," he said. "But we don't race in that area. We're just waiting for the final tally. Broderick's team is losing and they're out there trying to even the score."

"No, they're not," Sean said, limping up. "They're trying to murder her sister. How about some of you help us find her before the police arrive?"

"Pete and his team are out there," the guy on the ground muttered. "Call them and get them out."

"It speaks. I'm impressed," I said. "Call your buddies and ask where they are and tell them they're in a hell of a lot of trouble if they don't help us."

"We're not supposed to have our phones on while we race," Zombie #1 argued.

"But the race ought to be done by now. They've had time to hit the last marker." Zombie #3 had quickly sobered. He wore a worried frown as he punched his phone on.

I'd gathered these zombies weren't Broderick's minions. I'd like to have a word with "Pete and his team," though. Except these zombies didn't seem to be getting any replies to their calls and were starting to look as anxious as I felt.

"Didn't one of Broderick's team fall off a cliff the last time they were out there?" Zombie #3 asked uneasily. "Maybe we'd better check on Pete."

"I like this guy. Give him a hug," I told Sean, before trotting off to the nearest trail signpost and trusting someone would follow.

I hit Patra's number again as Zombies #1 and #3 wearily started up the path. Sean brought up the rear, talking into his phone. At this point, I didn't care if he called in the FBI.

Patra still wasn't answering her cell.

"Holy shit," Zombie #3 said as he stared at his phone. "Some bitch and her lawyer had Dr. Smythe arrested." He held up the image for his partner to see.

The news was displaying a photo of me in my party clothes. Oops.

* * *

Patra's perspective

"She went over the side here!" Pee shouted.

Patra ducked behind the shelter of tall rocks. She'd worked half way down the side of the gorge and found a crevasse surrounded by jagged boulders. If her herders had an ounce of rock-climbing ability in them, they could easily follow the same narrow path she'd taken. And they'd kind of proved that they were athletes already. She *so* wasn't.

Her sole advantage was that the ledge was only wide enough for them to attack one at a time.

She gathered stones in a neat pile in front of her hiding place. The fissure in the rocks wasn't deep and didn't give her much throwing room.

Breaking a stick from a half-dead shrub, she glanced down to the river below. Jumping into the rapids wouldn't be any safer than her narrow hiding place. If she kept her back to the wall, Pee Wee and friends were more vulnerable than she.

She could try climbing down, but she'd more likely end up sliding off one of those nasty looking boulders and still end up in the river. Nope, Custer's last stand was here.

"Come out, come out, wherever you are!" Pee sing-songed.

"I see her," one of the zombies shouted. "Over there, by the rocks."

If she'd been prepared, she'd have her knife with her. Damn. Ana was so going to kill her if she didn't make it out alive.

Patra yanked up her overall leg and began sawing at her pantyhose with the stick. She shouldn't have worn the mini-skirt to work. From now on, it was pants and knee-highs all the way. At least she'd left the hose on when she'd donned the overalls. "Hey, Pee Wee," she called. "Do *all* girls threaten your dick or just me?"

Ana's fighting tactics had taught Patra that testosterone-filled rage lacked logic. If she was really lucky, he'd get so mad, he'd fall off the cliff trying to race down and strangle her.

"You bitch!" Pee called back. "You're nothing but a lying spy just like your bleeding-heart father."

She didn't have time to look up to see if he'd found the path yet. "Lying spy? Wouldn't someone have to be spying on me to figure out if I'm a spy?" Was he talking about Leonard Riley? Or had Sam Adams not been guarding her back this morning as she'd thought?

"You can't cheat by hiding down there. Godless heathens are losers," one of the zombies crowed from somewhere just over her head.

"And your god says it's okay to murder in his name?" she asked, ripping frantically at the tear she'd made in the nylon. Maybe crowing would distract the jerkwads until help arrived. "I think I'd rather side with the peaceful heathens then."

"We're not murdering anyone," one of the nameless zombies said, apparently confused. "We just want to win this game."

"Oh yeah, let me throw you my last flag and you can all go home," Patra called, trying to sound confident.

"Flag won't reach us from there. You have to come out," the zombie argued. "This is a race, not hide and seek."

"If this were a race, I'd still be on the marked course and not on these rocks. Nope, you take Pee Wee and his henchman out of here, and I'll hand you the flag when I reach the parking lot." Keep them talking, she muttered another of Ana's axioms. The pantyhose leg finally ripped off. She pulled at the branches of the bush concealing her sanctuary, hunting for a pair of sturdy limbs while surreptitiously studying the path above her.

"Don't you morons know who you're talking to?" Pee asked, finding the path she'd taken and starting down it.

Crap. She hastily snapped off the best branch she could find.

"Her family just had Dr. Smythe arrested," Pete said, seeking safe purchase for his big boots. "Her father was a raving lunatic who encouraged terrorists. She's been digging through our files, trying to find dirt. And she thinks we're *idiots* and can't figure that out."

Her family had Dr. Smith arrested? Who in hell was Dr. Smith? Oh, Smitty, she guessed. The R&P zombies wouldn't be happy about losing their fearless leader. What the devil was Ana doing out there in the real world?

"You're lying about all except that last bit. I *know* you're idiots." She finished knotting one end of the nylon to a thick branch and started on the next. "You let your own bigotry blind you. Journalists are supposed to be objective and unbiased, and you're not even giving me a fair trial. C'mon, let's see which of us is right. If I win the race, you're wrong."

Had she pushed him to real rage yet? She peered around the bush. Sure enough, Pee was now sliding down the rocky path at a stupidly reckless pace. She finished the knot, and set a nice round stone in the sling of her mangled stocking. The angle wasn't as good as she'd like, but she'd take what she could get.

"Hey, Pete, check my phone." The voices of the zombies weren't coming closer. "He's right. Dr. Smythe's been arrested."

"You're not supposed to turn your phone on," another zombie protested. "It's against the rules."

Watching through the shrub, she could see Pee and his cohort in their red shirts continuing down the path. She waited until she could smell the alcohol on their breaths before she pulled back on the sling.

The rock hit Pee Wee right between the eyes.

***

A male scream echoed over the deserted forest trail. I broke into a run up the path the zombies had showed us. That hadn't been

Patra, but I knew enough about my sister and battles to be frantic. Patra never attacked unless cornered.

The rush of the rapids ahead was loud enough to guide me the rest of the way. I left the weary zombies in the dust. Sean increased his pace, but he was hampered by the limp. We arrived in a clearing near the cliff's edge to find a zombie wearing tattered skin, green eye shadow, and bloody rags blocking the path with a big stick. Cute.

Not subtle, Sean simply plowed his fist into the guy's jaw. Maybe he really did have a thing for Patra.

Green Boy went down, cracking his head on one of the rocks lining the path. I winced but kept running across the clearing. I could hear Patra talking now. A second zombie wearing a fright wig and black make-up turned in our direction. I raced straight at him, hands out, and shoved him backward, down the hill.

His scream wasn't pretty. Neither was Patra's.

The impetus of my shove had me off balance. Sean caught me and flung me toward solid ground before I could tumble down the hill. That was a damned tricky ledge.

"Patra, we're here!" I shouted. "We've got two down. How many more?"

Sean peered over the ledge and held up two fingers. I got down on my rear and started sliding down the rocky path. He grabbed the back of my army coat, presumably to keep me from taking chances on a crumbling cliff. I jerked a switchblade from one of the pockets. He'd have to learn that my army coat meant lethal business. I did not wear it without planning to use it. He probably wouldn't approve of the grenade in the inside pocket either.

Sean released the back of my coat.

"Pee Wee just went into the river. I think we've got the other two trapped between us," Patra shouted. "How about it, guys? Want to join Pee and Blackface down the ledge or want to shake hands with my sister and my new boyfriend?"

I would probably throttle Patra once I had my hands on her. A guy in a red shirt was further down the path, closest to Patra and holding a big stick. Another red shirt stood nearer to me. They both looked pretty ticked off.

"What did you do to stir the hornets?" I called back, still sitting on the cliff's edge but brandishing my rather nasty looking knife. I didn't comment on Patra's adoption of Sean as boyfriend.

The roar of a helicopter nearly drowned my question.

Sean, the impeccably correct, used one of the race flags to signal the 'copter, but I wasn't seeing landing space on a cliff.

"I called them names, stoned their ringleader, and you apparently had their fearless leader arrested," Patra called back. "Looks like you've taken out Evil Menace Numero Dos," she said with admiration.

I could see her now. She'd found a nice niche behind some massive boulders. "Is that a panty hose slingshot?" I asked in approval. "Good work."

The Redshirts glanced back and forth between us, probably trying to decide which of us was crazier. Apparently distraction defused their hormonal rage, and their brains kicked in again. Finally realizing the helicopter wasn't moving on, they glanced up at and swore at the military markings. Someone's 911 call had gone through. I was in no place to question why military and not police.

"The slingshot got Pee Wee right between the eyes. He was a little unbalanced," Patra said with regret. "Not sure if he hit the river or if he's on the rocks."

I could hear sirens in the distance. "Do we want the cops to talk to these guys or do you just want to go home?" I asked conversationally.

"We didn't do anything!" Redshirt shouted. "She was shooting at us. She's *killed* Pee..." He stumbled uncertainly over the unflattering name Patra had used.

"They're bullies," Patra said. "Loudmouth there is Broderick's tough. The zombies are with R&P. I'm betting they've sent a few other people over this ledge before. They're kind of good at it. I say let the cops have them. Throw me down a coat, if you've got one. I'm about to freeze."

Sean heard this last. He looked at my armed and loaded army jacket, and immediately doffed his fancy suede coat. "Catch," he called, flinging the coat and aiming at the boulders.

Patra caught it. "You're going to get really lucky," she called back.

Sean sighed and looked at me. "She's a baby, right? She doesn't mean that."

"Only if ten years difference matters," I told him. His look of interest should have ticked me off. It didn't.

I laughed as our two drunken bullies staggered up the hill, looking for a way to escape my knife. Athletic as they were, they chose to cut through shrubbery and find a different ledge than the one I guarded. I just wanted Patra safe. The cops could work off some energy chasing criminals.

"She's Magda," I warned Sean conversationally, as if we were in the front parlor. "Your virtue is in danger."

"You're right, I should leave Graham alone," Sean said in resignation as the Redshirts shoved their way through a bush and looked for footing on an outcropping of rock. "If all of you are on his side, I don't have a chance of surviving, much less learning anything."

"Graham's alive and on the side of the good guys. What more do you need to know?" I was probably lying. It wasn't as if I knew Graham was on any side but his own. I just preferred not to be caught between Graham and Sean.

I waved at the helicopter. A long arm waved back. I wanted there to be a diamond cufflink but I saw only a flight jacket before a ladder was lowered to Patra's ledge.

Twenty-five

"CRAP," I muttered as Patra disappeared inside the helicopter. I didn't need to test my phone's reception to call our resident spider. I recognized his tactics. "Graham's covering up again. Let's get out of here before the cops arrive to ask questions."

Sean didn't have to be told twice. We turned left instead of right, and took the long way around, avoiding the path the authorities would follow. The zombies and redshirts could help the cops find their friends once we weren't there to give evidence against them.

I briefly considered giving up the old Magda tactic of staying low so the bad guys don't know who you are or where you are until you'd nailed them. Except I wasn't interested in the puppets on the bluff. I wanted to nail Broderick and the puppetmeisters who had sent them. That required avoiding media attention—and keeping Patra out of the spotlight.

The police and park rangers had already disappeared up the hill by the time Sean and I leisurely made our way down and climbed into the MG. One cop had stayed behind to gather equipment. Since we came down from a different path, he rushed through his routine and left us alone. If they wanted to talk to us, they could check out Sean's license plate.

The pickup drunks had probably fled as soon as they heard the sirens. Drinking and driving made people nervous around the law.

In a blue funk, I sank deeper into the MG seat. Patra had nearly died today, and I wasn't any closer to the demons behind the attempt on her life, Bill's murder, or anything else. I could suspect orders came down from the upper echelons of BM, or that someone in the R&P had something to conceal, but suspicion didn't provide evidence. Like in our grandfather's death, we had no proof at all. How did I cut the head off a Hydra?

"How much of this is related to the murder of the speech analyst?" Sean demanded, aptly enough.

"Probably most of it," I said, glad to air my thoughts. "Bill's father worked for Broderick and died not long after Llewellyn in the same war zone."

Sean whistled. "If Bill's family has an inside track with Broderick, then BM isn't likely to kill one of their own, unless he knew too much."

"Broderick can and has killed its own. You just saw evidence of that today. You're over-simplifying and not seeing the nest of snakes," I protested. "Patra started looking into her father's death, trying to sell his memoirs, and suddenly, she's invited to interview for Broderick Media. How likely is that? She uncovers a tape possibly implicating Broderick's conglomerate with media incitement of revolution and someone recommends Bill Bloom to analyze it? The same Bill Bloom whose father used to work for Broderick in the same war zone in which her father was killed?"

"Well, when you put it like that..." he said reluctantly. "But if Bill was a plant, why kill him? Why not just have him hand over the tape?"

"Based on my psycho-analysis..." I said tauntingly. Sean shot me a dirty look, but all I had was theory. "I think Bill turned coat on his family. They didn't like his Hispanic girlfriend, he moved out, quit talking to them much. He'd probably been cutting himself off for some time, and his family just didn't realize his attitude shift until it was too late."

"And this has what to do with the price of eggs?" he asked.

"I'm *analyzing*, so shut up," I warned. "I think Bill recognized at least one of the voices on Patra's tape without even running the speech programs. He called his mother three times the day he was killed. If that was his father's voice on the recording, and Bill called his mother to verify his father was in that war zone, or to accuse his father of something, what would Carol Bloom do?"

"Complain to anyone who would listen about heartless sons, like any good mother," Sean said.

"Good boy," I said, patronizingly, ignoring his dirty look. "Carol had Bill's brother Ken clean out Bill's apartment after his death. Ken was thinking of *burning* those files—like he'd burned his father's files."

"Like the files that got burned after Patra and I rescued them?" he asked, catching on. "And Llewellyn's files got burned? Damn. We met Ken when we picked up those papers. Patra suspected he was the one who called the tail. But why didn't he just burn the files while he had them?"

"Because someone wanted to know if anyone might come looking for them. They wanted *Patra* more than the files." I was getting unhappier by the minute.

"You think *Broderick* had thugs planted to follow us? He had something to hide in Bill's place, and that's why they went after Patra today?"

"Snakes," I reminded him. "Nests of them writhing around each other. Carol also mentioned giving the boxes to R&P. I promised to do it for her, and she thought that's who Patra was. Did the R&P believe Patra helped find evidence against Smitty? I'm sure the Righteous weren't any too Proud when Smitty got arrested."

My phone rang and I grubbed around in my pockets until I found it. *Nick*. "Get the job?"

"I did, no thanks to all of you," he grumbled. "They wanted to know if my family will continue to garner media attention because my position is one that requires discretion. So after assuring them that we're the souls of discretion, I come out and discover Patra is in a helicopter, the street is full of news vans, and I suppose you're visiting another planet since you're obviously not here."

"Poor baby," I said, not quite soothingly. "I'm on my way. Patra will probably be there soon if Graham hasn't put her on a plane back to England. But anyone who hires you for discretion is not quite playing with a full deck. Let's tape his voice and compare it to the Brit on Patra's recording."

"I'm not speaking to you ever again." He hung up.

Sean sent me a questioning look. I smiled, probably wearily. "Nick isn't into paranoia." But I was. I needed the people on Patrick's tape identified pronto.

* * *

By the time we'd worked our way through rush hour traffic, the six o'clock news was wrapped up and most of the news vans had departed.

I eyed a lingering unmarked van with suspicion and dislike. "Friends of yours?" I asked, nodding toward the seemingly empty white Ford. The vehicle ought to have a dozen parking tickets if it had been there all day.

Sean studied the van and shrugged. "Not that I recognize."

Why disturb the snakes? I ignored the Ford but pulled my hood over my hair as we got out. I'd rather not have my photo plastered on Entertainment Nightly if it could be avoided.

I actually invited Sean in. He deserved a reward for his heroic efforts. He studied the mansion longingly, looked at me in my grungy army coat, then shook his head in regret. "I'm going back to look over Bill's files. They're the only physical clue we have. And you need to sit down with Patra."

"You mean someone needs to tie her up in the basement. Tried that once. I think she charmed a rat into nibbling her free." I waved him off, smiling as if I was joking.

I wasn't, except the rat had been human. Since Patra had only been ten at the time, Magda had arranged for him to be transported to Siberia for kidnapping and attempted child molestation. Honest, happy Patra had simply been puzzled that we hadn't been pleased that she'd escaped and won the game with her slimy adult friend.

She was older now, I told myself as I entered the house. Sean was a decent guy. She could charm him all she liked—not my problem. My problem was whacking off all the Hydra heads at once. Looked insurmountable from here.

"May I take your coat?" Mallard asked as I headed for the stairs. "The others are gathering for dinner."

"No, you may not take my coat. And tell Graham if I find cat hairs on it later, I'm buying a pit bull to guard it. I have to clean up. Tell Nick and EG to start without me."

Graham kept a cat. Now that I knew he was mobile, I also knew he was a sneak. What irritated me most was that the damned man still intrigued me. So I focused my concern on Patra for now. Where had he taken her?

"Shall I tell Miss Llewellyn not to wait also? She's still in her room but promises to be down shortly."

Now he tells me. I drilled Mallard with a glare and dashed upstairs to the massive chamber Patra had taken for herself. She opened the door before I could pound more than once.

She's taller than I am. Hugging her is awkward. But we did our best before Patra looked down at my grimy jacket, made a sound of disgust, and backed off. Since she'd changed into pale blue silk dinner dress, I understood.

"Who was in the helicopter?" I demanded immediately.

She spun in a circle, admiring the flare of the silk. "Pilot and a hunk in a suit. It was too dark to get a good look. Very weird and James Bondish, like something Magda would have arranged. I thought you'd sent them. You didn't?"

"No, I just warned Graham. Almost the same thing as telling Magda. Where did the helicopter take you that you got here before us?" I was dying of curiosity, but Patra seemed to be high on an adrenaline rush and not using her head at all.

"Helicopter pad on top of some embassy not too far from here. A security guard escorted me to the elevator, gave me directions to the Metro, and here I am." She finally stopped twirling to face me. "I owe you big time, I know," she said with only a little regret at the panic attack she'd caused. "What happened at the gorge after I left?"

"Sean and I scampered. We'll have to check the police scanners. Want to explain what the devil that was about?"

She made a puzzled moue. "Pee said I was a spy. Since I'd never met him before, I assume he'd been told I was a problem that needed to be removed. The zombies were mad about Smitty being arrested, but they didn't know about it until I was over the edge. They really seemed to think it was all some weird version of the game. I'll have to ask around tomorrow and see what I can find out about Pee."

I almost had a second heart attack. "While I admire your fortitude, I recommend you not return to Crap Media in the morning," I warned, trying not to scream and bash her head against a hard object.

"But that would take all the fun out of it!" she cried. "What can they accuse me of—not dying? I want to see their faces when I show up. Besides, I've already written the bones of an incredible exposé on BM. Sam said he could get the first segment onto the AP wire without anyone knowing. An exposé on BM coming from BM! Just think about it. It will be fun, and then I'll scamper, I promise. Hurry and change so we can hear all about Nick's new job."

My family was officially nuts. This was why running away had seemed my best move ten years ago. But I didn't want to run away from my grandfather's house. Which meant I had to learn to deal with adrenaline poisoning. Somehow. Strangling Patra probably wasn't an option.

I trudged over to my grandfather's study, locked my coat in a filing cabinet, and hit the intercom on the lovely old desk overlooking the street below. "Thank you," I said, possibly grudgingly, but I meant it.

"She's worse than Magda. Tie a bomb to her when she leaves in the morning."

Graham's deep dry voice always had the power to stir my blood. And lately, it had made me grin. In the matter of my family, we were almost in tune. For now. "I think she's carrying her own time bomb," I warned.

"I should have guessed that," he replied. "Smedbetter is the one you need to focus on. He has something on Broderick to land him that cushy job after he got put out to pasture. They don't exactly travel in the same circles otherwise."

Graham checked out before I could tell him I'd look into it. He knew I would, so telling him so was obviously redundant. Ernest Bloom had interviewed a General David Smedbetter in the article Patra had sent, and the initials DS had been in Patrick's notes well before that. I desperately needed to dig deeper, but family was waiting.

I didn't own much of a wardrobe. I might have to consider some on-line shopping soon. I showered and donned khakis with my best sweater to pretend I was trying, then dashed downstairs to hear the current topic of discussion at the dinner table.

This was the part of family that I loved. I almost wished Graham would join us. EG sipped her soup and held up her iPad so I could see the video on the rescue operation in Great Falls gorge. The zombies looked particularly foolish with their faces falling off as they tried to explain why two of their race members were so far off course.

The guy I'd knocked off the edge had landed in a bush and survived with a few broken bones. They were still searching the river for Patra's tormenter. Oddly, not a soul mentioned Patra's existence. It just appeared to be a race gone strangely awry.

Patra snatched the iPad, punched a few buttons, and produced a story on Smythe's arrest for murdering the lawyer accused of embezzling millions. Speculation was rife that Reggie had somehow stolen funds from Smythe or the R&P. Oppenheimer had disappeared from the picture, although one of the lesser rags had posted my glamorous dinner photo under *heiress*. Sweet. Not.

"What would it take to get Smythe to rat on Top Hat?" I asked the table at large.

Nick was really the only one who understood me, and he narrowed his eyes. "Not going there, remember? Patra's already been targeted just for digging around and turning up nothing. And if they could murder our grandfather in his own home and Reggie in a federal prison, we really don't need to be in deeper."

"We're getting deeper by the minute. Princess there wants to return to work tomorrow." I nodded at Patra, who ignored me.

Nick rolled his eyes. "Right. Of course, she does. Do we handcuff her or let her learn the hard way?"

"I'm not doing anything either of you wouldn't do," Patra said, helping herself to the grilled salmon.

Sadly, she was right.

"We need to hack the bad guys' phones the way Broderick Media does to the politicians they want to destroy," EG said, shoveling couscous into her maw while we passed her iPad around.

All our heads turned to stare at our youngest sibling. We hadn't told her anything. I suspected she was making a general observation based on her extensive reading of current events and her curiosity about the ugly world we lived in. But she'd nailed it.

Patra's eyes narrowed. Without a word, she produced her smart phone and checked her list of calls. She pushed it toward me. I glanced at the screen.

All of her calls appeared dangerous. Worse yet, she'd called Magda. That wasn't a big deal on its own. In light of what EG had just reminded us of... If Broderick's henchmen had hacked Patra's phone and knew who she was calling... They had damned good reason to push her off a cliff.

"I don't suppose this was an innocent conversation involving cosmetics?" I asked, holding up the phone with Magda's number showing.

"I reached voice mail. She must have called back while I was at lunch, and I didn't notice. I picked this up just a while ago." Patra took the phone back, put it on speaker, and punched up her voice mail box.

Our mother's voice spoke clearly and succinctly. "Dear,

Smedbetter and his coalition cohort, Whitehead, were up to their ugly teeth preventing media coverage of the Rose atrocity scandal in Kirkuk ten years ago. Broderick *owns* them. Do use safer channels to make your inquiries next time." In true Magda fashion, she hung up without farewells or so much as asking after our health.

The Kirkuk bombing had involved *Paul Rose*? Man, that had been covered up in the stories I'd read. But Kirkuk had been ten years ago, five years before Patra's father died. Paul Rose had been back home, winning elections, by then.

I grabbed the phone and trotted upstairs to Graham's office. His door was closed. For a change, he wasn't expecting me. That probably meant he'd found more important matters than monitoring our dinner table conversation. Stupid man.

I knocked. I took his answering grunt as an invitation to enter. He was in front of his bank of computer monitors as usual. He didn't turn to acknowledge my presence but manipulated his mouse, changing the many screens so rapidly that I couldn't process the images. I thought I caught a glimpse of our lawyer's office building, the prison where they'd kept Reggie—and presumably Smythe now—and Sean's newspaper office. The man had to be autistic to focus on all those screens at once.

I leaned over his broad shoulder and dropped Patra's phone on the desk. "Can you debug it?"

He stopped scrolling through his screens and picked up the equipment with interest. "Didn't take Broderick long, did it? Hacking voice mail is the usual method, but if he could plant spyware directly..."

His words trailed off as he hooked the phone up to a computer, pried through the innards, cursed, and started deleting files. The man was scary good.

"Your sister should know better than to leave her phone where someone can get at it," he said reprovingly. "And if she intends to snoop in company files, she needs a stronger password on her voice and email. They'll go for those next."

I didn't waste time inquiring how he knew her password wasn't strong. As long as I had him talking, I went for the more interesting question. "Why the helicopter?"

"I did my duty by Max by offering her the job in Atlanta. She didn't take it. If she intends to set herself up as a target in

Broderick's office, I might as well take advantage while I can. The helicopter was just payback for the information she's providing."

I clenched my fingers into fists rather than box his ears. As soon as he put the back on her phone again, I jerked it away. "You don't care whose lives you risk as long as you get what you want, do you? Including your own. Keep in mind that the world is full of petty dictators and evil overlords and you cannot singlehandedly stop any of them. Get a life."

I stalked out. I had no idea where that pithy speech had come from. Sounded like one I'd probably thrown at Magda in the past. Made me want to ask just what a life was supposed to be if one wanted to get one.

I returned downstairs and dropped the phone in front of the Brownie Surprise Mallard had just served Patra. I hadn't even eaten my salmon yet.

"He says get a better password and quit leaving your phone where others can hack it."

I skipped the brownie and went back to my office to email Magda. I hated doing it, but if Patra was determined to swim with the devil, I needed to know where the demons were hidden.

Twenty-six

TUESDAY night, after everyone had scattered, I studied the notes I'd gathered:

GENERAL DAVID SMEDBETTER: Retired Army, served in Iraq, commander of troops including Lieutenant Paul Rose's squadron in Kirkuk ten years ago. Promoted to general after Kirkuk and at command headquarters in Iraq five years ago when Llewellyn died. Currently on executive board of Broderick Media.

LT CHARLES WHITEHEAD: Former British Army, served in foreign theaters as communications director—read PR front man. Left the service after coalition forces under Paul Rose's command dropped a bomb on a Kirkuk mosque, killing hundreds of innocent civilians. Joined the British embassy staff in Kuwait shortly after. Arranged an interview between Smedbetter and Bloom five years ago from his Kuwait office.

ERNEST BLOOM: Broderick Media embed in Iraq five years ago. Died of apparent heart attack overseas, a month after Patra's father was shot. A member of R&P.

I detested Paul Rose enough by now to spin all sorts of conspiracy theories from these few facts alone. Kirkuk stank of cover-up. Rose came from a wealthy, politically conservative, well-connected family, just the kind of man Broderick would support. The good ol' boy network took care of each other.

I scrolled up the article Patra had sent me on Ernest Bloom's interview with General Smedbetter—dated a week before Patrick's death. Bloom puffed the piece to make the general sound like a war hero who enjoyed studying weapon history. Apparently Smedbetter was also an expert marksman and John Wayne on steroids. No mention of the mosque or Kirkuk.

A short time later, Patrick and Bloom were dead. Not too long after their deaths, Smedbetter was working for Broderick. And Paul

Rose was a damned senator. Money can buy anything. Don't let folk wisdom persuade you otherwise.

None of them seemed likely to have killed poor Bill. Reggie, maybe, but we had Smythe for that. Patrick... his death had to have been an execution we'd never prove. But Bill...

I added LEONARD RILEY to my time line. Journalist for Broderick Media for most of his adult life. Indicted in vice presidential phone hacking ten years ago, about the time Rose was blowing up a mosque and Dr. Smythe was founding the R&P. Riley went to prison for tapping the VP's phone line. Five years later, Riley was out and Patrick and Bloom ended up dead. Nothing connected the two events.

Leonard's résumé became a little unclear after he left prison. His credit report showed him as self-employed, what Magda would call a contractor, working for anyone who paid him. Currently, he had an R&P insurance card, so there was some connection.

Because of the initials in Patrick's coded files, I delved deeper. Smitty, in his vice presidential aide role, had the ability to give Riley access to the VP's phone during a war-time crisis ten years ago. Kirkuk? Riley took the rap for the tap, but Dr. Charles Smythe had been forced to resign. Instead of prison, he landed a cushy job at R&P.

I trolled through public records looking for more connections between Riley and R&P. Non-profit corporations file copious records if one knows where to find them. R&P had been no more than a disgruntled horde of taxpayers until about five years ago, at which point they'd been heavily funded and gone professional under Smythe's direction.

Bingo. Budget line item with their first filing five years ago—R&P had covered Riley's travel expenses and provided compensation for *publicity*. Publicity? That smarmy slug couldn't bum a cigarette with his spin doctor skills.

Around ten, Magda got back to me. Since I didn't know what country she was in this week, I couldn't calculate her time, but she sounded bright and cheery.

"Ana, so good to hear from you! What are all my little chickies up to these days?"

"No good, as usual. Patra nearly got herself killed by some of Sir Archie's goons. Has she been telling you about her latest endeavor?"

"I left her a message and then regretted it," Magda said with a sigh. "I tried to dissuade her from going after Broderick. Archie's organization is so invasive, that she'll never be able to pull out all the roots. Tell her I'm heading for Paris next, and she's welcome to join me."

"Really? And you think she'll just come running?" I couldn't resist the snark. I didn't bother to give her time to hem and haw. "I need more info on Lt. Charles Whitehead, General David Smedbetter, and a Leonard Riley. How did Smedbetter get from Iraq to Archie's empire?"

"I'm sure you know as much about them as I do, and I'm not encouraging Patra to dig into her father's death by providing further information," she said crisply.

Which told me right there that she suspected they were involved in his death. But I kept my mouth shut and let her continue.

"I do remember Riley as a creepy little man who ran errands for Archie's sycophants in Iraq," she said. I could almost see her frown. "I think he used to provide drugs and alcohol to most of the press corps, so he was probably spying. Wasn't he in prison at one time?"

I hid my glee that she'd revealed more than she knew. Riley *had* been overseas! Iraq... not precisely where Patrick was killed but relatively speaking, not too far away. "Yes, Riley went to jail about a decade ago for tapping the VP's phone. Typical Broderick stunt," I said casually. "Apparently Archie couldn't hire him directly once he had a prison record, but hired Leonard as a private contractor."

"Oh, yes, that's right. Has that phone tapping incident been ten years already? Graham caught the tap and turned the glare on Broderick instead of the war. That was back when Graham was still speaking to the world. How's he doing these days? Giving you any trouble?"

"He does his thing, I do mine. Riley's been following Patra," I said, diverting her back to the topic at hand. "I assume if he was running errands for the press corps, he probably had contact with Smedbetter as well," I said casually. "All the English speakers hang together."

"Well, you can't expect us to live in areas likely to be bombed, can you?" she asked tartly. "But Patrick was killed in Lebanon, Smedbetter was in Iraq, Whitehead was with the Brit embassy and not the military, and I wasn't in either place, so I can't tell you anything."

But willingly or not, she had told me Broderick's flunkies had been in the same part of the world as Patrick.

"Well, if you can think of any way of making Riley back off, I'd be appreciative. Graham isn't happy with lurkers," I said.

"Oh, just light a firecracker up his posterior, dear. You know how it's done. How's my baby doing in school?"

We'd had a fight over EG not too long ago, but apparently Magda had given up in favor of letting EG know her dad. We had a brief discussion on EG's fascination with bats, and then she got another call and had to cut off.

I know Magda loves us, but she was never the kind of mother who hovered and took care of boo-boos. She'd always left that to me and whatever nannies or ayahs she hired. I'd spent half my childhood resenting her and the other half imitating her. Strong personalities like hers had that kind of influence—which was why I was determined to give EG a different experience. Except that nature/nurture thing was pretty impossible to separate.

But at least we were talking to each other again, sort of. I needed to ask Magda about our African siblings sometime, but with the yacht insurance and lawsuits still up in the air, it didn't need to be immediately.

Someone had tried to kill my sister today. That took priority.

Anyone could have bugged Patra's phone. I had no way of knowing who had heard Magda's message about Rose's atrocity, but I was pretty certain that had been the lighted fuse. Orders had come down to cull her from the herd. Was Smedbetter in a position to give orders?

But a white Cadillac had followed Sean and Patra after they'd picked up Bill's boxes and a black Escalade of thugs had come gunning for them. And Patra had said the armed goon had wanted *her*, specifically, not just the boxes. To see what she knew about her father's papers? To see who else knew about Rose and the cover up?

And now they didn't care what she knew, they just wanted her gone?

My gut instinct was to put all the bad guys in one room and let them tear each other to shreds, but I didn't have that kind of power. I only had sneakiness on my side.

I emailed the speech analyst to ask if they'd identified any of the voices from the various files we'd sent them.

I emailed Sean to ask if any of Bill's audio files matched interviews with Smedbetter, Whitehead, or Leonard Riley. I wanted to add Sir Archibald Broderick, but Archie wouldn't leave his signature, or his voice, anywhere that would muddy his image. Tape #1143 was a rarity.

Tired, stymied, and overwrought after the day's excess of terror, I puttered around while waiting for replies. I was wound too tightly to sleep. The house above me was growing quiet as the inhabitants settled down for the evening. I usually returned to my room and worked on my laptop at this hour, but knowing someone could be staring into my window from the house across the street sort of ruined my relaxation technique.

So I amused myself by scanning one of Crap Media's scandal sheets for the past few months, under the assumption that easy reading ought to bore me into slumber.

The entertainment news nearly pushed me over the edge within minutes. Having grown up without American movies or television, I'd never developed the habit of watching them. So the busty bimbos and chesty gigolos pasted all over the front pages were meaningless names and faces to me. Tapping their phones and following their cars ought to bore any decent journalist into hara-kiri. Overdramatizing the speculation derived from said tapping and stalking was the work of a soap opera screenwriter.

But after a few minutes, my lizard brain clicked in, and I got focused. When I looked at Archie's scandal sheets all at once like this, a pattern formed. Chesty Gigolo attended a conservative rally and sang the national anthem to a roaring crowd and applause. Fine. Chesty wins some film award. Chesty goes to London. Chesty can't do wrong.

Busty, however, has a head on her shoulders. She sings at the liberal president's holiday dinner and makes speeches for a women's rights group. Suddenly, Busty's alcoholic mother hits the newsstands with stories of how her daughter broke her heart. Busty rallies the crowds to support gun control. Busty's teenage arrest for drunk driving hits the front page.

The pattern followed through all of the various Busties and Chesties on the front pages of the gossip sheets. I didn't know who gave a crap that the liberal entertainers got smeared with bad news and the conservative flag-wavers came out smelling like—pardon the expression—Roses, but if it sold papers, someone must.

So, in the midnight hours, I papered most of Hollywood with discreet inquiries and copied Patra on all of them. Let her really work entertainment news.

* * *

Patra's perspective

People swiveled to stare as Patra strolled through BM's offices on Wednesday morning. She'd dressed for stares. She'd dressed to demand respect. Wearing an Armani jacket and skirt with her Gucci heels, she strode through the cubicles with her head held high and her best smile on. She *liked* making them stare. She hoped it threatened the hell out of the monsters behind that spy mirror.

She carried weapons they'd never understand in her imitation Gucci shoulder bag. She intended to leave a strong impression before she left. She'd make them think twice about coming after her later.

She wasn't happy that she hadn't uncovered the evidence she needed to pin Broderick to her father's death, but she would never have a chance to expose him if she was dead. So her parting message had to be memorable.

No one said a word as she took the chair at her desk, not even the office manager who had to allow her to log into the system. So, she wasn't fired yet. She had no idea which desks her team mates had occupied, so she didn't know if the empty cubicles had been theirs.

She went online to check her personal email before she went to work subverting the system with Sam's aid. She nearly laughed aloud at the flurry of irate messages from her Hollywood contacts asking if she knew about Broderick's propaganda campaign.

What the hell had set them off? She read deeper and found Ana's message at the bottom of several— asking if they'd noted that left-leaning actors got smeared and right-leaning got promoted in the gossip rags. The examples the messages fed her provided enough material to write a book.

And one tiny clue amid the rants: *Beware the Righteous and*

Proud interviewers. They tape everything and manipulate your words to suit their purposes in their propaganda sheets. I thought I was talking to good Christians and ended up being toasted in hell.

R&P had interviewers?

She didn't have much time but she did a quick Google search. The organization had its own newsletter with a huge audience. The interviews they printed came from their role models—including Hollywood names. The R&P had the power to build a strong fan base.

Broderick's television stations and newspapers acted as a mouthpiece for the R&P. Media fed off each other. Any interesting interviews would be picked up by conservative pundits and Poo Manor.

R&P's journalists would most likely have taped their interviews and seemed the likely source of the audio files invoiced to Dr. Smythe. She didn't have time to dig deeper.

She IM'd Sam Adams: *Ready?*

You're sure your guy will hire me after this? he IM'd back.

Yep. She'd already had a talk with Sean. He'd agreed that anyone as enterprising as Sam Adams would be an asset to a real newspaper office. If nothing else, Sam could get their new computers up and running.

Send it on then. I'm taking out some insurance.

Whistling under her breath, Patra called up her personal online document folder and copied the first installment of the exposé she'd written. The article revealed times, dates, and events connected to BM's media propaganda and practices prior to the Iraqi revolution, taken from her father's files. She pasted the article into her BM word processing program and sent it directly to Sam.

The system required that he vet any articles passed for publication and forward questionable ones to his manager, but that wasn't happening today.

This method of bypassing the system wouldn't have worked for long if she and Sam intended to keep their jobs, but they didn't. So once was enough.

A few minutes later, while she pretended to work on her next Hollywood story, her office phone rang. She tapped one of her earbuds. All she got was one long, appreciative whistle. She grinned.

"Same to you, buddy," she replied, cutting off.

She closed up her computer and moseyed upstairs to have a word with a few of her least favorite execs. All she needed was a few curse words shouted into her recorder as she tendered her resignation.

Twenty-seven

AFTER walking EG to the Metro, I returned to my cave and began setting wheels in motion. I didn't care about Graham's research or any of my other cases today. I had one goal and one goal only in mind—bring down the menace who had attempted to kill my sister.

I worked through the papers Patra had rescued from Bill's files. Tapes #2844 and #3926 had the names of *Smedbetter* and *Smythe* on the file label. None mentioned Broderick or Riley. I emailed Sean a request for copies of those audio files.

Sean was apparently working along similar lines. He emailed the audio files back to me within the hour. I passed them on to the speech analyst in Seattle. With Magda's verification that Smedbetter, Bloom, and Riley were all in the wrong place at the same time, I couldn't dismiss coincidence.

I wasn't entirely certain how Whitehead, a Brit and an embassy employee, figured into any of this, but he'd been in Kirkuk and again in the Mideast five years ago. There had been a Brit accent on Patra's tape. I emailed Nick asking if there were any Whiteheads on the embassy staff here in D.C.—because his offer of a job seemed a mite too Machiavellian.

Dr. Smythe worried me, too. He didn't work for BM directly. He hadn't been in any war zones that I could determine. He was the connection to Riley, not any of the warriors. He'd killed our lawyer, which had nothing to do with anything as far as I could see. It had been some of his R&P people who had helped hunt Patra down, but he'd been busy being arrested during the zombie race.

I was hesitant about taking my next step. It would be tricky, and it would involve Graham. I didn't want to play all my cards at once unless I had a good chance of results. I liked as much information as possible before I blew up my world.

Patra sent me a cackling e-card of triumphant witches. I took that to mean she'd appreciated my Hollywood amusement, and that she was still alive. No one at BM had shot her down in cold blood. Yet. I got cold chills thinking about her working that nest of snakes.

It was too early in Seattle to expect the speech analyst to get back to me. I wanted loose ends tied up, and I didn't like waiting. I tapped my fingers on my desk, considered all the parameters, then, in an act of desperation, I emailed Graham with my query. I politely didn't disturb his privacy with the intercom the way he disturbed mine.

No was his instant reply.

I'd expected that, but I was still furious. It wasn't as if I asked things of him unless I was utterly desperate. Flat out refusal was just rude.

I'd already debated my alternatives if politeness didn't work. The one I liked best involved power tools. I slipped across the street, liberated a couple of battery-operated macho man toys, and dropped them into my canvas sack while the workmen were taking a smoke break. I was back in my cellar before anyone noticed.

I may have mentioned a time or two that I excelled in hiding while growing up. My introverted self craved privacy and my curiosity demanded answers, so I learned how to locate secret doors and hide from the best spies in town. I'd not had the time or incentive to hunt for my grandfather's secret passages, but I'd threatened to do so enough that Graham really should have been warned.

He'd been in my locked cellar office. That ticked me off enough to justify my next step. I'd chosen the cellar for my office because it's pretty hard to put secret doors in solid concrete walls. A normal person might assume he'd picked my door lock or obtained a key, except I'm not normal. I always left tape or a hair or other marker to know when my door had been opened. Even though CDs had been removed from my desk, the markers had never been disturbed.

Graham being Graham, he may have just found some sneaky way to put the markers back, but my privacy had been disturbed in too many ways on other floors. Knowing my mother and grandfather, I was pretty damned certain there were hidden passages.

I eased down the cellar stairs with my tool trophies and checked Mallard's kitchen and premises. He was gone, as I'd also expected. Graham's curiosity about my note would not be assuaged until he'd sent Mallard to do what I'd requested. He simply didn't intend to tell me about it, the secretive bastard.

Humming to myself, I tapped along my roof. No one had bothered adding acoustic tile or plaster board for a real ceiling. All I had over my head were the century-old boards and supports for the floors. When I found a section that sounded different from the rest, I flashed my light over it. Sure enough, there were the nearly invisible cuts giving evidence of chicanery. A trap door would allow anyone reasonably athletic to simply drop into my abode. Climbing out would be a bear for a short person, unless they came prepared with a rope ladder.

Someone tall and muscular could lift themselves up. I drooled just picturing Graham performing that feat.

Spiderwebs coated most of the dark corners since I didn't allow Mallard in here to clean. I'd set off a bug bomb before moving in, so I wasn't too worried about actual creepy crawlies. The area in question, however, was remarkably clear of dusty webs. Really, the deceptive bastard deserved anything I threw at him.

Just the idea of Graham lowering himself into my cave like GI Joe on a mission riled my temper. That man had to learn to play fair, or at least behave like a normal human being and ask permission. No more stealing CDs off my desk that weren't his.

Humming the Halloween tune EG was currently using as her security alarm, I ran up to her tower. She usually left her door unlocked when she wasn't there, in brave hope that Mallard might actually change her linens at least. Her room seemed relatively neat, so I assumed she'd rid the place of bats and Mallard had generously cleaned up. He really deserved more than we could pay him.

I dismantled her mp3 player with the Halloween theme song, unburied a few of her electronic toys, and returned to the cellar. I checked my computer but Seattle hadn't come through yet. I really wanted those voices identified before wreaking external havoc. As long as Patra was safe, I'd stick to internal chaos for now.

Standing on a chair, I ran a power drill into the boards over my head and created a hole large enough for the power saw. I used the saw to open a hole large enough to use as a handle. I yanked down at the old planks, but they wouldn't budge. I couldn't see hinges. I had to assume the door lifted up, not down—a nuisance which made my job harder but not impossible.

I turned on the mp3 and slid it through the hole, then wound up one of EG's toy bats and shoved it through. The stupid thing flew into a wall immediately but kept flapping around, banging into things—like more walls in the hidden passage.

I returned to the first floor and headed for what once probably had been a family parlor. In my grandfather's last bedridden years, it had been turned into a bedroom. It came equipped with a marvelous modern bathroom with a Jacuzzi and was now an unused guest room.

Sure enough, between the new closet and the new bathroom, I heard the sounds of spooky music and a banging bat. I opened the closet, flashed my light around, and found the seam for a door in one wall. Right about now, the weird noises in the closet ought to be drifting up through the passage and irritating the hell out of Graham. The image cheered me considerably.

With a little exploration, I found the pressure spring to open the hidden closet entrance. This was a new device, probably installed at my grandfather's request in the last decade.

Whistling along with the creepy music, I opened the entrance to the hidden passageway behind the closet wall. A handle carved into the wood floor revealed the escape hatch to my office. Metal circular stairs led upward.

Collecting my toys, including the flying bat, I started climbing. I located the door on the bedroom landing and opened it—one of the unused bedrooms. Graham had better be very glad it didn't go through my study. It was bad enough that this relentlessly masculine bedroom was next to the study and may have once been my grandfather's.

I wasn't exactly being quiet. I hummed along with the spooky mp3 music. And the wind-up bat in my hand kept squeaking. I had a suspicion Graham would be waiting with the latest assault weapon if I tried actually sneaking up on him. I wound up or snapped on a couple more toys when I climbed the next set of stairs to reach the door at the top.

I gauged the position as opening directly into his enormous office. He'd locked it, of course.

I took my power drill to the lock, then kicked it open, letting my mechanical bats and mice loose at the same time. I flattened myself against the closet wall as the creatures crashed into ceilings, monitors, desk chairs, and scampered off into hiding under desks. All to the mp3 tune of a weird TV theme song about monsters.

I was trying very hard not to laugh as Graham's irate curses flamed the air. Leaning against the hidden staircase wall, I heard a gunshot and a bat squeak, followed by a stomp and another squeak. The wind-up bat would be a little tougher to reach, but it would wind down eventually, possibly after taking out a monitor or two. I was nearly bent double picturing the chaos in Graham's tightly controlled universe.

"If I'd really wanted to be mean, I'd have used the radio-controlled airplane," I said from my hiding place. "I could have taken out your head."

"Dammit, Ana, did you steal back your inheritance so you can sue me out of this house or are you ready to get kicked out?"

I heard a muffled shot and a thump, presumably the squeaking bat hitting the floor. With more bravado than I felt after he'd dealt a mortal blow to my weak spot, I sauntered into his cyber-universe to survey the damage.

One of the bats was tangled in some wires near the ceiling. Since the only light in here was from the bank of monitors, I couldn't really detect what he'd done to that one. Looked like all the screens were intact, so mostly, I'd just annoyed him. What a pity.

"I'm ready to be treated like someone who has more intelligence than the average spook and who is as capable of protecting her family as you are," I told him, finally letting my anger emerge. "Patra is *my* family, not yours. If I want to fry the puppet-masters who pulled zombie strings yesterday, you have no right to interfere. Now, do I risk getting arrested to go after that phone on my own or will you help me?"

"Bill Bloom's personal effects are still in police custody," he intoned, actually turning to glare at me.

If he knew what his voice did to me, he'd use it more often. I just propped my fists on my hips and glared back. "You think I don't know that? That's why I politely asked if you could have them released. I didn't want you going all lionesque if I did it myself."

"Lionesque?" he asked with what almost sounded like amusement. "What in hell is that?"

"That's not the point. The point is that you're treating me like EG. If I want Bill's phone, it's because I have a very good reason for it. *You* might prefer hiding in this attic pulling strings, but it's not healthy, and I don't intend to fall into the same trap. If you can't provide what I need, have the courtesy to explain why, and I'll do it myself. Until now, I've done *all* the outside work on my own. I stupidly hoped maybe we could work together on some projects."

Wow, that hurt to admit, but sometimes my tongue flaps faster than my brain. I probably needed to make an appointment with my therapist, after I found one.

Amadeus Graham rose from his chair, towering over me. I refused to cower or scamper back down the stairs. My heart pounded erratically— more because this man and his abilities turned me on than because I was frightened.

"I am not hiding," he said reasonably enough. "I simply work better off the radar."

"No, you are regretting that you kissed me, you are regretting that you let us into your life, and you're trying to make me mad and drive us off," I retaliated.

Okay, I'd been harboring a *lot* of pent-up frustration.

"What I do is *dangerous,* Ana. If you can't keep your head down and stay out of trouble, go back to your Atlanta basement and send your family somewhere safe. I do not want to be responsible for their lives."

"Yeah, I got that already. Tough cookies. We can't all be that irresponsible. Hide behind your stupid excuses, but you know we were raised to be what we are. That's not going to change." Possibly to my regret, but I couldn't ignore the obvious any longer. "We accept full blame for our actions. Let me be your front. You can't do everything from here." This was not precisely how I'd meant this encounter to go, but my tongue had a mind of its own. So did my hormones, and they were just plumb insane.

Graham wore his shirtsleeves rolled up today. He crossed his muscled—bare—arms and took a step closer, aiming for intimidation. "You don't really think I'll put you in danger in place of myself, do you? I deal in information, not stupid mouse tricks. Until you figure out how to make information work for you, I'm not aiding and abetting your self-destructive tendencies."

"Information is worthless unless someone is prepared to act on it." I bunched my hands into fists and took a step closer so we were nearly toe-to-toe. He had me vibrating with far more than fury.

"Living isn't for cowards. We have to be prepared to die at any moment. I'd prefer to die for a good cause."

"You're not good to anyone dead," he said in a voice dripping with scorn.

"You're not good to anyone, period," I retorted. "Spiders trapped in attics have a very self-centered universe."

I turned on my heel and stalked out—the normal way, through the hall door. I was steaming. I'd stupidly hoped to somehow convince him to get Bill's phone for me. I really didn't want to break into a police station, and I knew Graham had contacts. Now all I'd done was make him curious. And furious, but that was a bonus.

I hurried back to my office and left my door open so I could hear Mallard return. Both of them really ought to give my deviousness some credit.

While I waited, I emailed Nick asking him to run a background check on all the personnel at the British embassy who'd interviewed him. If any of them had been in war zones with Whitehead and Smedbetter, I wanted their names. And their voices.

Seattle finally came through, with a hefty invoice for the rush job but also the identification I'd requested. They'd matched Smedbetter's voice on tape #2844 to the voice on Patrick's recording insisting that "escalation is the only solution," and "You have a wild card in your deck who needs to be dealt with. He's been snooping where he shouldn't."

Nailed him.

I did a little jig of triumph. We had no proof that the general might have murdered Patra's father, but chances were good that we had an instigator.

The unaccented American voice declaring that his *party* was prepared to support Smedbetter's request for escalation of the war, and that they'd acquired newspapers across Europe was still unidentified. That could be almost anyone on Broderick's staff, or even Paul Rose's. The smooth politician's voice and the use of the word "party" would indicate the latter.

As a bonus, Seattle had also matched the ungrammatical American voice on Patrick's recording with an unidentified interviewer on the Smedbetter tape. I played tape #2844 with General Smedbetter speaking to a reporter—it sounded like a newspaper interview about the general's interest in military weapons. Patra had sent me an article with Ernest Bloom interviewing the general on that topic.

Excitement blossomed.

If this interviewer was Ernest Bloom, he had been in the room when an American general and a media rep discussed starting a revolution to protect oil interests—and worried about a spy in their midst. Patrick?

Bill Bloom would have recognized his father's voice on Patra's tape—and called his mother, as well as Patra. It was beginning to look like the tape really had been the cause of Bill's death. One of the men on it must have learned of the tape's existence from Bill's mother or by tapping Bill's phone. That man would most likely be his killer.

Or had hired Bill's killer. Generals were accustomed to giving orders, not running over men with stolen cars. And I had a hard time believing media executives had the guts it took to run a man over in broad daylight. That had been a practiced maneuver by hired killers.

I heard Mallard coming in the kitchen door. I grabbed the army coat I'd brought down earlier and hurried to greet him. The corner of a plastic baggie stuck out of his jacket pocket. He looked startled to see me as he removed his hat and hung it on the rack beside the door.

"I think we need to throw a Halloween party for EG," I said cheerfully. "Funky lights, weird music, ugly cupcakes, the works. Dry ice, maybe? Do they bob for apples on Halloween? We can invite her class."

Disconcerted by this unexpected approach, Mallard straightened his tie and appeared to consider it. "Perhaps a professional party planner?" he suggested.

"You're so not up with the times," I said, brushing past him to head out the door. "All that stuff is available at the mall. I'll take a look. See you later."

I was up the stairs before he realized I'd picked his pocket. He'd made it so very easy, possibly intentionally. One never knew with Mallard.

Leaving our portly butler shouting futilely, I jogged down to the Metro and hopped on the next train going anywhere.

Twenty-eight

Patra's perspective

PATRA lingered in the ladies' restroom on the executive floor. There were so very few women on this level that she was fairly confident no one would intrude. She waited until she heard General Smedbetter in the corridor. She was pretty certain that was Broderick Jr.'s voice joining him. They didn't sound pleased.

She whistled a happy tune.

She had hoped her lovely wire story would lure the culprits from their lairs. From the rising anger in the hall, she gathered her story had hit the fan.

She couldn't wait to leave this hell hole and see how the news of Broderick's perfidy was hitting the real world, but she had one more task on her list before she left.

She turned on the microphone in her pen, edged open the restroom door, and recorded their voices.

The men entered an office and closed the door. *Bollocks.* She'd love to be a bug on the wall, but she hadn't had time to gather that kind of sophisticated equipment. Still, maybe...

She connected the pen to her phone and sent the small audio file to Ana and Sean with notes of the participants' names in hopes they could match the voices to her father's tape. Then with wickedness aforethought, she checked to be certain the coast was clear and entered the men's restroom. She left the pen behind a trash can. It was set to record with the sound of a voice. She wasn't certain how she'd get back in here to retrieve it, but it was just a wild chance anyway.

With the exposé she'd written working its way out on the AP wires, she figured it was time to make her exit. She took the elevator down.

Security met her in the lobby as the elevator door opened. The long tile floor to the glass door exit stretched past their burly shoulders like a barbed-wire no man's land.

* * *

After ascertaining that Mallard, Riley, or no one else followed me, I changed trains and headed for Bill's neighborhood. I'd prefer to experiment in a safer location, but the apartment would be the first place the thugs would look once I sent my message. If Graham wouldn't descend into the mucky world, I would.

Using my own phone, I texted Nick, Sean, and Patra to let them know where I was so they could collect my body if necessary. That's not what I told them, of course. I just said I was investigating a new clue at Bill's place.

The discovery of the spyware in Patra's phone increased the probability that it really had been her audio file that had cost Bill his life. The thugs had zeroed in on Bill within an hour of his calling Patra to say he had information. It was possible Patra's phone had already been hacked, but she'd just arrived in the States. My assumption was that Bill's phone had been hacked first. By whom was the question I meant to answer today. I expected that answer to lead me to Bill's killer.

Bill's apartment house had no security. I walked in without anyone paying a bit of attention, not just because I was wearing my grubbies and looking harmless but because no one cared. I wore leggings tucked into the cowboy boots I'd found at Goodwill. The boots were more comfortable than the fancy spike heels Nick had made me buy, but a little noisy on the stairs. I stopped on Bill's floor, ascertained his place was empty, and opened the flimsy lock with a credit card.

Inside, in the light of Bill's dirty window, I examined the outdated cell phone I'd retrieved from Mallard. Bill's contact list didn't hold many names, but I didn't need many if the spyware was in this phone. I'd done a little research and was utterly appalled at how easy phone spyware was to install. As a result, my phone was now loaded up with every anti-bugging software known to mankind.

Bill's didn't even have a password, poor trusting guy.

I figured his mother wouldn't know how to receive text messages, so I sent mine to all Bill's media contacts, including Carla at Intrepid. *Found Bill Bloom's files*, I wrote. *Hidden door in closet.*

Treasure trove!

What better way to bait a hook for phone-tapping criminals, right? As well as notifying half the news media in town as to where the treasure—and by default—Bill's phone was. If they knew Bill was dead, they'd probably wonder about the message sender, but that would just arouse more curiosity. I'd had a hankering all along to throw all the bad guys into one room. Throwing in the media as well might be even more fun.

I tucked my own wireless bug into a dusty corner and checked the speaker by tapping my toe and listening to my earbuds. Seemed to be working.

The day was unseasonably warm for this late in October. By the time I reached the roof, the sun beamed down, and my army coat was stifling. I kept it on anyway. I sat down in the shadows on the roof with my spyglass and my earbuds and waited to see who was ambitious—or desperate—enough to show up first.

***

Patra's perspective

Patra assessed the two security goons blocking her exit, the crowd of employees surging onto the elevators, and chose the path of least resistance. She stepped back into the elevator with the crowd.

If Poo Media was really good, they'd have security standing in front of the elevator on every floor. This wasn't looking pretty. If they wanted to maim her yesterday, they'd probably want to slice and dice her today if they knew about her lovely prank.

Her best bet was to be surrounded by witnesses. She texted Sam that she was trapped, figuring he was closest. Not that she expected him to do much, but both Magda and Ana had taught her to stay in contact with friends and family at all times. Kidnapping had been their main concern in third world countries. Patra hadn't really considered it in civilization.

She palmed her spray can, removed her Taser and other weaponry from her purse and tucked them into her blazer pockets. She stepped off the elevator on the floor expelling the most passengers, ready to aim and fire.

Two black-suited goons zoomed in on her like homing pigeons. She maced one, who went down grabbing his eyes and screaming curses. She zigzagged and placed a couple of slow-moving, lard-butted office jockeys between her and the second guard. She raced for better cover as the gas spread and burned eyes and panic broke out behind her. The spritzed goon shouted, but he was still stumbling and incoherent.

Patra could hear curses as the second goon stepped on toes and shoved bystanders to clear a path through the frightened crowd.

She dashed into cubicle hell and had nowhere to run but over people. And desks. Patra tossed a rolling office chair in the path of the goon still in a condition to chase her. More screams. One idiot jumped on his desk, bringing the flimsy platform crashing down and causing a domino collapse of fabric partitions. Jolly fun, if only she knew where to run.

Taser in hand and looking for an opening where she wouldn't shoot the wrong person, Patra thumb dialed 911. She had no idea what the cops would make of this chaos, but she was pretty certain assault and battery were illegal—as soon as she assaulted and battered someone.

More goons appeared in the doorway. Rats. Ignoring the gaping jaw of the office manager, she climbed up on his more substantial metal desk in the corner. Keeping her back to the wall, she aimed her Taser while reporting a terrorist in the Broderick offices to the police dispatcher. Trying to remember the office address while staving off furious, testosterone-pumped guards did not add to her peace of mind.

She shot the first thug who approached and watched in glee as he yelled and jerked spastically. She didn't want to kill the guy, so she let up on the trigger once he hit the floor. She hadn't secured one of the new multiple-shot weapons and had to pull the stun gun out of her other pocket. She loved well-tailored suits.

Two guards came after her at once, attempting to tackle her from the desk. Stupid. Her pointed-toe shoe clipped one in the balls. She stunned the other, then kicked him in the jaw as he staggered. Maybe she'd use her metal heel on the nose of the next jerkwad who approached. She was starting to steam, if only because all the sheep in the room simply stared helplessly while three big men attacked her.

As if the heavens heard her fury, the fire alarm screamed and sprinklers drenched the office.

* * *

Generally— I postulated as I huddled on the roof and waited for action— gorillas and Neanderthals ruled the world because they were stronger. They had learned they could get what they wanted with power, whether that power was guns, fists, wealth, or the law. But every once in a while, diminutive David's intelligence and knowledge could take down a powerful Goliath.

I prayed like heck this would be the case today, because the first car to the curb was a black Escalade. I maneuvered to the end of the roof where I could see the license plate, took a photo, and sent it to Graham.

Because nothing more interesting was happening on the street, I moseyed over to the far side of the roof and examined the alley. If you've ever lived in Kabul, you'd know to keep your eyes on alleys.

Sure enough, Leonard Riley—who probably had been in Kabul at one time or another— was sneaking down this one. I wished I had a water bomb.

Graham's return message said *DeLuca,* along with a lot of angry gibberish that I ignored. Maybe I should tell him I was on the roof so he'd send a helicopter after me, but I wasn't ready to leave yet.

Through my earbuds, I heard angry grumbling and thumps in Bill's apartment as the Escalade gang trashed what remained of the place. Dang. I needed names.

Leonard slipped in through the apartment house's back door, out of my sight. Seeing no one else, I cruised back to the front. A battered VW was pulling up behind the SUV. It could be a resident, but I bet most of them used the Metro and didn't own cars.

I frowned as a Hispanic female climbed out. I really didn't want Carla going in there with DeLuca's thugs, if that was Bill's almost-girlfriend.

I grabbed a pebble off the roof and flung it at her. Startled, she glanced up. I gestured to come upstairs. Stupid of me, and showed I was getting soft. In my old life, I would have just waited for the fireworks and taken no chances.

Through my earbuds, I heard Leonard enter the apartment before the VW owner reached the roof. I strained to catch his words through the cheap electronics.

"Who sent that damned message?" was Riley's first intelligent question.

"Don't know. Boss just got orders to come look," a deep bass replied.

"Nothin' here," a younger male voice said. "No hidden nothin'. No treasure."

Okay, sounded like this trio knew each other.

Unless one counted Riley, Deluca's people were hardly the legitimate media contacts I'd texted. Since that was DeLuca's SUV, I thought I was on pretty firm ground guessing DeLuca had tapped Bill's phone—or worked for someone who had. And Leonard was in on it.

The VW owner arrived on the roof. I gestured for her to be silent and pointed at my earbuds. "Carla?" I whispered as she approached.

Her eyes widened. "And you are?"

"Bill's associate. Just call me Linda." I really would have to change that name soon. "That's DeLuca's gang down there."

"You know how to text a gang boss?" she whispered in incredulity.

"No, but Bill's phone was tapped. I figure they got the message, which means they did the tapping." I held up a finger to silence her as Leonard started talking again.

"Son-of-a-bitch, someone else has already found whatever he was hiding," Leonard said. "How the fuck did they get the geek's phone?"

I heard footsteps, as if he was pacing. And kicking walls. I winced at a loud thump too near my spy gadget. He called and reported the loss to someone. A moment later, he announced, "The client has the girl cornered. If she's hidden the files, he'll find out, but my bet is on her interfering sister. Let's get moving."

I stuck my thumbnail in my mouth and chewed to keep from going ballistic. *They had Patra?* I'd go down there and rip off their faces finding out who their *client* was.

"DeLuca says we're not getting near that Maximillian place," Bass Voice protested. "He says it's bad juju. The general will just have to get it out of the girl."

The general. Smedbetter? My heart started pounding harder.

The general who was now an exec at BM, where Patra was working *right now?* I started texting Graham as fast as my thumbs would allow.

Then I stared at the screen and deleted it. We were *not* relying on that man again.

I saw Patra's screen name on a message and opened it while the thugs below argued. She'd sent me an audio file of Smedbetter. If she'd gone to work today to get that, she'd risked her life for nothing.

At least she was still alive, although if she was recording BM execs as this message indicated, I had to wonder for how long. I had to get over there.

Before I could tuck my phone away, a screaming text in all caps crossed the screen: GT YR ASS BK HERE NOW!

Graham. I whistled at the all caps. Graham never shouted. What was happening at home?

Through my earbuds I heard Leonard say, "Smythe is in jail. We don't have to worry about him getting to Bloom's files before us. We just need to eliminate them before anyone reads them."

It sounded as if he was talking on the phone again. Interesting. Leonard and the general had feared Smitty would find Bill's files first, and they didn't want the good reverend to have them? Why?

Because they feared blackmail?

BM might be the mouthpiece for R&P, but as far as I had determined, Smitty had never been a partner in war zone games. The sneaky reverend was the type to plant bugs in presidential offices. He collected information on powerful people who may have been in war zones. If Smitty had proof that General Smedbetter had ordered Patrick's death, or anyone else's...

Smitty was a stupid troublemaker if he thought he'd pin anything on any of Broderick's execs. No wonder he'd ended up in jail. They'd probably set him up for the fall. I'd tell his lawyer to check his phone for spyware. Someday.

Leonard was the imbecile who had the facts I needed. Leonard was a squealing coward. How could I work that?

Carla was watching me with puzzlement. Was she the only media person who cared enough to follow up on my text message? I glanced down to the street again and smiled. Sean's little MG had just pulled up. Bless his little heart. His newspaper had been in Bill's address book, but I hadn't texted Sean directly. I stoned him the instant he stepped out of the car. He glared up at me, not in the least surprised.

I punched in his phone number and watched him lean against his car and answer.

"We've got part of your Pulitzer story in Bill's apartment. Leonard Riley seems to be working with DeLuca's gang, General Smedbetter, and presumably, by association, Broderick Media. They're in there now looking for that treasure trove you're here to find. They've been worried that Dr. Smythe would get to the files before them. Isn't that interesting?"

"Because Smythe thinks Smedbetter killed Llewellyn or he's just nosy?" Sean asked snidely.

"Do you think I care? If Dr. Smythe is smart, probably both. Broderick's goons put spyware in Patra's phone, Bill's phone, and probably Smythe's phone. That's how Leonard's goons got to your newspaper office after you lost the white Cadillac."

"Wait a minute," he interrupted my hasty explanation. "How do you know we lost the Cadillac?"

"Patra said the car following you from the Blooms was a white sedan, not a black SUV. She said you lost him on the way to the office. She said the one that entered your garage later, carrying gunmen and arsonists, was a black Escalade. That vehicle you're parked behind is probably one of a fleet of DeLuca's SUVs, like the one that Patra saw at Bill's apartment. He has a limo service," I explained with as much patience as possible. I handed my earbud to Carla who grimaced but listened with me.

Sean caught on quickly. "I figured brother Ken called the R&P guys and the white sedan was theirs. So Broderick had nothing to do with the boxes."

"At that point," I agreed. "When Smitty's men lost you, they called their boss. Phone tap on Smythe relayed that info directly to Broderick or his minions. If they identified you, then your office would be the first place BM's men would head. They are apparently a bit superstitious about Patra's abode. Have your garage cameras verified the Escalade's plates yet?"

"Yeah," he said reluctantly. "Cops have questioned DeLuca, but he says it was rented out by a guy whose credit card failed."

"Yeah, Leonard and company. They're in the apartment now.

Want to let air out of some tires while I call the cops?"

"On what charges? Bullying?"

I didn't care if he was being snarky. I could see he was already working on the tires. Those big heavy vehicles lose air quickly. I know, and not because I ever owned one.

"Breaking and entering for now," I suggested. "Manufacture some murder evidence and Leonard will squeal like a teenybopper at a Justin Bieber concert. We just have to make it happen before Broderick's goons catch and kill him."

Listening to both me and the apartment, Carla had excitedly yanked out her phone and was hitting buttons. I didn't need her broadcasting just yet. I snatched her toy away and scrolled through the menu to find her phone number. Before Sean could comment on my assessment, I gave him Carla's number. He stopped messing with tires and hastily scribbled it on his palm.

"That's Carla. She's up here with me if you need reinforcements. I've got to go. Patra's in trouble, and Graham's probably pitching people off the roof. Love ya." I pushed off and met Carla's frown. "Sean O'Herlihy down there works for the *Times*. I can't tell you more than you just overheard except that the guys in Bill's apartment are most likely killers. Take care."

I handed her the rest of my spyware and ran for the exit, dialing up Graham as I went.

On the way down, I saw Leonard Riley getting away out the back door. Damn, I needed the little squealer.

Could I give up my mother hen instinct and hope Patra could take care of herself?

Twenty-nine

Patra's perspective

THE sprinklers and fire alarm—on top of the crashing desks, dividers, and goon chase— instigated full-out hysteria. Patra's cubicle-farm audience screamed and dashed for the door as if the apocalypse had arrived.

Patra didn't waste time standing on the desk in stunned astonishment at manna from heaven. She screamed *"Fire!"* Then she leaped down, maced a goon stupid enough to get in her way, and sent more waves of panic through the crowd. With chaos established, she blended into the mob pushing and shoving into the corridor. No way would the big goons break past an ocean of terrified office workers running for their lives.

"Single line!" she shouted, using her smaller size to sidle in between people to put distance between her and the Goliaths. She grabbed the arm of a secretary tottering on a leg brace and helped her along. "Don't use the elevators. Take the stairs," she called over her shoulder, verifying that her strategy was working. The goons had fallen farther behind.

Like good little sheep, the crowd did their best. A few frantic ones jumped on the elevator. A few more shoved for the head of the line and got pushed aside for their efforts. But mostly, everyone obeyed orders and attempted to calm each other down. Not until they were all filing down the dry stairwell together did anyone realize that they didn't smell smoke.

"Procedure says to file into the street until the fire department gives the okay," Patra shouted. The message echoed nicely in the shaft and was repeated up and down the stairs. If anyone recognized her, they didn't seem to care. It was an entertaining break in the gerbil wheel of their day.

With one hand, she texted Ana that she was okay, just in case

Graham was monitoring a police scanner. She hoped she was okay. She kept an eye out for Sam in the mob, but he worked on another floor. She had to assume the fire alarm was his parting gesture.

As the mob obediently filed out the stairwell door marked for the first floor, Patra left the secretary and the crowd behind. She slipped around the corner and down to the basement level. She'd rather not make it easy for any remaining goons watching the lobby. Sean's basement trick seemed reasonable in this situation. And she still had some mace left.

* * *

I muttered a very dirty bad word as I trotted after Leonard down a dark alley. I needed to reach Patra, then find out what had Graham shouting. The whole world could be blowing up, and I was sneaking after a sawed-off drug dealer with a grudge. I wore my armed camouflage coat, but from the looks of the lump under his jacket, Leonard had started carrying a gun.

Guns are for men of small intelligence and limited imagination, which certainly described Leonard. With a sigh, I accepted the role reversal and stalked the little scum.

He took the train I'd take if I was heading home. I got an uneasy feeling in the pit of my stomach and began hunting news stories on my phone as I stood at the back of the crowded car. Keeping an eye on Leonard and the news at the same time wasn't easy. Headlines like *Shocking Revelations* and *Broderick Media Accused of Murder* had a tendency to make my insides roll.

My eyebrows probably reached my hairline as I speed-read that last article *under my sister's byline*. Patra had set the hell hounds lose.

My sister was officially crazier than I was. Broderick was going to kill us all, even if the FBI reached him first.

She'd done her research, or her father had done his. A lot of the story dated back ten years and had to have come from Patrick's unfinished book. No legitimate media would have released this story without a warehouse of evidence. Could Broderick sue himself?

Patra had listed all the international media outlets owned directly and indirectly by Sir Archie. She listed dates of inflammatory articles and ensuing rebellions. And of course, since the story was written under her byline, she mentioned that her father had been murdered while in the same war zone with General Smedbetter, a Broderick executive, while investigating this story.

If that didn't set Leonard squealing, nothing would. Our biggest problem would be keeping him alive, if my suspicions of his involvement were true. Aiding and abetting the murder of Patrick Llewellyn to protect Broderick and his henchmen put Riley squarely between the Feds and a lot of rich madmen.

Maybe he could just confess to Bill's murder, and they'd tuck him away somewhere safer than the prison Reggie had been in. Except I really didn't think Leonard had the spine to murder anyone.

My text message buzzed again. NO FIRE, it read. I'M FINE.

I exhaled a small sigh of relief. Now I wasn't quite as torn between finding my sister and following Leonard.

Leonard got off and scurried for another train. I hastily tucked my phone away and followed. I'd wasted a few years of my life following Magda around. It wasn't as simple in a Metro station as in Baghdad, but I didn't think he noticed me.

The little sneak got off at Dupont Circle.

Traffic was worse than usual. So were the crowds. Leonard was short and it was easy to lose sight of him, but by now, I had no doubt of his direction. His intentions might be murky, but I had to assume the worst.

I caught sight of him taking the street behind the house undergoing renovation, the one just before our street. I didn't like the looks of the cars backed up at the intersection. Graham had been shouting for a reason. I didn't have time to see what it was. I had to stop a dumb bunny with a gun before he got himself and everyone else killed.

The scaffolding had been moved to windows on the side of the house, mostly out of view of the street since the houses were so close. I watched Leonard slink down the alley and in the basement door.

I stopped to ponder the situation. I didn't have a gun and couldn't nail the twerp if he appeared in a window. Not that I condone shooting people on sight, mind you, but I had a slight anger management problem. Some days, I'm simply tempted to murder, and this was one of them. My only solution was to follow him. I just didn't want to do it inside.

No workmen stood on the scaffolding. I peered between the houses to see if I could catch a glimpse of the street in front of the house, but shrubbery blocked most of the view. I thought I caught the red that might have been a news van. Graham could handle that for another few minutes.

I verified that the scaffolding seemed to be up to code and began climbing up it. Scaffolding really wasn't built to be a ladder, but a few judicious shinnies and good arm muscles can accomplish a great deal. It wasn't as if I was worried about my clothes.

I flattened against the wall when Leonard peered out the attic window. The maggot was carrying a P90! Personal defense weapon my foot and three eyes. That was an automatic assault weapon, except small enough to conceal. He could blow away anyone standing on our front porch across the street—and probably half a crowd with it. No one should be allowed to buy a gun like that. It shouldn't even be legal to make.

Apparently reassured that no workmen stood on the scaffolding, Leonard moved away from the window. I moved up. Using my army knife, I cut off a long length of the rope the workmen used for their safety belts. I'm pretty good at knotting nooses.

I fastened a second safety belt around my waist. I was pretty damned furious but not enough to forget all caution.

At the top of the scaffolding, I could see over the trees. Our street was mysteriously blocked by huge vehicles and a crowd. No wonder Graham was screaming. My gut tightened, but I had to stomp a termite first.

I knotted the other end of my noose rope to the scaffolding. Then I hefted a crowbar, and with the power of my frustration, helped the nice workmen remove an old window. Smashing heavy metal into glass created a satisfying racket and probably caused Leonard to poo his pants. After bashing out the frames, I flattened against the wall again, bracing my hand and my prepared rope above the attic window.

Stupid Leonard. He cursed and stuck his head out to see what had caused the noise. I was tempted to knock his block off with my crowbar, but I wanted him squealing down at the police station. Seeing me, he aimed the gun in my direction.

"Leonard, this is about the stupidest thing you've ever done," I informed him, counting on his not wanting half the world to see him murdering me now that we were above the trees. "If that gun goes off, you'll probably kill two babies in the next house and a news reporter on the street and the cops will really take off your head."

"You set us up, didn't you?" he snarled. "This time, the boss ain't gonna be so lenient with you. Get inside here before I blow out all them brains of yours."

"Which boss, Leonard? DeLuca? General Smedbetter? Archie? Do you really think any of them want to see my smiling face? Don't be stupid. You're fish bait. They'll feed you to the sharks if I don't first."

"DeLuca's my buddy. He'll back me up. C'mon, get moving. We're going downtown." He gestured again.

I leaned against the wall, holding the crowbar in the one arm he could see. I really didn't have time for this. But Leonard was the puzzle piece that would make the picture whole.

And who was out here getting the information? Me, that's who. Not omnipotent Graham. Our landlord could just suck up a few news vans a little longer.

"Leonard, old buddy, I'm trying to help you out here. DeLuca can't save you if he's running from the cops. They've already picked up your buddies at the apartment," I warned. "That's what happens when you work the right side of the law. I don't need friends in low places. I've got authority on my side. Your best bet is to work with the cops before you end up like all Archie's other enemies."

I was taking shots in the dark. Since he paled a little, I figured I'd come close to the mark. But as I'd said, men with guns have no imagination. They think bullets will take care of everything for them. Stupid, stupid, stupid.

He fired the gun at my feet to get me moving. I swore and nearly jumped off the scaffolding before I got my heart beating again. I glanced down. He'd taken out a few aluminum scaffolding poles, tilted the platform, and blasted a hole in the ground three stories down. I'd been serious about bullets hitting babies in the next house. That's the kind of weapon it was. I lost all sympathy with him.

Before he could really hurt someone, I whacked his gun hand with my crowbar. He hollered but clung to his precious P90. Not taking any more chances, I dropped my lasso over his head and yanked. This time, he had to release his weapon to grab the rope before I strangled him. I wouldn't have wept if his hands had slipped, but survival was probably Leonard's strongest instinct.

The P90 bounced against the scaffolding. I kicked it with my cowboy boot and sent it flying into the bushes below. Leonard cursed and tried to lunge after his substitute penis. My lovely knot caught him right below the ear, and he gagged.

I had the handcuffs out of my pockets and on Leonard before he knew what hit him. I slipped a wireless bug under his shirt collar while he was screaming. The cops probably wouldn't let me hear him squeal, but I intended to be there, one way or another.

When he refused to cooperate and answer my questions, I yanked the rope down around his arms and gave him a shove off the scaffolding. His yells as he dangled over the side couldn't be heard over the circus noise in front. I really needed to investigate that once I was done here.

I checked my knots to be certain they'd hold and called Sean. He was sitting at the police station with Carla. I told him where the cops could find Leonard and his gun.

And then I slid down the tilted platform to go home.

* * *

I was hot, cranky, and worried after nearly having a heart attack several times over. I was not in the mood to deal with Graham's fury. I'd wanted to stay and watch the cops bring down Leonard. I had to pray that Sean and Carla handled a scene that I'd created, and that *really* irked. I actually debated ignoring Graham's summons and going down to the police station to throw in a few accusations of my own just to get the ball rolling.

But noooo, I had to come running for our landlord just as if he were part of the family.

Leaving Leonard shouting, I shoved past the shrubbery into our street. That's when I fully comprehended what had Graham up in arms. Crikey! I gazed in awe at the spectacle filling our quiet, respectable neighborhood. Leonard's shouts were drowned in the commotion. I doubted anyone had heard the gun.

Satellite trucks and mobs of reporters with microphones and cameras blocked the narrow pavement and sidewalk. Idiots had set tripods over historic wrought iron fences and aimed long-range cameras at elegant mansions with security systems that were probably filming them right back. Cop cars with strobe lights were everywhere, trying to break up the gathering mob.

How very convenient for dangling Leonard. A policeman was already talking into his phone and running toward the shrubbery where I'd told them they'd find the dangerous weapon. Leonard was a little easier to spot.

I didn't have time to duck, prepare, or escape an armada of media. I was wearing an army coat, cowboy boots, and a long braid and didn't look anything like the celebrity images of me the media had caught a few weeks back. So, I'd caused a riot at an embassy dinner once. I shouldn't be recognizable now.

But some astute observer still spotted me. He elbowed a camera man who turned his lens my way. A talking head shoved a microphone in my face. Before I could retaliate, two over-eager reporters caught my arms and shoved me into their truck, sticking another microphone in my face.

"Is it true that Patra Llewellyn is your sister, Miss Maximillian? Does she have evidence that Sir Archibald Broderick murdered her father?"

Frazzled and so far beyond annoyed that another planet was involved, I didn't hear the rest of his inane questions. It wasn't as if I intended to answer them. He'd *grabbed* me. He'd *physically* hauled me into his van against my will, just because I'm small and unassuming. Maybe his giant ego thought I'd enjoy being the center of attention, or maybe he thought that he was protecting me from a crowd, but it was assault and kidnapping in my book.

While the camera whirled, I snatched the microphone out of butthead's hand and beaned him with it. Startled, he didn't fall but dodged out of my way when I elbowed him aside and took the driver's seat. I was operating on high anxiety and pure adrenaline. I had just dropped a gunman off scaffolding, and they thought they'd get away with kidnapping?

"You want to see what real media manipulation feels like?" I yelled.

They'd left the van running to operate all the equipment. With malice aforethought, I put the shift into gear, and we were rolling.

While the reporters scrambled for safety, I leaped out the wide open door.

The enormous satellite van full of expensive tech rolled straight into the smaller local TV news van in front of it. And kept rolling. That should solve Graham's problem. Eventually.

I ran for the house as the smaller truck angled into the street, connecting with a car. The semi-sized vehicle gathered momentum and rammed the next bumper in line. I was on the porch before the crashing, swearing, and screaming reached its peak.

Mallard held the door open for me. We nodded curtly, and I left him admiring the street scene.

Too angry and exhausted to take pleasure in the chaos I'd created, I dragged up to my shower. Let Graham steam in his own juices. This introvert had had all the personal interaction she could handle for one morning. I wanted food and cold drink and my dark quiet corner of the basement. Maybe I should be a spider like Graham, weaving webs in darkness.

I didn't need to inquire how the news vans had found Patra's address. I'm sure it was on her employment application and merely a matter of some enterprising clerk selling the information.

It was Patra I wanted to strangle. She had no right to expose us to the world with a byline on that article. In our family, discretion was second nature. As far as I was concerned, she might as well have pulled up her shirt and flashed the world.

She'd better stay out of my reach for a long time. I was too furious to even care if the cops had found dangling Leonard or left him to hang.

Once I was showered, clean, and cool again, I donned a T-shirt and my denim dress. I braided my wet hair as I wandered to my window to see how the van wreck was going. We were on a slight hill, and those big semi-sized satellite trucks carry a lot of weight. Cars and little Econolines had been shoved willy-nilly into the narrow street or up against fences. Security alarms wailed. Police lights flashed down the street, but the patrol cars couldn't get any closer. I could hope they'd collared Leonard but whether he was back at the precinct yet was a matter of debate.

A few smart cameramen were filming the melee. The talking heads were screeching at each other or their cell phones. People eased out of their houses to investigate. We seldom saw our neighbors so I studied them with interest. Looked like they were a motley international lot—made me feel right at home. Maybe we should have a block party.

Abruptly, a voice blared from a loudspeaker directly over my head. I nearly jumped out of my sandals and raced for the stairs before I recognized Graham's tactics. He'd probably have a Batman floodlight shining on Leonard by now except it was still daylight and there was no smoke.

The loudspeaker was playing tape #1143 of Sir Archie Broderick, Paul Rose, and the vice president of the United States being warned that the media was manipulating Congress in support of defense and oil industries. The part where Paul Rose warns that Graham is breaching national security was abruptly followed by a tape of Paul Rose introducing himself at a campaign rally, just in case anyone was tone deaf and didn't figure out who the speakers were.

Few of them would recognize Graham's voice, but I could see shock as the entire mob recognized Rose. And possibly the former VP's distinctive drawl. These were D.C. reporters, far more familiar with politicians than I was.

Now that he had their attention, our resident tarantula proceeded to play Patrick Llewellyn's tape of Broderick minions and a general discussing manipulating the media to foment revolution—supporting Patra's article if anyone recognized the voices, which they probably wouldn't.

Except bless Graham's evil heart, he produced an audio clip of General Smedbetter introducing himself, followed by the voice of the Brit PR flack Whitehead accepting a position as an attaché to the British ambassador.

I winced as Nick's new boss was greeted by Sir Archibald himself. Ouch. Maybe Tex would take Nick back.

The only voice identity missing from Patrick's original tape was the smooth-talking American politician. We'd no doubt identify him as one of Rose's cronies eventually. Rose seriously owed the evil triumvirate if they'd covered up the Iraqi scandal for him.

Contrary creature that I am, I was starting to enjoy the circus.

Cameramen climbed on top of their wrecked vans to get better pictures of the house. Downstairs in my office, a faint alarm shrieked. The cheap spy trap in the attic across the street had been set off. I grabbed my spy glass and scanned the windows, but it looked like workmen in the attic, taking in the street entertainment. No goons with holsters and no Leonard, thank heavens. If nothing else, the circus outside prevented Sir Archie or DeLuca from gunning for us—and I had Graham to thank for that.

He was doing his job, keeping us safe. My grandfather would be proud—or bust a gut at the chaos usually created by me and my siblings. Maybe our antics were starting to grow on Graham.

I still had to figure out how a D.C. gangster like DeLuca came into play and why Smitty would murder Reggie, though. It didn't seem to fit the big picture, although it looked like poor Bill was the connection between the loose ends.

Watching the world go by wasn't the kind of physical release I needed from the frustration of this maddening day. I still didn't have all the answers, but I was betting Graham did. I picked up a water gun I'd removed from EG's possession and filled it up.

My phone rang and Patra's number appeared on the screen. Holding my breath and trying not to scream, I answered.

"Your spider in the attic is totally whacked," she said in greeting. "I'm in a bar across from Poo Manor, watching the news reports. I don't think I'll go back to the house. Where are you?"

"In said house," I growled, "surrounded by howling animals ready to eat us all alive—because of *you*. Go away, little girl."

She chuckled. "I'm probably out of a job, so I guess I'll have to. Maybe I'll visit Magda in Paris. I speak passable French. Think anyone there will hire me?"

"I'm sure Magda will be delighted to introduce you to Chaos International. What if I ask Graham if that job in Atlanta is still open?"

"That would be *great*," she said.

I could almost see her perk right up. I'm not entirely certain why I'd made the suggestion given the bedlam she'd created, but I'd rather she was safe with us than with whatever Magda was doing far, far away. I was reluctantly starting to appreciate the advantage of allies.

The loudspeaker broke into a rock version of the national anthem, complete with screaming guitars. With a sigh, I headed for the stairs to Graham's lair to pull the plug.

"Find Nick at the embassy," I told Patra, still carrying the phone. "He's probably been fired and will need a shoulder to cry on. I'll get back to you after I figure out how to warn EG and head her off," I said. "And if life is really good, Leonard Riley is singing down at Bill's precinct. You probably should avoid that area for now, but give Sean a call. He might still be there."

"Oh, I'll do better than that. Sam's here with me. I'm sending him back into BM to pick up a recorder from the men's room. While all the good little sheep followed the leader to the street, Sam opened some kind of line into BM's archives. He's downloading as fast as the cable will allow before security gets back to their desks. Expect fireworks."

"I'm in awe. Let's adopt him. Gotta go." I clicked off and stuck the phone in my denim pocket. Graham's office door was closed.

I opened it anyway. Our insane landlord wasn't in his web. His monitors were broadcasting footage of the madness below as well as the herd of BM employees and fire engines in the street at Patra's workplace. I'm sure his scanner was picking up police calls to Bill's apartment and possibly screams of rage at the British embassy. I took a quick look around at the monitors in hopes of seeing General Smedbetter and Sir Archie running for their lives, but there was no footage of the airport.

Figuring he couldn't have got far, I headed for the gym.

Graham was stripped to boxing shorts and gym shoes and whaling the tar out of the heavy bag. Sweat streaked down his broad back, so he'd been at it for a while. The man was as frustrated as I was if he hadn't even bothered watching the crowd reaction to his coup de grâce.

I'd changed into a dress and sandals so I wasn't ready for fun and games—not his kind anyway.

My kind, I could handle. I squirted him with the water gun.

Thirty

THE water gun didn't stay in my hand for long. I hadn't expected it to. It accomplished exactly what I'd wanted—Graham's full and undivided attention.

He continued to grip my wrist even after the plastic toy flew across the room. Despite the sweat, he wasn't breathing heavily, but when he dragged me up against his muscled chest, I could feel his heart pound.

"I can't decide whether to thank you, pop champagne, or beat the bottle over your head," I said, before I stood on my toes, wrapped my arms around his neck, and kissed him.

He reacted with gratifying speed, wrapping his big arms around me and hauling me against him. His mouth was hungry, as hungry as mine. So okay, now I knew adrenaline junkies got high on lust. My skirt rose high as I wrapped my legs around his hips and hung on while he spun my head into new dimensions.

We were both breathing heavily by the time the loudspeaker silenced. Sirens screamed in the distance. Men yelled. Horns honked. A few unmonitored security alarms continued shrieking. Graham returned me to the floor. I took a deep breath and stepped back.

"Whatever we've got going is a very bad idea," I warned.

"Probably," he agreed with unnecessary alacrity. He reached for me again. "But I appreciate your way of expressing gratitude."

I dodged and grabbed the water gun. "Until you're ready to accept us as more than flies in your web and come down to dinner like a human being, we're just not doing this. I'm aware that I'm as nuts as you, but at least I'm trying. You're not. So stay in your attic and spin dangerous webs, if you want. I have to go back down and deal with the real world. I just wanted you to know that we recognize and value your efforts."

I backed out and left him standing there with water running off his chest. A magnificent sight. My knees still trembled and my female parts screamed in protest, but I didn't do casual sex anymore. I'd tried it. It wasn't satisfying. Usually, I could do it better myself. Graham was a whole different set of problems, and I just wasn't ready to deal with them yet.

Mallard was down in the kitchen watching the news on his flip-down kitchen computer, humming to himself, and preparing an enormous lasagna. I could smell peach cobbler cooking. I didn't remember having lunch, so I snatched an apple.

"Life is complicated," I said, trying to get my head and my priorities straight.

"For complicated people," Mallard agreed. "I will be happy to fetch Miss Elizabeth Georgiana."

"You think you can escape past that madhouse?" I nodded in the direction of the front of the house.

"Certainly. They are too busy untangling their vehicles to bother with the street behind us. Is Miss Patra safe?"

"Miss Patra needs her panties smacked, but from all reports, yes, she's safe and unemployed. I'd meant to ask Graham about that CNN job, but I'd better wait until he cools down." Literally as well as figuratively. "I'm assuming Nick is safe, although he may be ticked. He should be home for dinner. I need to run down to a police station and offer a few clues."

"Very good. I'll hold dinner until you've returned. There's an excellent ham sandwich in the refrigerator. Don't be too late."

My jaw probably dropped. Mallard never made sandwiches for me. I had to be usurping Graham's lunch. I nearly whistled in awe as I stole the magnificent creation from the refrigerator shelf—on a baguette, with ripe tomatoes and curly lettuce. And some kind of fancy cheese, and mustard. I really could get into living like this.

"Bless you," I mumbled through chewy fresh bread.

Mallard merely smiled as he admired the news footage of Senator Paul Rose dodging cameras.

I was more interested in catching criminals who ran over honest hard-working geeks than caring if a politician got crucified by the media.

Looking dowdy but semi-respectable, I scanned on-line news articles as I took the train to Bill's precinct. Carla hadn't added anything new to her website, but a few of the rowdier independent news sites had some hilarious footage of the melee in front of our house. They particularly liked videos of the national VIP news anchors, trailing wires and mics, awkwardly scrambling to escape crashing vehicles and dodging the excited mob in the street.

Several news websites carried a few paragraphs here and there on Graham's revelation about Paul Rose and Broderick Media being involved in murder and revolution, but his loudspeaker voices didn't come equipped with videos of train wrecks. Images painted a thousand words and all that. Voices apparently generated a big yawn. But with a few of their secrets out in the open, the baddies had no reason to burn out Patra anymore.

The more legitimate local news websites were slow to add material, but they had a few headlines about Archie being implicated in a political scandal and possible affiliated crimes, nothing in depth. Yet. They'd screw their rival to the wall as soon as they had enough evidence not to get sued.

I smiled in anticipation. With Patra's friend Sam downloading BM archives, we were in a lovely position to eventually give them Archie on a skewer.

Of course, the D.C. media stayed far, far away from the favored local presidential candidate. For now. Not my concern. I wanted Bill's killer.

Sean was pacing the floor and shouting jubilantly into his phone when I arrived at the precinct. He hugged me. He actually hugged *me*. Usually, he just wanted to hit me.

I left him feeding his latest news scoop to his office and walked up to the officer in charge. Sergeant Duvalle Jones was a burly, unsmiling man who looked as if he'd been at the job for a while, if the size of his belt and the wrinkles around his balding head were indicators.

"I'm here to press charges against Leonard Riley. He shot at me."

"Miss..." He glanced down at his papers. "Miss Devlin?"

Well, I couldn't lie to a police officer, especially after Sean, the rat, had given my real name. I produced my passport. "Yes, sir. Mr. Riley was stalking my sister, also."

"That wouldn't be Miss Patra Llewellyn, the lying, thieving bitch, would it?" he asked with a heavy shade of irony.

"The very one," I said brightly. "I see you've spoken with Mr. Riley."

"More like he's shouted loud enough for the heavens to hear him. Come along, Miss Devlin. This could be interesting." He gestured to a rookie standing nearby and we sauntered into the bowels of American authority.

Guess if I meant to stay in D.C., I'd better start cultivating the natives.

I'd learned the sergeant's name, marital status, and opinion of the Washington Redskins by the time we reached the back rooms where they were holding Leonard. I offered Jones a tip on how to get good discounted 'Skins tickets—compliments of Nick and Tex—and in return I learned that the police were holding DeLuca's goons as well, since they had outstanding warrants.

Despite every attempt I made to disguise the fact, I was Magda's daughter right down to my toenails. I left the sergeant smiling and sat down at a battered metal desk while another officer wrote up the charges. Somewhere in the back, Leonard screamed for his attorney.

"Does he actually have an attorney?" I asked with interest, scanning the documents the printer spewed out before I signed them.

"DeLuca will send someone down here eventually," Detective Azzini said with a shrug. He was younger than the sergeant, with clipped tight curls, mocha-colored skin, a cleft chin, and high cheekbones. D.C really was starting to feel like the international homes I'd known.

"South African ancestry?" I asked politely as he typed on his keyboard.

He glanced up with narrowed eyes. "Why?"

"We used to live there. I recognize the name and the cheekbones." My phone rang and I checked the caller ID: Patra. She'd sent a link labeled "archieleaks." I clicked on it and pages of indexed document files appeared before my wondering eyes. I needed a tablet with a bigger screen. I scrolled down, found a link labeled DeLuca, and smiled.

"I don't think DeLuca will have time for bottom feeders today," I said with satisfaction, handing him the signed papers. "Are you interested in DeLuca or would you prefer that he go to a bigger precinct?"

"Interested in DeLuca? What, you're simply going to hand me a criminal who's eluded the law for decades? Who the hell do you think you are?" he demanded, finally paying attention to little ol' me.

"Anastasia Devlin, just as it says on my ID. I come from a rather large, well-traveled family with connections. If you'll check the local news, you'll see an article or two about Sir Archibald Broderick. That would be my sister responsible for the possible end of his reign of terror. It seems she's downloaded a few of Archie's files and DeLuca's name is in them. Want to see what they look like?"

"There's a reason Riley shot at you, isn't there?" he asked, appraising me.

I smiled briefly at his recognition that I might be more than the dowdy shrimp that I appeared. "There usually is. But shooting unarmed people is never justified. Still, Riley has the answers to a lot of questions more important than he is. I'd be ready to drop charges if he'd implicate the men who set him after us. I think this file link in my hand might aid that cause."

We negotiated. It seemed the good detective was in line for a promotion, and nailing DeLuca would almost certainly seal it. I gave him the link to the DeLuca file. He gave me permission to wait around while they interviewed Leonard. We both studied the files and came up with lots of questions. Bigwigs were called in who added a few more queries based on years of experience. We invited Sean to join in as a reward for his good deeds and patience.

By the time we were done, we had a super interview prepared for lovely Lennie. The cops thought I was nuts for sitting around while they interrogated him. They obviously hadn't searched him yet because the listening device I'd planted on him still worked.

Sitting next to Sean in an empty office, we shared my set of earbuds. Listening to Leonard squeal, I wanted a bucket of popcorn. Stereo wasn't necessary. As loud as Leonard was wailing, the wireless transmitter probably wasn't necessary.

Given all Riley's D.C. criminal connections, stalking Patra had fallen way down Detective Azzini's list of inquiries, but I'd insisted on having Leonard questioned about Patra's father.

After Riley related his part in that long-ago story, I was sick to my stomach. "They'd better keep Riley locked up until they have Smedbetter behind bars," I said as the little pig laid the blame for his murderous overseas operations on the general, Broderick, and the victims themselves. Nothing was ever Lennie's fault.

"Broderick and pals had Llewellyn assassinated because he knew too much about Archie's involvement in promoting warfare for kickbacks?" Sean asked in disbelief. "Megalomania, much?"

"Assassination is pretty easy over there," I said reluctantly. Even though I'd suspected this outcome, I was saddened that a good man had been removed from the world by people with too much money. "Leonard didn't even have to get his hands bloody. All he had to do was give a kid a euro or whatever was in his pocket. Whack, the deed would be done. When you live in war zones, with killing all around, life becomes pretty meaningless. People are just obstacles to be removed."

I chewed my fingernail and pondered Riley's answers. "I think Patrick knew more than Leonard does."

"What's that supposed to mean?" Sean was jotting notes for his Pulitzer-prize winning article. Or to tell Patra, hard to say.

"Patrick started investigating General Smedbetter after the military blew up a mosque in Iraq. I think Paul Rose's battalion was involved. I smell cover-up. Leonard wasn't in Iraq at the height of the war. He was busy being sent to jail for tapping a vice-president's telephone. Years later, Smedbetter might have told Leonard a story about Patrick holding info on Archie, but that didn't really justify assassination."

I stopped and tried to put all my theories in order. "I think Patra's dad was sitting on evidence that the *general* wanted buried—like who ordered the bombing of Kirkuk and why. Ernest Bloom was an embed in Smedbetter's command at the time Patrick was over there. Bloom may have talked with Patrick or overheard too much or simply started acting too suspicious. He presumably died of a heart attack right after Patrick, but I'm betting he got whacked. Heart attacks are simple to fake when you have no medical facilities for examination."

I pondered the problem while Sean jotted notes.

"Didn't you say Bloom was present when Smedbetter, Whitehead, and some possible Rose rep talked about buying media to foment revolution?" Sean asked, following my thoughts pretty accurately. "Bloom could easily have overheard worse."

"Yep," I agreed. "Chances are good, if Bloom was any kind of reporter at all, that he'd learned about the cover-up of Rose's fiasco five years earlier. He sounded pretty cynical on that recording. If he started rocking the boat—" I had no proof of anything.

Sean whistled and tuned in more intently to the interview with Riley. The detective was more interested in a crime boss than in the ancient foreign history I'd asked about, but they'd moved on to Smythe now.

"Smythe is a blackmailer!" Leonard shouted in the other room. "He collects information and uses it to get what he wants."

"What the Righteous and Proud wants," I murmured. "That makes sense. Smythe gave Bill Bloom a lot of recordings and had the voices identified so he knew whose arm to twist. He didn't need Bill's audio files, but he wanted to know who was interested in them. That's why he let the files sit around and had you and Patra followed."

"But you said it was DeLuca's men—not Smythe— who set fire to the files in my office," Sean said, tapping his pad with a pen. I should buy him a digital tablet if I ever collected my millions. I should buy myself one.

"Because *Archie* ordered the audio files burned," I whispered. "Smythe was probably twisting his arm with the contents of those files."

"Why Archie?"

I hushed him as the detective apparently produced our printout from the DeLuca file. Leonard started muttering as he heard the incriminating evidence Patra had sent.

"DeLuca was told to silence Smythe," Leonard admitted grudgingly. His voice was low enough that Sean and I had to press the ear buds tighter. "And he needed to get rid of Brashton. Made sense to do both at once."

I gripped Sean's arm. Here it was, the answers I needed.

"So *DeLuca* actually killed Brashton?" the detective asked, cluelessly.

Leonard snorted. "Smythe is just this little shit the big guys were using. He ran errands like me, except he got paid better. The R&P nuts actually tried to save DeLuca's gang by offering them jobs and *insurance*. DeLuca thought that was hilarious, but the guys kinda liked having the insurance ."

"That's not answering the question, Riley. This document shows you and DeLuca grew up in the same neighborhood. You were buddies. When you went to jail, DeLuca took care of your family.

You get out, and you run errands for him. And he runs them for Archibald Broderick and Broderick Media. Where does Smythe fit in?"

"I don't know how they got to Smythe, okay? They just do that. I gave Smythe a baggie from DeLuca and told him to take it to that lawyer Brashton with the message that this was the last coke he'd supply, and after that, Brashton was on his own. No one really searches ministers, so Smythe played the church card."

And so Reggie the Snake had died by innocent minister. I sighed and released Sean's arm. The picture was almost whole. I was still furious, but there wasn't much I could do about an organization that had infiltrated every particle of society. Or drug addicts who took drugs in jail from crime bosses. DeLuca had no reason to care if Reggie sang like a canary. I had no doubt that the mysterious "they" Leonard kept referring to was Top Hat, not DeLuca's gang. Leonard probably didn't even know Top Hat existed.

"Did you know that the baggie contained cyanide with the drugs?" the detective asked, calmly ticking off another question.

"I did not," Leonard said indignantly. "All I do is carry out orders. I gave Smitty a bag. He took it to Brashton. Stupid schmo probably thought he was doing the addict a good deed."

"And how did DeLuca figure poisoning Brashton would eliminate Smythe?"

Nice detective. I hadn't known enough to ask that earlier, but I listened now.

"He didn't, for sure. DeLuca knew what was in the baggie, so he just took out a little insurance. If Smythe tried to blackmail him or his pals, DeLuca would just have to mention poison and who'd seen Brashton last. That damned rich chick ruined everything by setting her lawyer loose. DeLuca didn't want to cut our connection with R&P. That health insurance is nice for guys like us."

Rich chick! I started to giggle. I covered my mouth but I was practically shaking with near hysteria. Bribery by health insurance. Smythe was one damned smart man.

I almost didn't mind that Smythe would probably walk if Leonard's rambling story was confirmed. Brashton was dead, our yacht was gone, and behind it all was the mysterious organization called Top Hat that had ties to Paul Rose—and apparently a gang boss. It all made sense in a convoluted sort of way. Reggie Brashton the Snake had been a loose cannon who needed to be eliminated. They'd probably feared he'd left evidence on the yacht. None of this had anything to do with us, personally, except we got screwed out of half a million dollars.

"We have witnesses that DeLuca arranged for the death of one Bill Bloom," the detective said a little while later.

That was a bit of a stretch. I'd stuck in that question. The detective had looked up Bill's file and learned Bill's apartment was where they'd caught Leonard's goons. He was willing to put two and two together.

Leonard cursed. "Little creep worked with Smythe for a while. DeLuca got paid to take him out. That's when word came down to silence Smythe. No idea what that was all about."

That was all about learning Bill had Patra's tapes and had turned raging liberal, or at least anti-R&P. And then someone listening to Bill's audio files—my bet was on one of Archie's menials like Smedbetter— and realizing Smythe was a perennial blackmailer. Snake's nest, just as I'd said. So a five-year-old murder to cover up an even older scandal had blossomed into today's mass havoc. I wanted to believe in karma, but I wasn't seeing justice yet.

"Do you know if DeLuca spoke with anyone at Broderick Media before or after Mr. Brashton's demise?" the detective asked smoothly.

"DeLuca got his orders from Smedbetter, just the same as I did. You'll have to ask him," Leonard snarled, confirming my suspicion. "Look, I told you everything I know. I didn't do nothing. When am I gonna get outta here? You said I could walk."

"For your own safety, it might be better if you stayed in our custody a while longer." We heard the detective flipping his pages for more questions.

As if on cue, an alarm shrieked through the entire building. A loudspeaker intoned, "Evacuate the premises immediately. I repeat, emergency evacuation, follow procedures."

I sighed and took Sean's arm as he hurried for the exit. "Bomb threat," I warned. "DeLuca has found his loose-lipped little shit."

Sean snickered as we ran for the door. "He wouldn't really blow up a police precinct would he?"

"No, but Broderick might if he thought Leonard could nail him, and he was getting darned close by implicating Smedbetter."

The street rapidly filled with cops and prisoners. The news vans would be here shortly. This routine was getting really old. I knew better than to hang around for the bad guys to find me. I headed for the Metro station.

Shots from a rooftop echoed off the old bricks. Shrieks of horror split the crowd as they backed away from the toppling victim.

Bye-bye, Leonard, I thought as I ran for safety, tugging ever-curious Sean after me.

Thirty-one

"I LEFT my car over at Bill's apartment," Sean said when he realized my goal was the Metro. "Let me give you a ride."

The curls falling over his forehead didn't conceal the concern in his eyes. I patted his muscled bicep reassuringly. "You are a seriously annoying man, but a good one. If your foot is hurting, you can give me the keys, and I'll go get the car for you."

He sighed and glared down at me. He knew me too well, kind of like an older brother. "Turn off Magda and get real again. I will fetch Patra or whoever it is you're after now. I owe you for this story. It's huge. It's ginormous. If it doesn't win us a Pulitzer, it will be my own fault. So where do you want to go?"

Ambulance sirens screamed down the highway. The police station didn't blow up. I cast a look over my shoulder to the mob milling in the street. Cops were running for the rooftops, but they wouldn't find anything. DeLuca's men would have their exits planned.

Rest in peace, Leonard.

It was late and I needed to go home.

"You need to be at your office more than I need to be anywhere," I told him. "Go on, fetch your car, call Patra, and the two of you write your prize-winning story. I need time to locate everyone. I can do it easier on the train than clinging to your dashboard. We might make a good team, but you're a scary driver."

"We make a lousy team," he argued. "You're going to get us all killed one of these days. If we're safe for now, if you don't need me to take you anywhere, I need to go back and check what happened at the precinct and verify that it was DeLuca's thugs who killed Bill."

"We're never safe, not as long as megalomaniacs and monsters run loose," I pointed out. "All we can do is take them down one at a time. I'm sorry Leonard didn't have time to contemplate changing his ways, but even DeLuca had to know his personal rat would squeal. There wasn't any way he could let Leonard continue spilling secrets. Without Leonard following me, the train is safe enough, go on."

Sean accompanied me and made sure I got on the train. I wasn't about to linger with DeLuca's goons hanging around. If they'd shoot DeLuca's old pal, then they'd happily go after me, if they knew who I was. So far, they really didn't—which was why grandstanding was seldom my modus operandi. I was still furious with Patra.

I texted Patra and Nick to see where they were. We needed a family confab. And after today's events, I wanted to make certain they were still alive.

Patra called back, her voice brimming with excitement and laughter. She was already at Sean's office, downloading info into his computer with his permission. It sounded like she had Sam with her, and they were hosting a Pulitzer party.

"Is someone singing *ding-dong, the witch is dead*?" I asked in suspicion.

"Broderick is about to have a house dumped on him," she explained. "My exposé today was only the tip of a very large iceberg. We have Archie so nailed that the FBI is hunting for him right now. Apparently only Homeland Security gets to hack phones in this country, not media, and they're totally ticked. Besides, Archie's connection with a crime boss bears a lot more scrutiny. We shouldn't be having this much fun without drugs and alcohol."

"I take it you'll be dining on carry-out and won't be home tonight," I translated.

"Will I still be allowed in the house?" she asked, with just enough trepidation in her voice to be believed.

"I may strangle you, but the house is as much yours as anyone else's, for now. I kind of provoked Graham, so he may have changed the locks. We all need to get together and talk sometime, though. The repercussions from today's events could be..."

"Entertaining?" she suggested.

"Not precisely the word I had in mind. We need to protect EG from the wrath of our enemies, and we may have created one or two today," I reminded her.

"Why do you think Magda keeps moving around? But I don't think anyone will touch us after we're finished here. I'll be there tomorrow. Any word on that CNN job?"

"Not yet. That's on the agenda. Just let me know you're alive. I need to find Nick."

Nick answered with a weird mixture of resignation and awe. "I'm with the FBI. I may still have a job, maybe. I'll get back to you." He clicked off.

Okay, that was interesting. I couldn't decide if the day was improving, but I wanted to think positively. With everyone but EG accounted for, I headed home.

Home, I hoped, if Graham hadn't locked the doors or criminal gangs hadn't burned it down or the media raided it.

It had been a lot quieter when I'd lived in my Atlanta basement. But quiet had its limitations.

I got off at Dupont. The sun had set and the street lights were just coming on as I discreetly slipped up the alley behind the house. I kept a sharp eye out for vagrants or footsteps following me, but instead I heard odd screams and...*cackles*?...echoing off the old mansions. I couldn't resist checking the front. Easing through the vine-covered archway, I lingered in the shadows between houses and studied the situation.

The worst of the traffic snarl had been cleared, but the BM story was still ripe and juicy, and a lot of news vans hung around. Or had been hanging around.

As I watched in amusement, men with microphones shouted and ran for their trucks. Women shrieked and covered their heads. Even as I poked my head out to see better, one of the remaining news vans screeched away from the curb—with a colony of *bats*? swarming after it. I stared in disbelief at the black cloud of flapping wings swooping and swirling in the twilight beneath the street lamps.

A loud, crackling cackle split the air, and another van hit the gas, careening down the street and out of sight. Mesmerized, I slipped through the gate and leaned against the corner of the house to watch as van after van hit the road. The mob that had spent the afternoon watching the news trucks was running for cover.

I glanced up toward EG's tower. I was pretty certain that was Mallard in her open window, waving a towel to set our resident bat colony free.

But the cackling loudspeaker... Only one person that I knew of controlled the mechanical equipment.

A spooky wail emanated overhead as I entered through the

front door. All we needed was a skeleton dropping from the sky and tombstones in the yard and we'd be ready for Halloween.

Sounding more like a little girl than her usual Wednesday Adams self, EG flung her arms around me when I entered. "Mallard says we're having a party! Thank you, thank you! I want skeletons and spooks. Can we have it in the basement, please, pretty please?"

Maniacal laughter rang through the house.

* * *

EG and I enjoyed lasagna and peach pie in lonely splendor on Wednesday night. Fairly oblivious to all the commotion her half-siblings had created throughout the city, EG happily discussed Halloween preparations. The candelabra didn't once offer a protest.

I'm the one who raised an objection to EG's suggestion of live bats in the basement.

"Mallard chased them all away, anyway," EG said mournfully. "He's calling pest control in the morning."

"If only pest control eliminated two-legged pests," I murmured, but if EG heard, she ignored me. The candelabra might have snorted.

I sent EG to do her homework after dinner, but I was too wound up to concentrate. I went to my room and called up news websites on my laptop. A passing reference to one of the Hollywood stars I'd warned last night caught my interest, and I linked to an entertainment page.

The whole site was furious rants and threats of lawsuits regarding Broderick Media's tapping of telephones and insidious slanting of the news. Hollywood was forming a lynch mob. I clicked on one or two familiar names, but they all just said they'd received an anonymous warning and had taken their phones to their computer people and discovered the spyware. I'd warned them it was probably Broderick's minions. They could find their own proof.

I looked but couldn't find any interviews with Archie proclaiming his innocence, and if anyone knew to talk to Smedbetter, I didn't find evidence of it. The media was having too much fun smearing Archie's stupid TV stations and gossip rags to dig into the real story behind the story.

I just wanted to know that my family was safe. I waited until midnight and finally gave up and went to bed.

* * *

No news vans littered the street on Thursday morning when I walked EG to the Metro. Apparently the breaking stories over Broderick and DeLuca were more appealing than chasing maniacs with bats and dead lawyers. I was good with that.

Construction crews swarmed over the house across the street, and not one of them carried an assault weapon that I could see. Given the crushed fences and rutted lawns along my path of destruction, I was kind of relieved not to meet any neighbors.

Both Nick and Patra texted to say they'd be home by dinner. No word of what they were doing. Once I was back in my office, I emailed Graham to ask if the CNN job was still open in Atlanta. He emailed back an application form, smartass.

I called Oppenheimer. His assistant said he was down at the courthouse and would get back to me. I didn't know if it was necessary any longer, but I checked on Lemuel, the witness against Smythe. He was talking to the FBI, too. Fine, then, everyone was safe. I could get back to work.

I didn't know what my work was. We'd broken Broderick Media wide open, which probably ought to be the end of Graham's research, not that he was saying so.

Out of idle curiosity, I fed Patra's stolen archieleaks files into the Whiz and began searching for names from other suspected Top Hat members. No surprise, Paul Rose was a Broderick investor. The Righteous and Proud—theoretically the umbrella group for the humble religious types who knew nothing about investing in megacorporations— had also privately funded their mouthpiece. Probably with Smythe's blackmail money.

I hoped the FBI was smart enough to start putting pieces together, but I had my doubts. Once this latest scandal blew past, Senator Rose and his cronies would be back with boatloads of cash to invest in more media to spin pretty stories so the politicians would look good in front of cameras. It was the American way.

Nick came home and collapsed in bed. Patra sent me a photo of Sean sleeping on his desk. There might be a decade difference in their ages, but not necessarily in their maturity. I wasn't touching whatever happened between them. I texted back and asked for a photo of Sam Adams, my hero. She sent me a shot of a skinny, long-haired nerd hunched over a keyboard.

I resisted going upstairs and hunting Graham down. The ball was in his court, as they said in the gym I'd once attended. Maybe I should find another public gym instead of hiding out in Graham's. I'd learn more about the outside world, but it was really hard to resist the temptation of running into Graham again.

I dug into a couple of cases from other clients that I'd been neglecting. I have some very good international contacts who help me with translations. That side of my business had been growing lately. I wouldn't see replies until tomorrow. Not everyone can be a night owl.

Mallard brought me gumbo for lunch, and a newspaper. I almost dropped my teeth, but I remembered my manners.

"Join me?" I asked.

"Another time, thank you," he said gravely. "I'm preparing a repast for this evening. Please dress for dinner."

I blinked and stared after him as he departed to his hideaway. A *repast? Dress for dinner?* Had hell frozen over? Only a few weeks ago he'd been chasing us out of his kitchen with a kitchen ax when we'd tried to make our own meals.

I ate my gumbo and returned to my computer. Broderick's dirty deeds had made headline news, naturally. I scanned the article. It concentrated on phone tapping and bribery and not the real skullduggery like chasing employees off cliffs and killing people who knew too much, like Patra's dad and Bill. But this was only part one of the series, so I could hope for more—so could Archie and his cronies.

A small paragraph said Sir Archie was out of the country and unavailable for comment. Yeah, I'd bet.

To keep me entertained, I received an email from Sam Adams with an audio file attached. His message just said *from the boy's room.*

The file quality was bad. I could hear a toilet flush, so he meant a real boy's room. A voice echoed against hard walls, and I strained to make out the words.

"I've got a place in Cambodia. Weather is good, servants are cheap."

I didn't recognize the voice under these conditions, but the speaker's clipped accent sounded like General Smedbetter.

"Offshore account?" a plummy voice with a British accent asked. "Cambodia won't do you any good without money, and I'm not counting on collecting my pension."

Smedbetter and Whitehead smoking in the boy's room. Fascinating. What was the British attaché doing in Broderick offices? Cohorts in crime was my guess.

"Several accounts," Smedbetter agreed. "You'll be taken care of. Take the keys in the desk. The house in Mali will be ready. Better get out tonight and use your other ID."

The voices trailed off as they left to collect keys and fake passports and plane tickets. Crap, just what I'd figured.

This had probably been recorded yesterday. I hoped Sam had sent the file to the cops. Just in case, I sent it to Graham. I'd played Lone Ranger for as long as I cared to and didn't want to get involved again. I was pretty sure the cops were already looking for General Smedbetter after Leonard's confessions, but they wouldn't understand yet how dangerous the man was. He was an American military hero, after all. Not going there.

Instead, I met EG at the Metro and took her clothes shopping so we could dress for our *repast*.

I hate malls, so I'd done my research. The boutique consignment store I'd located was all that I'd hoped. EG went wild in the children's section, and I found a dinner dress that I could live with—just a sleek, knee-length silk in deep vibrant Microsoft blue. I added some imitation sapphires set in silver and a matching clasp to keep my mass of hair out of my face if I got brave enough to let it down.

I was daring fate, and I knew it.

EG went for purple everything, including a pair of cowboy boots. I allowed her the purple lace tank top atrocity but not the mini-skirt that went with it unless she bought leggings. She agreed to leggings if she could wear the cowboy boots. I was no fashion arbiter. If that was her idea of dinner wear, I was fine with it as long as she was decent.

We also added to her school clothes with purple jeans and a purple sweater. I hoped that was an improvement over black.

We could hear Nick and Patra in their rooms, rummaging about, as we carried our treasures up the stairs. Had Mallard told them to dress for dinner too?

"What are we celebrating?" EG whispered, understanding the implications of everyone being home and getting dressed.

"Patra getting fired?" I suggested.

She snorted with laughter and ran down the hall to her cave.

I dislike the fussiness of silk and stockings and heels, but I'd learned from the best, and could appreciate the need to celebrate occasionally. Life is dangerous and often dreary and survival ought to be recognized with good cheer. We'd certainly survived a hurricane this past week.

I opted to twist my long black hair into a loose stack on top of my head and clip it with my fake sapphires. With more hope than good sense, I added just enough eyeliner and mascara to emphasize the exotic tilt inherited from my mother's Hungarian ancestors. I wanted to look good—just in case.

My gown had long sleeves but not much back. I probably needed a shawl or some such flummery. I wore the fake jewels and turned up the heat instead.

I met Nick emerging from his Ali Baba cave. He'd spiffed up in a tailored navy suit and designer tie. He offered his arm. I accepted.

"Do we know what we're celebrating?" he asked as we descended.

"Your deployment to Outer Mongolia?" I suggested.

"No such luck," he said cheerfully. "Seems the ambassador has been suspicious of his chief attaché for some while. Patra's archieleaks files provided the ammunition he needed to turn Whitehead in to Brit intelligence. I'll be assistant to the replacement attaché."

"Very good placement," I said, squeezing his arm. "I don't suppose the Brit equivalent of Homeland Security can nail Whitehead for anything, can they? Do we even know what he did beyond encourage Archie's minions in their cover-ups?"

"Phone hacking, providing information warning BM of events that might have proved detrimental to Broderick interests overseas, the usual chicanery as far as I know. He was on retainer to Broderick Media in the UK and acted in their interests when necessary. Stupid stuff."

"And the walls come tumbling down," I said in delight.

We entered the dining room to discover five place settings prepared—Waterford crystal, the Lenox china, and the best silver, with enough pieces to feed two armies.

Patra and EG were staring at the name cards placed at one end of the table.

Thirty-two

THE antique dining room table was large enough to hold a dozen people, easily. We usually sprawled up and down it with our computers and newspapers and books. Mallard had set all the name cards near the head of the table, where Nick normally sat.

A fabulous bouquet of hothouse flowers replaced the bugged candelabra. Mallard had truly gone all out.

"Do I *have* to sit here?" EG asked, indicating the card across the table from where Patra stood.

I circled around next to her. My place card was on her right. The head of the table was to my right. Nick was directly across from me. We both looked for a card at the fifth setting, but there was none. I wasn't holding my breath, but I did offer a smug smile and check to make certain my blue gown showed what little I had in the way of curves when I sat down.

Mallard arrived carrying a silver platter of dazzling appetizers. We took our seats across from each other without quarrel. He poured wine and offered EG sparkling water. Even EG quit whining and politely placed her hands in her lap and waited instead of diving into the mouth-watering creations in front of us.

We waited some more. I wanted the candelabra back so I could smack it and tell it the food was getting cold. Fortunately for our resident spider, Mallard's appetizers were already cold. Otherwise, I would have said to heck with manners and dug in.

Mallard returned, solemnly bearing a wide-screen laptop as if it were the pièce de résistance. He removed the china and silver at the head of the table, opened the laptop, and stepped back, as if awaiting more orders.

The screen lit up. Graham, wearing white tie and a tux, filled the center, looking like some really ripped version of James Bond. In the background wasn't his usual spider's lair but what appeared to be gold tapestries and a polished desk. Not that anyone else at the table but me would recognize his image. They might recognize Graham's voice from his intrusive habits though.

"I regret that current events prevent me from joining you at dinner as planned," he intoned. "Elizabeth Georgiana, your purple plume is very fetching."

We all stared at EG. She was definitely wearing a plume in her purple-streaked hair. The damned man could see us!

"I thought as long as you were dressed for a celebratory occasion, I might offer a little information that may or may not please you to add to the festivities."

He didn't smile. With his dark hair properly combed, the scar along his hairline was barely visible. Nick and Patra were gaping. I scowled and forked an appetizer off the plate.

"Please, go ahead and eat," he said dryly.

"Darn right I will," I told him. "And don't think this counts for anything."

His eyes crinkled as if he almost smiled. "Of course not. Heaven forbid. To feed your insatiable curiosity, I provide this." He switched the screen from him to a video but we could still hear him. "This came in from the coast of South Africa."

We watched an enormous yacht bucking waves in a torrential rainstorm. It was hard to make out anything through the gray waves of wind and rain. An unidentifiable newscaster began speaking.

"It's been reported that Sir Archibald Broderick has been washed overboard from his yacht, the *Titan3*. The reports are as yet unconfirmed. SOS signals have been received and the ship's crew are reporting they're taking on water. Navy ships are on their way."

EG was clueless and happy with her cheese puff, but Nick and Patra gasped in horror.

"Convenient," I said dismissively. "He's probably meeting Smedbetter in Cambodia. Broderick has homes scattered around the world. They won't find him, even if they're looking, which I assume this video will prevent."

"Perceptive," Graham said, flashing back to himself. A shadow crossed behind him, so he wasn't alone. I memorized the background so I could search for it later. "Tying up another loose end..." He changed the image again.

This time, we saw a large group of people with candles kneeling outside the prison where Brashton had died. The news announcer intoned, "Members of the Righteous and Proud are praying tonight for the health of their leader, Dr. Charles Smythe, who is said to have suffered a heart attack while awaiting trial for murdering Reginald Brashton."

Graham silenced the announcer to interrupt. "He was offering to hand over all his audio files in exchange for a manslaughter charge. The authorities are considering it, should he survive. I've advocated a witness protection program."

"What are the chances it wasn't a heart attack?" I asked, reaching for another of the pesto bruschetta. The platter had almost been wiped clean already. This was better than popcorn but the entertainment left a bit to be desired. EG was glancing down at her lap. I suspected a hidden tablet.

"Tests are being run," Graham agreed. "Smythe has been removed to an undisclosed location. Nicholas, there is a bug in the attaché's desk lamp. The feed goes to security and is filtered for sending to the ambassador. Use it wisely."

Nick flicked a finger to his forehead in an informal salute, not offering a single snarky comment. I sent him a glare.

"Patra, the CNN job is yours, if you want it," Graham continued. "It involves travel, which I understand isn't a problem for you."

"I'm in," she said cheerfully, tipping her wine to the screen. "Do I have you to thank?"

"Your intrepid reporting has been noticed," Graham said dryly. "Although expect your Hollywood connections to be more important than your father's revelations."

I breathed a sigh of relief. Hollywood was a safe place for Patra. Politics was not.

"He's hooking you," I whispered in warning. "You're going to owe him."

Patra and Nick shrugged. Graham continued smoothly, "I'll leave you with one final note."

The screen flashed to an image of Oppenheimer filing a motion before a judge. How the devil did Graham get his spy cameras inside a courtroom? The damned man knew exactly what our lawyer was doing despite my efforts to keep our inheritance battle undercover.

The judge pushed a file across his desk. "I find judgment in favor of your client in the case of the yacht, counselor. It's apparent the funds to purchase it came directly from your client's inheritance. We still cannot rule on the remainder of the monies until the audit has been completed."

I gaped, then remembered to cover my mouth as the judge banged his gavel and handed over a legal-looking document potentially gaining us another half million dollars. We'd done it! We were millionaires!

"Enjoy your dinner," Graham intoned, shutting off the courtroom.

Before I could respond, he lifted his arm to close his laptop—and flashed his diamond cufflinks.

I lifted my wine glass in toast. Patra shrieked in excitement. Nick straightened his tie and clinked his glass to mine.

A million dollars wouldn't buy back our house, but our landlord had become our ally. Almost. I could live with that for a while longer.

Author Note

THE Family Genius mysteries were conceived in the tradition of tall tales with a soupçon of satire and a dash of wicked humor. Do not expect reality, or even *CSI*.

The timeline for Ana's stories takes place over a period of roughly a year—an election year. Unfortunately, I'm not capable of writing fast enough to produce an entire series of books within that same interval. So the series will not take place in real time. Current events and technology will remain static even though changes have multiplied since I conceived the original concept— and occur rapidly every day that I write. Anyone with a modicum of political knowledge will realize that ten years after 9/11/01 does not correspond with a Senator Paul Rose—or anyone similar— running for office. All characters are fictional and entirely the product of my warped imagination.

Author Bio

With several million books in print and *New York Times* and *USA Today's* bestseller lists under her belt, former CPA Patricia Rice is one of romance's hottest authors. Her emotionally-charged contemporary and historical romances have won numerous awards, including the *RT Book Reviews* Reviewers Choice and Career Achievement Awards. Her books have been honored as Romance Writers of America RITA® finalists in the historical, regency and contemporary categories.

A firm believer in happily-ever-after, Patricia Rice is married to her high school sweetheart and has two children. A native of Kentucky and New York, a past resident of North Carolina and Missouri, she currently resides in Southern California, and now does accounting only for herself. She is a member of Romance Writers of America, the Authors Guild, and Novelists, Inc.

For further information, visit Patricia's network:
http://www.patriciarice.com
http://www.facebook.com/OfficialPatriciaRice
https://twitter.com/Patricia_Rice
http://patriciarice.blogspot.com/
http://www.wordwenches.com

Manufactured by Amazon.ca
Bolton, ON